THE
HIDDEN
PLANET

PAUL LEONARD MORRIS

PublishAmerica
Baltimore

First printing

ISBN: 1-4137-5913-0
PUBLISHED BY PUBLISHAMERICA, LLLP
www.publishamerica.com
Baltimore

Printed in the United States of America

To Sophia Grace and Angelina Rose,
two of this world's greatest treasures

I gratefully acknowledge and thank my son, Christopher, for reading and editing my final draft and finding all those typos, grammatical errors and misspellings that I am so apt to produce and that neither my spell checker nor I could find.

I also appreciate the help of my brother, Manny Morris, Sharon Bovaird, David Levy and Susan Schwartz (a.k.a. Susan Silver), who were kind enough to read my manuscript in its raw form and share their thoughts and ideas with me.

The most important question a human being can ask is: *Is the universe friendly?*

—*Albert Einstein*

PROLOGUE

THE NEW YORK TIMES
February 25, 1972

CRAFT TO BEAR MESSAGE ON ITS SPACE JOURNEY

Pioneer 10, the United States vehicle to be launched Sunday into a trajectory designed to carry it past Jupiter and into the cosmos, carries a message that states, in scientific symbols, who sent it and where they live.

The message, etched onto a 6-by-9 inch aluminum plate anodized with gold, represents the first direct attempt by man to communicate with intelligent beings elsewhere.

It was devised by Dr. Frank D. Drake, director of the National Astronomy and Ionosphere Center at Cornell University, and Dr. Carl Sagan, who heads the university's Laboratory for Planetary Studies.

The message symbolically uses the energy difference between two basic states of the hydrogen atom as its units of time and distance. It shows the earth's position in terms of 14 pulsars, or celestial sources of radio pulsations, identifying each in terms of its characteristic rhythm.

The inhabitants of earth are depicted in drawings of a man and woman alongside the spacecraft. Other symbols represent the position of the earth within the solar system.

THE NEW YORK TIMES
March 3, 1972

PIONEER 10 BEGINS A FLIGHT TO JUPITER

The U.S. Pioneer 10 spacecraft launched toward Jupiter today after a 25-minute delay because of an unexplained technical problem. The upper third stage was added to the Atlas-Centaur rocket to give the spacecraft extra boost to enable it to escape earth's gravitational pull at a record velocity.

NASA officials say that the craft should reach Jupiter in 21 months: the craft's 11 scientific instruments are expected to provide new data on Jupiter, the asteroid belt between Mars and Jupiter and the physical boundary where the solar system blends into the rest of the Milky Way.

The spacecraft engineers hope that the small radio will continue transmitting until 1977, when craft should be flying past Saturn. The craft should escape our solar system and move out into the Milky Way in 1980…

Twenty-Five Years Later

Pioneer 10 hurdled through space; the golden plaque at its base reflected the light from a nearby double star. Indifferent to the impact of space debris, the craft continued on its journey—a slave to the forces of gravity surrounding it. Pioneer 10 had come a long way and those who launched it had long since lost interest in the purpose of its mission.

The ship seemed to swerve and slightly change course. Then it veered from its path and moved as though being towed by some mysterious force.

As the projectile approached, the planet's warships scrambled to intercept the craft and monitor the space in its vicinity. "There are no life forms in the vessel," said the captain of the lead ship, signaling back to the planet.

"Keep following and send a patrol to search for other alien vessels in the vicinity," was the order from an unquestioned authority. The escort vessels continued to follow Pioneer 10 to its imposed rendezvous.

As the unmanned spacecraft came closer to the city, an unseen tractor beam slowed its speed and altered its direction, like a giant hand pulling on a child's balloon. The twilight from the setting double sun danced on the dome of the tallest government building like pixies dancing on the dew. The dome slid open to receive the shiny new visitor. As Pioneer 10 entered, the dome closed behind it leaving the city in the same peaceful state it had enjoyed before the unexpected intrusion from Earth.

The gleaming walls of the city glistened in the double-sunlight. The atmosphere of the planet was too thin to sustain creatures of human kind, so the inhabitants lived within the artificial confines of the black, gleaming city. The city was an interesting mixture of modern materials, workmanship, and design, yet it had a feeling of tradition about it. Beyond the confines of the constructed zone lay a barren, rocky landscape, which looked as though it had never been occupied by intelligent life. Looking back toward the city, the skyline was punctuated by its tallest structure, a temple-like edifice, an anachronism in a city of modern splendor.

The alarm was sounded, but heard only by those who were responsible for receiving objects into the city. The reception team approached. They looked human in appearance except that their uniformity gave them a manufactured effect. All were exactly six feet tall, with precisely the same shape and build. They wore neatly-fitting garments of a perfectly balanced gray, exactly halfway between black and white. The outer garments were of a simple, functional design with a somewhat military look to them.

They all appeared to be male and the only exposed parts of their bodies were their heads and hands, which were both hairless. Their faces were distinguishable but all had similar perfect features, with no blemishes or imperfections.

The receiving room was round and open, with no objects covering either the floor or the walls. The walls and floors were sleek with a very functional look of buffed metal.

The reception team seemed to share a look of both puzzlement and delight at the same time. They carefully lifted the craft into a carrying vehicle and guided it along corridors, up and down ramps toward the building exit. They moved cautiously out of the building and through a connecting passageway. Corridors connected all the structures that held the inhabitants and passageways to protect against the inhospitable environment of the atmosphere that lacked life-sustaining oxygen.

Finally, the crew came to a room with large double doors. Each of the three members of the team thought of a number, which presented in the correct sequence opened the doors. They entered a room, barren of all comforts, but perfectly suited for the examination of objects. Scopes, lights and probes that the technicians used in their work were present in the room.

Another team of three entered the room as the first team left and proceeded back to their stations awaiting the arrival of the next unexpected object. The new team, appearing similar to the first in stature but were dressed in metallic garb. Though sleek looking, the attire did not reflect light, which could interfere with their examination, but did reflect the rays produced by their instruments. This group, consisting of two females and a male, did not speak but got straight to work, which entailed a detailed examination of the object. Each knew what to do and seemed to be a specialist at their job. One used a scope to measure radiation and any possible explosive potential of the craft. A second inspected the surface using special lighting and magnifying equipment. The third probed each crevice and orifice collecting any samples of matter that might have accumulated before and during its trip through space. The examination took about thirty minutes and, though concerned, they all seemed satisfied with their findings. Two of them turned to the third one, who called the chief scientist by pressing one of the six points of his badge. "Einstein, you must see the craft yourself," he said into his communicator

Soon one of similar dress, but somewhat taller, entered the room. Unlike the others, his badge contained a ruby on each point. "What have you found?" he asked.

The leader of the crew stepped forward and answered. "The craft is made of crude composition metals; there is no danger of radiation and the explosive potential is zero. Its plaque clearly shows that the creatures that launched it are very similar in appearance to our species. Also, the location of their planet indicates that it is from this galaxy. And what leaves us most curious is that they are obviously not concerned that whoever intercepted this probe would also be able to easily find their planet."

"Let me have a look for myself," said Einstein, coming around to the base of the craft to make a closer observation. He stared at the engravings on the plaque. "Oh—I see. This is very interesting," he said, knitting his brows in thought, "and very curious," he added, "very curious indeed. This is clearly a matter of planetary security; Number 2 must be notified immediately."

Craft to Bear Message On Its Space Journey

Pioneer 10, the United States vehicle to be launched Sunday into a trajectory designed to carry it past Jupiter and into the cosmos, carries a message that states, in scientific symbols, who sent it and where they live.

The message, etched onto a 6-by-9-inch aluminum plate anodized with gold, represents the first direct attempt by man to communicate with intelligent beings elsewhere.

It was devised by Dr. Frank D. Drake, director of the National Astronomy and Ionosphere Center at Cornell University, and Dr. Carl Sagan, who heads the university's Laboratory for Planetary Studies.

The message symbolically uses the energy difference between two basic states of the hydrogen atom as its units of time and distance. It shows the earth's position in terms of 14 pulsars, or celestial sources of radio pulsations, identifying each in terms of its characteristic rhythm.

The inhabitants of earth are depicted in drawings of a man and woman alongside the spacecraft. Other symbols represent the position of the earth within the solar system.

FLIGHT TO JUPITER IS SET FOR SUNDAY

Unmanned Craft to Fly By Within 100,000 Miles

By JOHN NOBLE WILFORD
Special to The New York Times

CAPE KENNEDY, Fla., Feb. 24 — Exploration of the distant outer planets by spacecraft is scheduled to begin Sunday night with the launching here of an unmanned Pioneer 10 on a 22-month, half-billion-mile journey to Jupiter.

Technicians conducted final tests today on the 570-pound spacecraft and its Atlas-Centaur rocket, which has augmented power to drive Pioneer 10 away from the earth at an unprecedented escape velocity of 32,000 miles an hour.

If successful, Pioneer 10 will be the first man-made object to venture beyond the orbit of Mars, through the hazards of the asteroid belt and to within 100,000 miles of Jupiter, the largest of the solar system's nine planets. The encounter with Jupiter should come around Christmas, 1973.

As it flies by, the spacecraft is to radio scientific data and the first close-up pictures of the planet and then, with a boost from Jupiter's gravity, eventually shoot out of the solar system altogether.

A Crucial Mission

The mission, and a companion flight scheduled for 1973, becomes even more crucial to the nation's space plans now that it appears that the exceedingly ambitious planetary "grand tour" project is dead.

Unless Congress overrules the White House and the National Aeronautics and Space Administration in the next few years, which is unlikely, plans for launching multiplanetary probes reaching out to Pluto will be shelved for budgetary reasons. The nation will thus pass up an exploring opportunity that comes only once every

179 years.

In the latter half of the decade, the outer planets—Jupiter, Saturn, Uranus, Neptune and Pluto—will move into a rare orbital alignment that would make it theoretically possible for a single spacecraft to fly by all five, using the gravitational force of one planet to speed up its journey to the next.

To take advantage of this alignment, NASA's Jet Propulsion Laboratory at Pasadena, Calif., had outlined two missions—one in 1977 to Jupiter, Saturn and Pluto and another in 1979 to Jupiter, Uranus and Neptune. A new spacecraft designed for the necessary lifetimes of 10 to 12 years was being studied.

Victim of Budget

But these plans fell victim of the space agency's decision to keep the next budget at a $3.4-billion level, while beginning development of the $5.5-billion space shuttle.

"I'm still very disappointed we are not able to go ahead with the grand tour," Dr. James C. Fletcher, the NASA administrator, said in an interview recently. "It would have captured the imagination of Americans."

Dr. Fletcher said, however, that the project would have cost up to $1-billion and "neither Congress nor the scientific community felt the same enthusiasm I had for it."

The space agency instead is planning a series of less expensive Jupiter-Saturn missions, probably relying on a modified version of the Mariner spacecrafts that have been used in Venus and Mars exploration. Dr. Fletcher says a Jupiter-Saturn decision will be made in a few weeks.

According to a proposal submitted by the Jet Propulsion Laboratory, two such spacecraft could be built and operated for about $300-million. A 1977 launching would enable the spacecraft to fly by Saturn for close-up photography in 1981.

Other American planetary missions in the decade include a Mariner flight by Venus and Mercury in 1973-74 and the landing of two Viking life-detection instrument packages on Mars in 1976

CHAPTER ONE

"Howard," called his assistant, Kevin Briggs, from across the office, but Howard Cooper's mind was elsewhere.

As publisher and editor of his own small-town newspaper, he kept late hours, but these days it seemed as though more than the responsibility of his business was keeping him from home. At forty-seven, he and Maureen, his wife of eighteen years, seemed to have fallen out of love. Their children, Christine, sixteen and John, eleven, kept them busy enough, though, that the issue of their marriage problems could be conveniently ignored.

Howard was an idealist of sorts, but luckily, his practical side usually got in the way. He always managed to at least muddle through whatever came in his direction; most times, he did a lot better than muddle. In fact, he always seemed able to rise to the occasion, regardless of how great the challenge.

"Howard," persisted Kevin, again to no avail.

The offices were small, but adequate. It was one large room in the front, a back room for the printers and a small office for Howard. The sign above the doorway read Cooper's Coop. The guys who worked there called it The Bull Pen. Howard paced a lot when he was in it and sometimes threw a rubber ball against the wall. He said it helped him to think.

The offices were on the ground floor and had a large window that faced the street. Right inside the window, in plain view, was an old nineteenth century printing press. Everyone told Howard that it was a waste of space, but he liked it. He told them that it was one of Ben Franklin's original presses. Of course, no one believed him except his son, who would brag about it at school. His sister, Christine, made fun of him for it, but he didn't care. If his dad said so, that was good enough for him.

"Howard!" called Kevin again, this time getting up from his desk and walking into Cooper's office. Kevin was Howard's assistant editor and number one reporter.

"Ha—what—sorry, I guess my mind was on Mars or something," said Cooper, now looking straight at Kevin, while removing his feet from his desk.

"That's okay. Maybe you're familiar then with the aliens in the flying saucer that old Mamie Johnson thought she saw last night."

"Thought she saw a flying saucer, did she?" responded Howard, now completely back from his mental sabbatical. "Well, write it up then like a good reporter. And—ah, don't forget to phone our friend Bob Jones out at the air force base. We don't want to get in trouble with the military. You know what sticklers they are about these things. Can't have our friend Colonel Bob reading about this in the paper before he's officially notified. But you know it's just amazing how these military types operate. They swear up and down that UFOs don't exist and then they go whacko when you don't tell them about a sighting. I can't figure it out."

"Okay, chief, whatever you say," replied Briggs with a smile.

"Don't be a smart ass, Kevin; it's too late at night for that kind of crap."

"You got it, boss."

Cooper just gave Briggs that look. Briggs just smiled back.

Howard had a good relationship with most people. If you were straight with him, everything was fine, but when his finely tuned bullshit meter went off—watch out. It was that simple.

Unfortunately, things weren't as simple for Howard at home. "I guess you can't treat women the same way as men and expect the same back," he once told Kevin. As usual, Kevin just smiled. "Hell Kevin, you don't have those kinds of problems, do you? You're single. You treat all women like shit, and they love you anyway!" Kevin continued smiling. Howard was too smart, though, to actually believe that it was that simple. He just liked to give Kevin a hard time.

It was getting late and he didn't want to go through the same hassle with his wife as he did last night and the night before. Howard got extremely involved with whatever he did. "There are just a very few things in life that really have meaning to a person, and he is bound to get very involved with those things," he often told his wife. This was the way he tried to explain his actions to her.

Howard dialed the phone. "Maureen? Oh, Chrissy. Put your mother on, honey."

"Maureen, I'll be home in a little while, maybe an hour or so. I have to just finish this piece I'm working on about the incident down at the high school.

18

"That *is* as soon as I can," Howard said firmly, as Maureen tried to get him to leave earlier.

Howard hung up the phone thinking how difficult she had become, recently. Also, that she never used to mind when he worked late. "What the hell is buggin' her," he wondered aloud. Maureen was nearing her forty-third birthday and Howard realized that the reality of middle age could be frightening for a woman. *Hell it's frightening enough to a man*, he thought. But her demand on his time was still an annoyance to him. Maybe after eighteen years of marriage things either got better or they got worse, but they never seemed to stay the same. *So I guess they are getting worse*, he concluded. Nothing improves unless you work at it and neither of them appeared to be putting in the effort lately. *Entropy*, thought Howard, he remembered that term from college physics; it meant that in the natural order of things, everything falls apart, unless it is maintained somehow. Marriage was no different and he knew it. The problem lay in the fact that neither of them seemed to care enough to do anything about it. It appeared that the bloom was definitely off the rose.

"I'd better finish this piece and get home," he finally said to himself.

Within an hour, he had finished the work, left and got into his car. He lived fifteen minutes from the office. It was getting dark and the sun, setting behind the trees, was casting strange shadows in the road. He remembered that night, back in the seventies, when he was dating Maureen, when he almost didn't make it home. It was about a forty-five minute drive from Howard's to Maureen's place. They had gone to one of their favorite bars to have drinks and something to eat and dance to a small town band that only played on Saturday nights. Howard had drunk a bit too much, and after leaving Maureen, was quite tired during the late night drive back home. Just like this night, there were shadows cast on the road, only that night, he began dozing at the wheel and the shadows appeared as objects. At one point, he started hitting his brakes because he thought he saw a log in the road, but it was just a shadow and the incident helped to wake him up for the rest of the trip. He was more careful with his drinking and driving most Saturday nights after that.

As he drove through a deserted stretch of road, he thought he heard a strange whirring sound coming from a field that lay behind a row of trees surrounded by thick brush. His reporter's curiosity almost got the better of him, until he remembered Maureen. He hesitated, then drove on, logging the event in the back of his mind.

Christine opened the door for Howard when he arrived. "Daddy, you'll never guess who called me."

"Who, honey? Where's Mom?"

"Dad, you're not listening!"

"Yes I am, honey. I'm sorry, I just wanted to tell your mother that I was home."

"MOM, DAD'S HOME! Now, don't you want to know who called me?"

"Sure."

"Bob Johnson. He's the captain of the football team," she said, beaming.

"You mean Mamie Johnson's grandson?" he said, putting down his jacket and looking for the latest edition of his *Field & Stream* magazine.

"Yes, that's right. Dad, you're not listening to me again. Can't you come into the living room so we can talk like adults."

"Well, that's just great, honey," said Howard, still looking around for his magazine, as he proceeded into the living room. "But don't get carried away with yourself," he said, now settling his six-foot-two-inch, 190-pound frame on the couch and giving her his full attention. "Remember, sixteen is still just a little too young to be getting serious, even if he is the captain of the football team. In fact, particularly, if he is the captain of the football team. You know how those guys love to brag about their exploits."

"Daaad, I'm not somebody's exploit, whatever that means. Besides, did you know that Romeo and Juliet were only thirteen when they fell in love?"

"Yes. I know, sweetheart, and look what happened to them."

"Oh, Daddy, be serious. This is important to me," she said, plopping herself down on the couch next to him.

"I'm sure it is," he continued, trying to look into the kitchen, to see his wife. "But just don't become overwhelmed by this guy," he said, again looking straight at her. "If he thinks that you're under his power he may try some—funny stuff."

"You mean like you used to do?" said Maureen, coming up from behind him.

"Maureen! What are you saying? Be serious. I don't want our daughter to get the wrong idea."

"You mean the right idea, don't you?"

"Maureen!"

Chrissy held her mouth to stifle a laugh. "It's okay, Daddy," she said, getting up and walking away. "But please don't forget that I am no longer a child."

Howard made a face and shook his head.

"Are you hungry?" asked Maureen.

"That's a safe bet," grumbled Howard.

He ate his meal quietly while Maureen busied herself around the kitchen. "Where's John?" asked Howard, as Maureen picked up his empty plate from the table.

"He's upstairs doing his homework, I believe."

"Do you think he would like some ice cream?"

"I think we all would. Why don't you see if John would like to take a ride with you?"

"Ah, leave the kid alone. I don't want to disturb him if he's doing his homework. Besides, I need a little time alone to think."

"Time to think?! Don't you spend enough time thinking as it is?"

Howard got up and started toward the door. "I won't be long, I promise." Maureen's response was a cold blank stare.

Howard was actually less interested in ice cream than he was in checking out the strange whirring sound coming from the field he passed on the way home. The way to the ice cream parlor, took him by the same field. He didn't hear anything this time, but he left his car to look around anyway. As he stepped out of the car, he felt a pleasant sensation pass over him as if he were being mysteriously drawn forward. As he walked through the bushes toward an open area, he experienced a strange sense of being alone. It was a clear night and all the stars were visible as he gazed up toward the heavens. Even the full moon seemed brighter as he looked out over the field. Yet he was puzzled that the bright moonlight did not help him see what appeared to be a very large object less than fifty feet away. He was struck by the lack sound of any kind. It seemed as though whatever was in the field, if there was anything, had scared all the wildlife away. Even the insect sounds were gone. It was as if something had cast a dark pall over the area he was trying to see. He walked forward to investigate this phenomenon further. But still he could not see any strange objects. He paced around for a few minutes, but failed find what he was looking for. Then he remembered Maureen and the ice cream. He turned to leave, but again he experienced that same pleasant sensation drawing him forward. He laughed to himself as he thought of Homer's Odyssey and the Song of the Sirens that lured unsuspecting sailors to their doom. Then a strange chill passed through his body and the hair at the back of his neck stood up; he felt almost breathless, as an eerie presence seemed to surround him. He felt as though he were being engulfed by the very darkness itself. He panicked as he felt himself being drawn into what seemed like the center of a small cyclone, whirling him up into space at a breakneck speed. He tried to wake himself, as though in a dream, but the reality of the situation could not be denied. He stopped struggling just as his consciousness dissolved into the blackness of the night.

CHAPTER TWO

Howard felt as though he were watching a science fiction movie from the inside. At first, he thought he was dreaming, or rather the way you feel when you wake from a realistic dream and don't know where you are. He was not bound in any way, but when he tried to move, he could not get beyond a certain point. He could not see the boundary, which felt like a thin membrane, which he could not penetrate with all his strength. He thought that this must be the way a dog feels when stuck behind an "invisible fence." His breathing was easy and comfortable, the temperature of the air around him felt like a pleasant 72 degrees and his "cage" contained a pleasant odor, not like perfume but rather like flowers on a pleasant spring day. He still wasn't certain that he was not dreaming, though it felt so real it must be happening. The more he struggled, the more frightened he became, but then as though he were on some tranquilizer, he would relax again. A feeling of dread suddenly came over him as he felt like a fly in a spider's web, all wrapped up nice and comfortable and alive, so that momma spider could have some nice fresh meat to feed to her hungry babies. He felt helpless and that frightened him even more.

He could see and hear everything perfectly. There were a half a dozen creatures around him performing their functions in a very mechanical way. Cooper watched them with fascination. Their movements were so effortless, so precise, so directed. No motion seemed wasted. They seemed to Howard as the most efficient creatures that he had ever seen. Although they were human-like, they were obviously not human. They looked too perfect, as though a very sophisticated robot maker tried to create a likeness of a human, without the flaws. It looked as though these creatures were designed to perform particular functions, specific to each individual. The parts that were the most helpful for their particular tasks seemed to be the most developed.

The one lifting things had the largest hands and arms. The one moving around the most was built for speed and maneuverability. And the one directing the operation had the biggest head. It was engrossing for the newcomer to behold and Howard was spellbound. He could not believe what he was seeing.

He tried to communicate with the creatures, but they just ignored him as they went about their work. They seemed to not hear him at all. No one even turned in his direction when he spoke, they looked past him, as though he were some cargo or wasn't there at all. He saw a table and wondered if that was where they would perform some kind of weird experiments on him by sticking probes in all the orifices of his body.

The room was confined and full of gadgets. Howard thought it was like a computer center, or a modern factory, or the control room of a ship—a ship— "A space ship. Holy shit! Wait a minute," he exclaimed, "this is obviously a dream. Must have been sparked by that report of a UFO that Kevin told me about. Wow, wait till I tell Kevin about this one, we'll have some laugh about it."

Howard pinched himself and tried to act cool, but somehow he knew that he wasn't dreaming. He was there. This was real. However, he had to redefine reality now. Howard tried to pull himself together, to regain his composure. As long as he was here, he would get as much out of it as he could. After all, he *was* a reporter. And this certainly was news, if he ever got back to report it.

Howard tried to comprehend the situation. His mind went back to the war. He was just out of college. He was serving as an intelligence officer, gathering information in an unsecured village in Vietnam, when the Vietcong overran the area, netting him in the process. He was hooked up on a bamboo pole with five other Americans and hauled into a Vietcong stronghold. They were interrogated individually and thrown into bamboo cages. This allowed them to watch the fun. The Vietcong were amusing themselves with games of death, and Howard and some others were obliged to watch the "merriment." The Vietcong were forcing the prisoners to walk back and forth along a three-inch-wide log while they would shoot blunt arrows at them. The object of the "game" was to see if they could knock the prisoner off the log and into the water where sharpened bamboo sticks awaited the hapless American. If the fallen prisoner was lucky enough to avoid a fatal wound, he was forced to go again until he died from sudden or gradual loss of his lifeblood. The one who knocked the prisoner down won money, a fatal knockdown won the top prize. The barbaric and inhuman proceedings were indelibly etched into Howard's brain. He stood there helplessly watching his friends and comrades being mercilessly tortured to death. But as bad as it was, he knew that he was the lucky one.

The marines swept through that night and found him huddled in the corner of the cage, dazed and half out of his mind fighting against the horror of his comrades' deaths and the fear that he was next.

It was ironic in a way, he thought. He was captured now too, but this time he had no idea what lay ahead. *If this is real and I ever get back, this should make great copy for my paper or at least the National Enquirer,* he decided.

Howard noticed one of the creatures moving toward him. Howard's face held a look of anticipation. He wondered if they were going to communicate with him and or grab him for some horrible experiment. As the creature reached Cooper, its arm went out and it pressed a button somewhere above Howard's head. He heard a low hissing sound, smelled something strange, felt a floating feeling and all went black.

Howard awakened to find himself in a room with a spectacular view of a strangely bleak and desolate landscape. There were no trees, no bushes, not even grass. The landscape was quite barren, except for large boulders and various sized rocks strewn about. There were also mountains and craters visible, which made Howard think of how our moon or some large asteroid might appear at close range. Everything outside the building had a reddish, brownish gray look to it. The starkness of the view was contrasted by the brightness of his room.

All the walls in the apartment were transparent. This alarmed him at first, for he felt like a goldfish in a tank. However, as he went from room to room, he soon discovered that the "glass" was transparent in only one direction— out of the apartment, and opaque in the other, like a two-way mirror. He had to conclude that no one could see into his apartment from the outside, though he was certain that *they* were watching him. He reached into his pocket and found his penknife, they let him keep his clothes and apparently the possessions he had on him. He took out the blade to see if he could cut or at least scratch the surface of the wall. He could not do either. He poked and stabbed the wall, but the results were similar.

The furniture in the room looked plastic but felt like the softest leather. He thought of attempting to cut that too, but decided against it, fearing they might think him deranged and discard him for another more "stable" human specimen and that would mean that they would either kill him or not talk to him, both alternatives being unacceptable.

It was all very strange, but nice, in an eerie sort of way. *I guess it just takes a little getting used to and, at least it appears by the looks of things, that they're not intending any physical torture*, he thought. The only things that resembled food were liquids, which were tasty like creamy fruit drinks of different flavors, which seemed to be both satisfying and nourishing. He wasn't afraid of being poisoned. Why would they take him all this way for that? Since he had no choice, Howard decided to settle in.

A couple of days had passed and Howard was getting restless. He judged the time by setting his watch to the sunrise, which he could see from his window. A day on this planet turned out to be twenty-four hours just like on Earth. The walls had no shades, but a control knob in each corner enabled him to adjust for light that entered the room. He found books that he could not read, their language and alphabet were different and a device like a TV with programs that he could not understand. The only thing he could do, besides sleeping and thinking, was to listen to their version of music. This was close to our classical music with strange passages that sounded atonal to Howard. He believed that they were ripening him up. He figured it was their version of psychological warfare. They wanted him to be settled down from the trip and anxious to communicate. At this point Howard was willing to talk to anybody. And, he would soon get his wish.

He went to sleep that night determined to either contact one of these aliens or somehow escape from his current accommodations to take a further look around.

Howard awoke the next day, showered and prepared himself for whatever the day had in store for him. He found a device in the bathroom that looked enough like an electric razor that he tried it out and it worked. "Umm, as close as a blade," he said, laughing to himself. Everything in the bathroom was similar enough to what he was used to for him to figure out its purpose. He concluded they must be primitive in some respects due to the absence of a bidet. *Well, I guess it's safe to say that this planet is not inhabited by Frenchmen*, he thought, quite pleased with his own humor.

He heard the sound of men's voices, which startled Howard as he paced his rooms trying to think of what to do next. He walked toward what he presumed was the entrance and saw two men that appeared human looking standing just outside. They were both about six feet tall with muscular builds, dressed in identical uniforms of gray. They reminded Howard of West Point cadets. Even their bearing seemed military in nature. He wasn't quite sure how to proceed in allowing them in. But as soon as he faced them the door slid open and the two greeted him in a rather warm and unthreatening manner.

I wonder if they're human, Howard thought.

"Please follow us," they suggested in an American accent that Howard found quite familiar.

They must have learned their English down my way, he observed.

They moved up and down ramps and through corridors and made no conversation as they walked. Howard noticed that the "glass" wall motif was present everywhere as he passed through the city. The city itself reminded Howard of Emerald City, from the Wizard of Oz movie. The ceilings were so high it gave one a feeling being outdoors. They passed open places where people could congregate, yet there was no one loitering about. Those that he saw, seemed quite busy and content. Everyone smiled and seemed genuinely friendly. There were many gadgets, pieces of equipment and paraphernalia around. Yet, nothing seemed out of place. Order, purpose and contentment. How do they manage it? What's their secret? he wondered.

Eventually they came to a room with double doors, which opened as the three reached it. Howard was asked to enter the room and wait. As he did, the other two left. He looked around. It was a medium sized room with a small group of seats facing a blank wall. The room had a comfortable feeling to it and as Howard was about to seat himself, he felt someone's presence. "I'm Number 2," said a stately-looking female. Howard had not seen or heard her enter; she seemed to have appeared from out of nowhere, which startled him. She did not look threatening in any way and she appeared to be human. Yet, she made him feel uncomfortable. He wondered why. She seemed so serene. Too serene perhaps, maybe that was it. It seemed strange, out of place, unexpected. She seemed somehow too cool. Something was missing. Was it her humanity that was lacking? Was something missing from her essence? Howard could not tell, it was just a feeling he had.

"How are you doing today?" she continued. "Have you slept all right? Has the nourishment been sufficient? Are your accommodations adequate?" She appeared to be sincerely concerned.

"Yes, everything is okay and I feel fine. Thank you for asking." Number 2 smiled benignly. "By the way, where are we? And what kind of...*beings* are you?" Howard tried to choose his words as carefully as possible.

"We are people like any other."

"People huh, that is comforting. If I may say so, it is surprising that you and your people look so much like us humans, just about identical in fact."

"That should not surprise you. How many beings from other planets have you seen?"

"None before you. In fact the humans from Earth did not even know that there was life on other planets."

"Is that so?" she said, seeming quite interested in this line of conversation.

"For your information all the beings in this galaxy that we have encountered look more or less like you and me. It is just that some are more *aggressive* than others. However, as far as looks are concerned, we all look somewhat the same."

"What do you call yourselves? And where are we?" Howard continued.

"We do not call ourselves by any name."

"Why is that?"

"It's not necessary, and it could be dangerous."

"Dangerous? How is that? And where are we?"

"Dangerous, for reasons you Earthlings obviously need to be made aware of," she replied. "And what is this obsession with where we are?"

"Well," said Howard, "if you were plucked off your planet and flown to…God knows where, wouldn't you like to at least know where you were, and who your captors are?"

"Well, I can certainly understand your desire to know these things. If it makes you feel any better you can call our world the Hidden Planet and our people the Hidden People. It is not really our name, but that's what the rest of the galaxy calls us. And I am Number 2, second in command to the leader of our society."

"At least you have names," Howard said in frustration. "Okay, so you won't tell me who you are or where we are. Will you at least tell me why you kidnapped me and brought me here?"

"I'm afraid Rondo, our leader, has reserved that pleasure for himself."

Before Howard had a chance to consider her remark, the wall behind Number 2 began to open. A bright, almost blinding, golden light shined out, revealing a male figure. The light that shined from behind the figure cast a radiant glow around his whole body like the aura of a saint. Somehow, the man, or at least the aliens' version of a man, almost seemed to have been created from the light. It made the figure appear god-like. Howard was enthralled and stood gaping in awe of the vision in front of him. As the figure slowly descended from the platform, Howard began to see the shining object that radiated the light.

"This is Rondo, our leader," said Number 2. He was taller than the others and wore a long gray cape over streamline clothing that was form fitting and functional with no more than a neat collar to break its line. On his feet were black boots that looked like patent leather. His hair, unlike the others, was not closely cropped, but was slicked back and was squared off at the neck. He had an air of importance about him, though his manner and expression were friendly and unthreatening. Howard felt though, that the man could be menacing if that were his intent. At this moment, his sharp-featured face did not betray his purpose.

Howard was about to greet him, but Rondo spoke first. "This is yours, is it not?" asked Rondo, pointing to the shining object behind him on the platform.

Howard could see the object more clearly with Rondo out of his line of vision. "It looks like a spacecraft. Could I have a closer look?"

"Whatever you require."

Howard mounted the platform and slowly approached the object. The light, from the plaque on its base, was almost blinding. Howard had to position himself so that he could get close enough to read the engraving without casting a shadow on it. The beauty of its golden surface astonished him. "Oh my god!" he said, realizing what was before him. Howard remembered seeing a picture of the spacecraft in the New York Times the day it was launched. "God that must have been at least twenty, twenty-five years ago," he muttered under his breath. He remembered how the engravings of the nude man and woman caused quite a stir in the early seventies. The irony, as Howard's present situation clearly demonstrated, was that no one seemed to give a damn that we had perhaps etched an invitation to our own destruction, complete with directions. *Yes, oh yes, they were so right, those brilliant scientists,* Howard thought. *Their plan worked. Oh how well it worked. The only thing is, if they had taken the time to consider what the possible consequences of their great cleverness might be. It took genius to develop the atom bomb also, and it put us in danger of extinction from within. Well,* his mind continuing on a rampage, *let's look on the bright side, the way the situation looks now, we may not be around long enough to blow ourselves up!*

Howard stopped his internal rant long enough to consider, *well maybe these Hidden People are just curious, they seem friendly enough,* somehow though, his gut told him otherwise.

He looked at Rondo but said nothing. Rondo's face was expressionless. Howard tried to muster all his negotiating skills. He was, de facto, the negotiator for humankind and it scared the hell out of him. He wanted Rondo to make the first move, show his hand. Maybe Howard was wrong. *After all, these "people,"* he thought again, *seemed friendly enough.* He had to know where they were coming from before committing himself, but the ball was now in Howard's court. "Well I'm sure glad it was your people that found our probe," he said, trying hard not to betray his fears.

"Are you certain?" shot back Rondo with a look of irony on his face.

"Only you can tell me that," answered Howard clearly shaken.

Rondo smiled a peculiar smile. Howard could not quite figure out what it meant. "What is your game?" asked Rondo, changing his expression to one of inquisitiveness.

"I'm not quite sure what you mean," answered Howard honestly.

"Well, if I must spell it out. What is the true purpose of this probe?"

Howard still didn't know what Rondo was getting at. However, he was getting more nervous by the moment. He didn't know what statement would render him useless to these people and be the cause of his own demise. He also knew that he had little choice but to tell the absolute truth. These folks seemed too clever for one to deceive them or even play with them. "The purpose of this probe is to contact other forms of intelligent life in the universe. I must admit, though, I doubt if anyone expected results so soon— if at all."

Rondo looked at Howard. "Then why bother?" he challenged.

"Fair question. I guess we just got carried away with ourselves," he said, forcing a smile. "You know how these scientists can be."

"We are getting nowhere with this," returned Rondo impatiently. "Let's get to the point of this interview. Your people have found our planet. We cannot permit this violation of our security, whether by accident or design."

"But surely you don't think that a civilization as primitive as ours, compared to yours, could do your world any harm?"

"Perhaps not directly."

"How then?"

"By communicating the information to others," said Rondo, looking at Howard intently.

"But we do not know any others, that is why we sent up the probe in the first place," answered Howard in a pleading tone.

"Perhaps. But even if you didn't have communications with anyone when

30

the probe was launched, you may have it now or in the future. Especially with this flying advertisement traveling around the galaxy, who knows what new "friends" you might have already attracted without your even knowing it! And how can any people be expected to trust a race foolish enough to do what your people have done. You do realize that this probe is nothing less than an broadcast to those in the galaxy who would like nothing better than enjoying the process and spectacle of your annihilation, don't you? Not to mention, that any civilization advanced enough to analyze the probe, will quickly realize that the people who sent it are clearly primitive, in terms of technology and therefore not very able to defend themselves from the invasion of a superior force."

"I guess we thought that any race of beings that were intelligent enough to decipher the probe would be of a benign nature."

"How naive—I've heard enough! This interview is over. Take the earthling away," he said into a communicator worn like a watch on his left wrist.

The doors swung open and the two that brought Howard entered and took him back to his room.

Now back in his room, Howard's head was spinning. He needed time to think. There was too much at stake for him to try to address these issues off the top of his head. He and mankind were in big trouble and Howard knew it. He wished by some miracle that he could say exactly the right thing so that he could save the Earth, even if it meant his own life would be forfeited. In desperation he clung to the faint hope that maybe, this was really, still, just a dream. Howard raised his fist to the sky. "GOD IN HEAVEN, WHY CAN'T I WAKE UP?!"

He slept in fits and starts, when he slept at all. He felt he needed to sleep. He needed to clear his mind. As he lay in his bed, something flashed in his mind. It was an editorial. It was published soon after the space probe was launched. The title was "Should Mankind Hide?" It dealt with the issue that creatures advanced enough to intercept and decode our space probe would surely be more advanced than us. The rational was that since we just moved into the space age less than two generations ago, the odds are that any civilization advanced enough to understand our message and act on it, would be further evolved technologically. And why should we believe that since we earthlings spend much of our time and energy killing and trying to dominate each other, and would probably try to do it to another civilization less advanced than ours, that they would not do the same to us. Why would we believe that some alien civilization would show benign and altruistic behavior toward us, when we find it difficult, very difficult, to show that kind of behavior toward even our own kind?

When Howard did sleep, he dreamed of the world being annihilated. He saw the landscape strewn with burned and rotting corpses. He could see the destruction all around. He could hear and feel the howling wind that brought the smell and taste of death with it. The dust blew and a screen door slammed with an unnerving clatter that seemed like it would never end. It was horrible. The land was barren, save the debris and remnants of a living world. He felt alone and desolate. He awoke with a start. He sat upright in his bed and stared out into the darkness of the room. "How can I prevent this? How can I convince them not to destroy us? Redeeming value!? Yes, I must convince them that we have some redeeming value. What other hope is there?" Howard thought for a moment then put his head in his hands and began to sob. "How naive I am, redeeming social values—" he berated himself. "Rondo is right, we are pathetic. There is no hope, no hope at all—" Exhausted, Howard finally drifted off to sleep.

The morning brought with it a beautiful sunny day. Howard peered out through his transparent walls. Though the temperature in the room was controlled, he could almost feel the warmth on his face and body and hear the birds singing inside his head. He just stood there transfixed by the moment. But his mood soon turned to melancholy as the reality of this strange planet, with its humanoid inhabitants flooded back into his mind. He did not know where he should direct his thinking. When he thought of home, he felt lonely and depressed, his strained relationship with his wife did not seem so bad from this vantage point. When he thought about these strange people, he felt angry. He was not angry with them, but at that stupid projectile, that "bullet in the brain of humanity," that we launched. He needed to know what was happening, and what was going to happen. He paced the floor of his room. He began throwing things. He picked up what looked like a smooth polished stone and flung it at a "glass" wall. The wall remained intact but he felt his mind shattering and going to pieces. He began walking around in circles. He felt trapped, like a rat in a cage.

Suddenly they appeared at the door. They were the same two that escorted him the time before. He wondered if they would be angry, if he would be punished.

"What is the problem?" the one on the left asked as the door opened.

"I must see Rondo," demanded Howard.

The two conversed, then one of them spoke into a transmitter of some kind. They conversed again and the same one spoke to Howard. "Number 2 will see you."

"That will be fine," said Howard.

They went the same way as before but entered a different room. This room was smaller, with a table and comfortable chairs around it. The room had a warm intimate feeling to it. The walls were covered with something that looked like dark expensive wood paneling but felt like leather. The floor was soft but smooth. The air in the room smelled like flowers and was quite pleasant. As he sat down in one of the chairs he could just barely make out the strains of music coming from somewhere in the room. It was very relaxing, he felt quite at ease. Just then, Number 2 entered.

"How is your mood?" she asked.

Howard didn't reply.

"I heard that you were acting as though you were upset."

"Of course I'm upset. What would you expect after what Rondo said to me?" Number 2 looked like she was about to speak, but Howard beat her to it. "What exactly are your plans for my planet?"

"You will be informed when the time comes."

"You mean when it is too late, after the fact!?"

"Whatever you wish. Before or after, it makes no difference to us."

"Well it makes a great deal of difference to me. I would like to have the opportunity to try to prevent this thing from happening."

"I'm sure you would," said Number 2, "but I highly doubt that it is possible. We do not enjoy destroying things and especially other creatures. Because we are a highly rational people, we do what we know is necessary, and unavoidable, even if it includes those things that are unpleasant. We do have a right to defend ourselves, would you not agree?"

"But we have not attacked you."

"No, not directly. But the foolishness and irresponsibility of your people have gotten you into a quandary and I doubt that you are wise or clever enough to get yourself and your planet out of it."

"Well maybe it isn't unavoidable," pleaded Howard.

"If that is the case then the burden of proof lies with you. And I do not envy you the task."

Howard racked his brain. Maybe there was something about them as a race that would help him. Something about the way they think or their background might hold the key to his salvation. He knew he was grasping at straws, but what choice did he have. "Why me," he began, "of all you could have chosen, why did you pick me?"

"That's simple. It was somewhat random. We wanted someone who knew what was happening, you publish a small newspaper. But we did not want someone too well known as to create too much of a clamor amongst your people. You fit the criteria. You were the lucky one."

"I can't argue with your logic," he admitted. "Can you tell me about your people?"

"What would you like to know?"

"How many of you are there?" Howard asked.

"About two million," she replied.

"We have some cities bigger than that."

"Well as you can see by now we all live in a self-enclosed area and so we must maintain our population below a certain number. Our survival depends on it," she said.

"Do you have the same kinds of problems that we do, like crime, war, hunger and disease?" he asked.

"No," she replied.

"Why is there no war on your planet?"

"For two important reasons: one is that we are self contained so if we create any openings to the outside we would lose our oxygen to breathe and second we are genetically programmed not to do bad things like fighting or hurting each other? Let me ask you, why is there constantly war on your planet?" she taunted.

"I believe that it is the nature of man," he responded.

"Precisely!" she said.

"So you never had war?" he asked.

"Not any longer. We did in the old days."

"How did you rid yourselves of it?"

"War is caused by greed and the need for power. We do not suffer any longer from these vestigial traits. There is no private ownership of anything. Everyone has what he needs. Everyone wears the clothing that he is supposed to wear. There is no need to accumulate anything, particularly wealth. In our land there is nothing to buy, because no one hordes or wastes anything."

"Sounds like Communism. That was tried in our world. It seemed to have helped some people in the beginning, but then it failed. Economically and socially, it failed. I guess if it works for you and has for a long time, then your people must be quite different from us humans."

"That may be true, but that is not the reason. You see we started out with a nature quite similar to yours. That is when we had similar problems."

"Well what happened?" asked Howard anxiously.

"We changed our nature. That is how we solved our problems." Number 2 paused.

"Are you going to make me guess how?"

"Why not, you're doing so well up to now."

"There are only two possibilities that I can think of. One is mind control and the other is gene engineering."

"Not bad for an earthling," she said, smiling mildly. But don't think it was simple. It wasn't. The scientific or genetic part was easy compared to the social aspect. Have you begun this type of work?"

"Yes," said Howard, "but we have hardly scratched the surface. And you are definitely right about the social or moral issues. It seems as though we spend more time arguing about them than progressing the state of the art. How did you deal with the ethical aspects?"

A gleam showed in Number 2's eye. She seemed genuinely happy at the opportunity to tell their story.

Howard looked at her. He wondered how human these people really were. *Do they have sex to reproduce*, he wondered, *or do they hatch from plastic eggs?*

"We were confused and misguided," she began, "as your people are now. We longed to free ourselves from crime, violence and war, we had at that time already conquered disease. But to free ourselves from the social blight we had to strike at its heart. You see greed, jealousy and avarice were rampant. And it was part of our nature, like yours I suspect. The subtle changes we made in the law and enforcement methods were just like putting a small bandage on a serious wound."

"Sounds familiar, we call them Band-Aids," said Howard.

She went on. "We knew that we needed to take more serious and extreme steps to change the situation. We had gone through economic, social, and technological revolutions. We needed a biological revolution. We needed to change our biology. We went as far as we could with psychology, it just scratched the surface. We had to go in and make major repairs. We had to..."

"Change the 'nature of the beast,'" Howard interjected.

35

"Yes, I believe you put it well. We had begun our work in gene engineering in earnest at that time and we soon conclude that it was indeed the only answer. Many people protested, but we had to go forward. We had a plan.

"We limited our initial studies to turning off the aggressiveness in our nature. When we located the genes that were responsible for our aggressive nature we had to restrict the birth of newborn babies to only those who were artificially inseminated. You can imagine what an outcry that created. There was chaos in the first years. Our people had to get used to not conceiving children 'the old fashioned way.' Many of our people actually liked the idea, for obvious reasons. The time of morality in sex was gone. The new generations had no problems. They just learned the new ways from the onset.

"The method was fairly straight forward. We would extract the egg from the mother, obtain sperm from the father, alter the genes in both, fertilize the egg with the sperm and implant the egg into the mother's womb. When you think about it, it may have been very different from the old way, but it was also more precise, and with a higher degree of certainty. The most difficult thing was to keep couples from having children the natural way. We had to resort to sterilizing all the males as soon as they reached puberty. Before sterilization, though, we collected enough sperm from each of them to father more little ones than they would ever have the need or desire to raise. Besides, we began restricting the number of children families could produce, anyway. But let me not get off on a tangent," she said evenly. "The real problem was those damned natural children that would slip by our notice until it was too late. We had a hell of a time getting those young males just at puberty so that we could collect their sperm before sterilizing them. We were forced to issue 'permission' cards to all young males who conformed to the sterilization law, which would allow them to have sex."

"Like needing a driver's license for proof of age in order to drink," added Howard, amused.

Number 2 went on without comment. "Unfortunately, even with strict penalties imposed, and with dubious benefits to gain, the practice of natural sex continued."

"Why was that such a problem?" asked Howard.

"You see," continued Number 2, obviously pleased with the question, "the plan was to allow the existing generations to die out until only those individuals that were made un-aggressive by the process, would be left."

Howard immediately thought of Moses and the Children of Israel roaming

36

the Sinai for forty years, until only the new generation, untainted by the sins of old was left, to enter the Promised Land. "So you wound up with a bunch of *Stepford Wives?*"

"What does that mean?"

"Uniformity, no emotion."

"Emotion, only when appropriate and as you can see, we are not all alike."

Howard glanced at her perfect figure and wondered if she were making a pass at him. *Nah!* he thought, it couldn't be.

Number 2 continued. "The idea was that it would be easier to control the work in the beginning stages if we concentrated on only one aspect of the gene project while we experimented, in this case aggressiveness. Then we went ahead full bore when we felt confident that there was little danger of misusing this awesome tool."

"What were the biggest problems that you encountered?" he asked.

"The biggest problem that we anticipated was the reaction of our people. We had to get this matter of birth control completely under our direction before moving ahead with our plans. The difficulty that we did not anticipate was the severity of the problem of the unaltered children. Instead of making the altered ones super people, it was the unaltered ones, at this stage at least, that had the edge. In fact, the unaltered ones could have become the de facto super race. The new breed, for the most part, lacked aggression, which would have put them almost at the mercy of the older regime. Therefore, we were forced to separate the ones that were not altered from the rest of society. There were two main reasons. One was that left to their own devices the aggressive group would eventually take over our planet. You see, unlike your world, we only have one nation, with one government. And two, by not taking strong measures others would be encouraged to remain unaltered in order to have 'super' children of their own."

"The midwife business must have been booming with all those illegal births," laughed Howard.

"I would think that you are right, but since I wasn't around at the time, that little detail escapes me, but to continue. We had to exile these 'super kids' to their own separate community, with their parents, until they died out. We were determined not to hold up the progress of our plan."

"What happened to these 'super kids?'"

"They lived out their lives fairly comfortably, but not in the mainstream. After all, it was not their fault that their parents were either misguided or unresponsive to our program. And naturally, it was the parents that protested the most, though they only had themselves to blame. They sentenced themselves and their children to a life estranged from society. And the irony of it was that these parents could have had there own children—but altered of course. Well once this problem was under control we could safely get on with the business of completely altering the species. We had to proceed with great caution, since we were dealing with altering life itself. We realized early on that specialization was necessary. We felt comfortable with what we were doing because it was for the good of all the people and no particular group was benefitting more. We calculated, as closely as possible, how many individuals were needed for each job. We gave ourselves some room for error and the unexpected of course. The problem of fashioning ourselves at the management end of the spectrum was the most difficult. The higher up the management ladder we went, the more difficult the task became. We had to blend just the right amount of emotion, sensitivity, aggression, imagination and humility to come out with the 'perfect' manager. Naturally, it took a great deal of trial and error. We got better from generation to generation."

As he listened Howard could not help but imagine an occupational cookbook: start with one lawyer, add one part oration, two parts aggression, one part understanding and a hell of a thick skin. Bake for fifty minutes at 425 degrees and presto, a politician.

Number 2 continued her story. "At this point we saw our purpose as maintaining life on our planet and increasing its quality as much as possible. We were eventually able to replace all the parts of the body, except the brain. It was not that we couldn't replace that mysterious organ but that we neither needed nor desired to replace it. We found that not only could we not match the power of the brain, the way we were using it at the time, but we had not even scratched the surface in understanding and use of its infinite potential. So, we had something far better in its natural state than we could possibly invent or create artificially. But our studies of that gray mass we carry around in our heads were not wasted. We found that it was mainly our emotions and beliefs in our capacities and abilities that kept us from realizing our true mental potential. So we just taught ourselves better how to use the brain we already had, and the problem was solved.

"The mechanics that I have described paved the way for the work of using the tools we had created to enable us to form the society we wanted. We could at this point create the temperament for the infant that we wanted to fill a particular job, by engineering his genes. As the child grows to maturity, it is tutored in the work chosen for it. Just past physical maturity, at the age of twenty-five to be exact, the young person's brain is transferred into an artificial body, also suited for his or her work. Though the process is not painful, it is disorienting." Number 2 smiled, remembering her own experience. "Initially it's like waking up from one dream to find that you are in another. There is a short period of adjustment, but that's basically it. I assure you though, it is less difficult than say, one on your planet getting married, going away to college or beginning a new venture. You see our lives are a great deal less complicated than yours are—by design. We do not inundate ourselves with an unending stream of mixed messages as you earthlings do. Be successful and aggressive, but remember, be nice to the other guy," she mimicked. "Our lives are not like that. They are directed and therefore simple. And we do not get bored, as I'm sure you must be thinking. Boredom is a punishment we used to inflict on ourselves. It isn't even part of our repertoire of feelings any more. We could no more be bored than you could—say, hang by your tail! It doesn't exist for us."

Number 2 paused to let Howard absorb what she had said up until then. Then she continued. "The new bodies are of course synthetic, though you probably could not tell the difference," she said, preening ever so slightly. "It is the lack of imperfections, actually, that gives it away. We grow the skin, bone, muscle, organs, connective tissue and other parts. We then connect it at a microscopic level. "We build the body just before planting the brain into it. We then make all the appropriate connections and test the circuits, so to speak. The procedure works quite well. We only encounter complications in less than one percent of these 'body replacements,' as we call them. Hardly ever is there a fatality. Our life expectancy is greatly enhanced by this procedure. We enjoy a life span of five hundred years, on the average. Our bodies can last a great deal longer than that, but even with the medication we take to preserve our brains, five hundred years is about as long as they function. Actually," she added pensively, "we could probably prolong its function beyond that point, but five hundred years seems adequate, even for us. And of course, we remain lucid to the end. Just so you don't think that life here is all work and no play, we do maintain our pleasures. In addition to the ones that you would probably be familiar with, we do get our clics."

Howard looked at her and smiled. "As in get your *clics* on Route 66?"

"That sounds about right," she returned, going along with the gag.

"By the way, what exactly is clic?"

"It's a rather pleasant feeling."

"Is it as good say, as having an orgasm?"

"Precisely!" she exclaimed. "Did you know that the experience of an orgasm is actually pain in a psychologically positive mode? Just as you could not tell the difference between cold and hot, if you were not looking, pain and pleasure cannot be distinguished except that they are interpreted differently in the brain."

Howard looked at her dubiously.

"Let us suppose," she continued with a knowing smile, "that you were having sex with a ravishing female and just as you were about to experience your climax she dug her nails into your back. Would that give you pleasure or pain?"

"I see what you mean," said Howard. "By the way, if such a female is available I would be pleased to meet her," he added.

"I believe that we have talked enough for one day," said Number 2, ignoring Howard's final remark. "After all, I'm sure you don't want to wear out my brain. I only have three hundred years left."

"Alien humor," said Howard under his breath.

"I do have one more important question to ask."

"What is that?" asked Number 2.

"From the way you describe things now, there would seem like there is no evil or evil doers among your nation."

"So why would that pose a problem?"

"It is not so much a problem as it is odd."

"Odd—in what way?"

"You see, in my business, running a small newspaper, I need to know a lot of things and since I do not have the budget to hire many specialists, I must know these things myself. This would include science, metaphysics and the like. At any rate it is my understanding that nothing exists in the universe without its opposite and I assume that we still are in the same universe as my planet," he said half joking.

"Yes," she said, eyeing him suspiciously.

"This means if there exists good, then there must also be evil, God and the Devil, up and down, man and woman, darkness and light, and so on."

"Yes, what is your point?" she asked.

"If your people only do good, then where is the evil?"

"Maybe you have come along to fill that slot," she smiled.

Howard suddenly looked uncomfortable and was feeling sorry that he had brought up the subject in the first place. *Sometimes I get carried away with myself,* he silently lamented.

"That is enough for now," she declared. She then nodded her head toward Howard, got up, turned and left the room.

Right on cue, the two escorts appeared and took Howard back to his room.

Howard lay in his bed speculating on his future and watching as the light from the twin suns played tricks with the shadows in his room. He thought about how married life would be for one of these creatures. They had no problems of infertility, frigidity or impotence. "But, God," he said aloud, "imagine being married to the same woman for five hundred years!"

Suddenly he heard a young female voice at his entrance. He quickly jumped up and put his pants on. He couldn't wait to see who it was. "Maybe Number 2 sent me that girl who digs her nails in men's backs while having sex."

He walked to the entrance with anticipation. He stood peering at her as the door slid open. She was young and pretty with firm-looking breasts, full lips and sensual thighs. Howard noticed how fresh she smelled, like a bouquet of flowers. He undressed her mentally, while she just stood there saying nothing, as if participating in his fantasy. She wore what looked like a white Roman toga, fastened at the waist with a cord. She appeared to Howard to be in her early twenties. He was certain that he was in love. "Hello. Who are you?" he asked. Not that it really mattered.

"My name is San321," she said sweetly, "but you can call me Sandra. May I come in?"

"Why—yes," he said, beaming.

She smiled warmly, making him feel more relaxed. His heart, however, still beat like a drum, as he wondered with anticipation, why she had come. He smiled back at her, nervously. Just then, a space ship, flying close by, caught his attention. He quickly turned his gaze back to her.

"I have volunteered," she said, "to serve as your guide and companion."

"I guess they plan on keeping me around for a while," he said smiling. *Might as well enjoy it while I can, since there probably won't be any Earth to go back to, even if I were able to leave here,* he thought. "Mind if I ask your age?" he said.

"I'm twenty-four," she answered glumly.

Twenty-four, he reflected. *I'm old enough to be her father.* He laughed to himself thinking how he wouldn't even consider having a relationship or relations with a woman that age, if he were home and single. *Well, I guess I'm single now!* he thought.

"How old are you?" she returned.

He considered lying, but changed his mind. "Forty-seven," he said, hoping that it wouldn't matter to her either. But he began to feel quite foolish as a rather large grin came to her face. "What's the matter? Why are you laughing?" he asked, feeling quite self-conscious.

"I'm not laughing. I'm smiling."

"Whatever. But why?"

"Don't feel bad," she said, "There's nothing wrong. I just wondered how it felt to be over twenty-five and still have your real body."

"Well, you ache a little more than when you're twenty, or even thirty, for that matter, but otherwise about the same. But why the concern? You won't have to worry about that pretty soon."

"But that's the point. I'm afraid of having that operation. What they call— body replacement," she said shuttering.

"But don't you want to live six or seven times longer than normal?"

"But that's just it, I won't be normal. Sure I wouldn't mind, if I didn't have to go through with that—operation."

"I guess the idea could be pretty frightening," he admitted, not knowing if his statement made it better or worse.

"Well it frightens me to death! And I won't do it!"

"Will they force you?"

"I don't know. I'm afraid to ask. I'm afraid to let them know how I feel."

"Does this have anything to do with your volunteering for this 'assignment?'"

"Everything," she said, as she fell to him and began weeping. "I hoped that you might understand."

"Yes, the others did seem different somehow. I could not quite put my finger on it. You seem so much more like a real human than they do. Do you think that something else is lost when they replace your body?"

"Yes," she said pointedly, "those I know, of similar age, who have not yet gotten the operation, are somehow different from those who have. My friends think that it is my imagination and others say that I am just a coward or that I am too sensitive. I am sensitive, that is why I can tell that something is lost during the process. Something is missing from those who have it done. They act the same, but I can *feel* that something essential has changed, at their core, their essence."

He held her, lost in her world and forgetting his own pain for the moment. His intentions alternated from father figure to suitor. He fell for her and he found her very attractive. He knew that it would be very hard to resist her passions. He was torn. Was this some sort of setup? What could they be after? She seemed to be on the level. Or, was it all an act? Were they watching the whole thing? What was their game? And did it really matter after all?

CHAPTER THREE

The doorbell at the Cooper residence rang three times before Maureen could open it for her impatient visitor. "Oh, hi, chief," she said sullenly. "Anything yet about Howard?"

Police Chief Dick Lynch looked evenly at Maureen. "May we come in?"

"Sure, Chief," she said, opening the door just wide enough to allow him and Officer Larson to pass.

The Cooper house was a modest colonial, white with four bedrooms upstairs, two and a half baths and a partially finished basement. Howard always wanted a pool table and a sit down wet bar but just never got around to it. The house sat on a half acre with an in-ground swimming pool and a high hedge surrounding the property. They lived on a quit street, that is except for the Fourth of July, when the fireworks were going off well into the night.

They entered the hallway and headed toward the living room. Maureen stared blankly as they went by. Lynch was a hulking fellow at six-three, 250 pounds. Men like him often went a little more out of their way to act polite toward non-combatants, especially women and children. Larson was younger. Though also built a little larger than average, he was not at all intimidating like Lynch. He also had a more relaxed, natural way with people.

Maureen asked them to sit when they got to the living room. Lynch wanted to stand but thought it would make Maureen more comfortable if they did as she asked. Maureen sat on the loveseat facing them. As Lynch spoke, he leaned forward. "Some kids found a set of keys in the open field off Elm Street," he said, handing them to her.

"These can't be Howard's," she answered without being asked.

"Are you sure?"

"Howard always had a habit of twirling his keys around his index finger after leaving the car; it was just a something he did," she added

44

absentmindedly.

"But are they Howard's?" he asked again, trying to be patient.

"Oh my God, yes, Chief—they are!—But how can they be Howard's if he's gone and so is the car. How do you drive a car without keys?"

"I don't know, but I'm sure we'll find out soon enough."

Maureen's mind drifted to Howard and how happy they were when they were dating. How they went to the drive-in every Friday night and made love in the back seat, and never got to see the show....

"Maybe someone kidnapped Daddy," interjected Christine.

"But why would they take the car without the keys, or why take the car at all?" asked Maureen.

"Maybe some Martians came down and took Daddy and his car away in a space ship," offered John with pride.

"Don't be stupid," said Christine, using her most condescending tone on her eleven-year-old brother. "There are no such things as Martians. You're so dumb"

"How do you know? There could be aliens; we talk about them in school."

Maureen's mind began to drift again, back to Howard. It was always Maureen and then his work. Then it became more his work and less her. *Why do marriages get weaker and devotion to work stronger as people get older?* she wondered.

"—the only alien around here is you!" continued Christine. "Mommm, shut this brat up, please? Before I send him to Mars, with all his alien CRAP!"

"Christine, watch your language. Sorry, Chief. Children today," she said, with an embarrassed smile.

"Well, we'd better be going," said Lynch, starting to rise from the couch.

"Chief, do you think Howard will show up?"

"I'm sure he will," he said, sitting back down, "they usually do. He hasn't even been gone forty-eight hours. Maybe it's his mid-life crisis. Some men at this age just have to find themselves. And they're bound to do strange things at these times. I'm sure you'll hear from him soon."

"But to leave like that—it's just not like Howard. And what about the keys, don't you agree, Chief?"

"I guess you're right—it does seem a bit strange—but who knows."

They sat silently for a moment. "We have to go now, we'll just let ourselves out."

"Thank you for your help, Chief." Lynch nodded.

They walked to the car without speaking. The sun was almost down, but it was still glaring. Lynch paused by the passenger door to put his sunglasses on. He wore the mirrored type, which only increased his intimidating presence. A squirrel chased another across the loan and two small birds dive bombed toward the hood of the car but pulled up in plenty of time to avoid the collision.

They got into the car and drove off toward the station house. "Do you really think it's his mid-life crisis?"

"Not really, Bob."

"Then what?"

"I hate to admit it, but it beats the crap out of me! Doesn't mean I'm giving up, though, just because I'm stumped. Facts, that's what we need, Bob, facts! Now, I want you to do three things for me starting tomorrow—" Just then a souped-up Chevy and its young driver zoomed passed. "Son-of-a-bitch! Did you see who that was, Bob?"

"No, but I can follow him, Chief."

"Oh, never mind," he said in frustration, "we have more important things to take care of. First, I want you to check around the area where the keys were found, and I mean thoroughly. Second, start looking for Cooper's car—any similar make and model. Maybe it was stolen and repainted or something. And third, ask Mrs. Cooper—no never mind, I'll take care of that myself. I'm going to take personal charge of this investigation."

Larson dropped Lynch off in front of the station house and continued home. Lynch went into the station, nodded to the officer on duty and walked directly toward his office. As he opened the door, he turned back to the officer. "I don't want to be disturbed unless it is absolutely necessary." The officer silently nodded his acknowledgment. Lynch felt that he could think better at night, especially when he was not bothered. Sometimes he would doze off, but that would just help him think more clearly. The brief snooze helped refresh his mind.

"Now let me see," he started. "Cooper was last seen by his wife two nights ago, when he took the car to go out for some ice cream. That was between 8:30 p.m. and 9:00 p.m. Then bluey: no more Cooper, no more car, and a set of his keys are found in an open field. Huh, pretty strange. He was well liked. His marriage seemed basically okay, and there has been no ransom or suicide note found."

Lynch stretched, shook his head, got up and walked out of the station house. He drove directly home and forgot the matter for the evening. The next morning he drove himself to the Cooper house to talk to Maureen again. He opened the gate in their fence, strode up the walk, straight to the front door and rang the bell. As she opened the door, he could see that she was in better spirits than the day before.

"There are just a few more details that I want to cover with you, Maureen, so that we can get as good a start on the thing as possible," he said as she led him toward the living room. "The sooner we get going in the right direction the better."

Maureen had sort of a dreamy look that morning. She was fresh from the shower and looked quite attractive in her light summer dress. Lynch caught himself thinking about her in *that* way. *Women always seem more alluring when they are vulnerable,* Lynch thought.

"Is there anything unusual going on in your life or Howard's at this time?"

"Nothing in particular."

"I know this is difficult, but do you think that Howard is seeing another woman?"

"Anything is possible, of course, but I would be very surprised."

"Is your relationship okay?"

"Not great, but okay, but then, whose is? Let's put it this way, he wasn't complaining."

"I see. He wasn't writing any special article that could get him in trouble, like investigative reporting into drug trafficking or anything like that?"

"Not that I know of. And I still can't understand about the keys."

"Well," said Lynch, "he could have made up a second set and not told you about it. But was there anything else, anything at all?"

There was a long silence, while Maureen fidgeted. Lynch looked at her patiently, not saying anything. "Well there was something, but only if it's kept off the record."

"I decide what's on or off the record."

"Then I have your word?"

"You have it. What is it?"

"Wait here." Maureen left the room and return minutes later with a bound notebook, like grade school children use. "It's Howard's—diary—or something. He writes things in it—notes to himself," she said, opening it up to the last entry and handing it to Lynch. Lynch read: *Whirring noise in open field off Elm, check for UFO evidence and sightings.* "What do you think?" she asked.

Lynch had a strange, serious look on his face, but said nothing. He rose, keeping the same expression. "Can I have this?" he finally asked.

"I can't," said Maureen. "Howard would kill me. There's a lot of personal stuff in there. Besides, you have what you need."

"Okay, but make sure you hold on to it. Keep it in a safe place, in case we need it later."

"Fine, Chief. What do you think happened?"

"I'll call you as soon as we have anything."

"Remember, you said it was off the record. I don't want Howard embarrassed about this UFO stuff."

"You have my word. And—don't tell anyone else—even the kids." He left, got into his car and headed back to the station house.

As he entered the station, the officer on duty stopped him. "Chief, Bob is waiting for you in your office."

Lynch opened the door expectantly and walked to his desk. "What is it, Bob? I hope it's good." As Lynch sat down, he noticed that Larson had a slightly bemused look on his face. "Well what is it, Bob?" he repeated.

"Well, Chief—"

"Spit it out, man! And what the hell is that lump of metal that you have there?"

Larson stared down at the round, metal lump on the hand truck. "Well," he began haltingly, "I can't swear what it is, but I found it next to the curb near where Cooper's keys were found. I didn't pay much attention to it the first time we were out there, but you said check everything. It's pretty heavy. In fact, it's very heavy. That's what caught my attention." The lump was round and about thirty inches in diameter.

"What the hell is this thing?" ask Lynch as he came over and tried to push it. "Jeeesus, this thing must weigh a ton."

"Two thousand nine hundred eighty-six pounds to be exact."

"Twothousandninehundredeightysix—p-o-u-n-d-s. That's as much as a—car!"

"Cooper's car to be exact. I checked it out, too."

"Someone is going to be in a great deal of trouble, if they are trying to make a fool out of ME!" Lynch shouted, his voice rising in intensity as he spoke.

"What do you think is going on, Chief?"

"I don't know yet, but when I do someone's balls will be sitting in my out basket!"

Larson started to leave with the hand truck and the metal lump. "Leave that here, Bob. I don't want anyone else to know about this. Got that?"

"Yes, Chief." Larson started walking out, but turned at the door. "Anything else you want me to do on this case?"

"No, Bob, I'll handle it from here. And by the way, good job!" Larson left pleased.

Lynch sat for a moment, then got up and walked out of his office. "I'm going down to the newspaper office, if anyone wants me!" he shouted as he left. "And I'm walking, I need the air," he said, mostly to himself.

He marched into the front door of *The Daily Pride* as though he was going to catch them at something. Everyone nodded politely at him, almost as though he were expected.

The newspaper staff consisted of, in addition to Howard, Kevin Briggs, reporter and for the moment acting editor, a part-time reporter named Ed, who also ran the press and a printer's devil. Lynch went right over to Briggs. "Hi, Chief. Anything yet on Howard?" he asked with concern in his voice.

Lynch just stared at him for a moment. "Would you mind stepping into Howard's office, I'd like to talk to you in private."

"Certainly, Chief," answered Briggs, slightly puzzled. "What's going on?"

Lynch sat in the chair behind Howard's desk, with Kevin in the chair, facing him. He eyeballed the reporter again. "I hoped that you might be the one to shed some light on the situation, Kevin."

"I don't know what you're talking about, Chief."

"Well someone had better know what I'm talking about, because I'm getting real pissed off!"

"Well, I'm sorry that you're pissed off, Chief, but I don't know any more than you, and probably a lot less."

Lynch let out a frustrated breath of air, and looked slightly apologetic. "Well, unfortunately, it sounds like you're telling the truth. I guess I was a little rough with you."

"It's okay, we all have those days."

"That's true. But that's not the problem. Problem is, the way things look, someone is perpetrating a hoax. And if they are, and you guys are mixed up in it, maybe to sell more newspapers or somethin', the law, meaning me, is going to look mighty unkindly on it. But, if you are tellin' the truth, like you claim, then we are looking at some way-out-shit going on here. I mean, way out shit! Like flying saucers, and little green men and all that crapola? Now I don't exactly believe in all that nonsense. But it sure as hell is pointing in that direction. And I guess if somehow, and some way, this turns out to be the situation, there is no way that this momma's child is going to take the rap for not at least following it up to some kind of dead end or other hard conclusion."

"Well, if I can be of any help, Chief—"

"Two things you can do. First, if you tell anyone about this *your ass is grass*. Second, you can tell me anything that might have transpired around the time of Howard's disappearance that might have some relevance."

"Well if you're talking about why Howard disappeared, as I said, I can't really help. If you're talking about flying saucers, there was a reported sighting in the area the day before Howard disappeared."

"That's right," said Lynch, rubbing his chin. "I remember reading about that a couple of days ago. Wasn't it old Mamie Johnson who reported it?"

"That's right."

"Well I don't know if she can be of any help. Did you talk to her?"

"Yes I did, and you're right. She just said she saw something that looked like a flying saucer. No other details—wait a minute, there's some air force colonel—er Robert Jones, he supposedly knows something about these things. At least we have to report every sighting to him before it comes out in the paper."

"Bob Jones! Shooot, I know that old son-of-a-bitch. Haven't seen his ugly mug in a 'coon's age. I guess ol' Bobby and I might as well have a little talk. Well, Kevin, Bob Jones may just be the dead end I need. No one's going to complain after I get an official denial from the military, will they?"

The morning air was sweet, one of those days when you're glad to be alive, even if you're normally not. The sunlight was almost blinding, and you could feel the warmth on your chest when you stood out in it. As Lynch's Ford Bronco sped down the interstate, he yawned and stretched holding the wheel with his knees. "Damn military people," he said to himself, still yawning, "always start so damn early in the morning. Christ, I'm glad I became a civilian when I did!" It was six o'clock and Lynch's meeting with Colonel Jones was for eight. That gave him two hours to cover roughly one hundred and ten miles.

The two went back all the way to grammar school. But when Jones went on to prep school, the two saw less of each other, mostly holidays and summers. Jones was admitted to the Air Force Academy. Lynch's ambitions were not quite as lofty. He joined the marines right out of high school and went on to do two tours in Vietnam, reaching the rank of staff sergeant, before he retired and joined the local police force where he eventually made it to chief.

Lynch could never figure out how Jones made it through the academy. Getting in, he could understand, Jones' family had pull, but he wasn't that bright in school, as Lynch remembered. *The son-of-a-bitch always knew how to get his way, though, he always knew how to look good, a real image guy,* Lynch thought, *I guess that can get you through almost anything.* Lynch did Jones a couple of favors over the years, never hurt to have a police chief for a friend. So, old Bobby owed him one, at least.

Jones made "bird colonel" at forty-one, which was quite an accomplishment in the Air Force. He was an ambitious man. *He always knew what he wanted,* thought Lynch. Even as a kid, Jones always talked about flying and being a big shot in the Air Force.

As Lynch drove down the long dusty road leading to the base he wondered what the next seventy-hours held.

Colonel Jones was handsome enough as it was, but seeing him in uniform, got women particularly excited. At forty-five he had one of those faces that made him look mature at twenty-two and would likely keep him looking great through his sixties. At six foot one, one hundred and eighty pounds he was a lean, mean, fighting machine. He was a strict disciplinarian, and he didn't take shit from anyone. His father was a businessman with many political contacts and his mother was a full-time housewife and a part-time alcoholic. He had an older sister, who doted on him, as did his mother. The two women relied on each other and spoke every day. His father also favored Robert and sister's doting was her primary way of winning approval from her parents. Rooting for brother Bob was the most popular sport in the Jones household. Sister's resentment had to be swallowed graciously.

Bob was politically shrewd and very ambitious. He was not a man to be taken lightly, and he usually wasn't, but he always seemed to act the gentleman and say the right thing.

"Chief Lynch is here to see you, sir," spoke the voice over the intercom.

"Send him in, Sergeant," responded Jones.

Lynch entered slowly with a warm but weary smile.

"Dick, how the hell are yer?" asked Jones, accentuating his down home Texas twang. "Keepin' all them housewives in Arlington happy, are yer? You old cunt hound!"

"Jesus, look who's talking," shot back Lynch.

Jones just smiled back. "Shit, I sometimes regret not having a job like yours. You bein' out on your own all day, fuckin' around and checkin' under some dainty lady's bed to make sure that some old boogieman ain't hiding out there, waiting to jump her bones. I bet some of them can get mighty grateful for the extra service you show them." He laughed again, harder this time.

"Stick it in your ear, Jones. Looks like middle age hasn't mellowed you out much. You're just the same old delightful son-of-a-bitch I always knew."

"Well some things just never change," he said with a note of sarcasm. "Besides, why mess with a winning formula, I say. Anyway, what's all this hollering about UFOs? Did one of the locals have a close encounter with his third bottle of muscatel or something?"

"Not exactly. I'm sure you know about the recent sighting, but you get those all the time I'm told. Whether or not you check them out is something else again." Jones gave Lynch a funny look. "But it's more than that this time. Right about the time of the sighting, our newspaper publisher, Howard Cooper, disappeared, under some hokey circumstances. Let's put it this way, if there were a flying saucer and it did kidnap Cooper, it would explain a great deal of what happened.

"Hum, that's very interesting," said Jones, rubbing his chin. "Would you like some coffee?"

"Sure, black," said Lynch.

"So how can I help you?—Sergeant," he said into his intercom before Lynch could respond, "two black coffees please, and hold all calls for anything short of World War III." He looked up at Lynch and smiled slightly.

"I'd like to know what you know about UFOs," said Lynch.

"Is that all?" he asked with a note of irony in his voice."

"That's all," replied Lynch in a similar tone.

"Well I'm sorry. If that's what you came for, you are going to have to leave disappointed."

"Why?"

"Because it's classified, that's why."

"I have a top secret clearance from the Marine Corps."

"Look," said Jones, losing his patience, "your clearance has probably lapsed. Besides, you don't have a need to know and my balls could be in the meat grinder if anyone got wind of my talking to you. And remember, loose lips sink ships—"

"—And the cow jumped over the moon, and fleas have balls, and money talks and shit walks! Please, spare me the nursery rhymes. I have a need to know." Beads of sweat stood out on Lynch's top lip, which he unconsciously wiped with his sleeve. I have an important man in the community missing, under very strange circumstances and who knows what will be next. It's localized now and it's in my bailiwick, so I need to know!"

Just then, the sergeant walked in with the coffee.

Jones picked up his coffee, slowly sipped a little, carefully put it down on his desk and looked straight at Lynch. "You have a hell of an argument there, but I just can't discuss it. Frankly, it's out of my control," he said, almost whispering, to imply that Lynch was hearing a secret.

Lynch mimicking Jones, put his coffee down just as slowly, leaned forward and in the same whispering tone said, "Fine!" Then his voice returned to its normal pitch and volume as he rose as if to leave. "I'll just tell my story to someone else. I'm sure there are plenty of interested parties inside the military and out. And the next occurrence of a similar nature will not be the privileged information of Colonel Robert Jones. If you hear about it at all, it will be in the papers. And won't your superiors just be curious to know why you didn't know this information first? They may figure that you're *losing your grip*. Perhaps, someone else would be better qualified to handle this important assignment."

"All right, all right, keep your shirt on. You're just bound and determined to get my ass in trouble, one way or another, aren't you?"

"I wouldn't say that, Bobby," said Lynch, determined. "Just doing what they pay me to do, that's all."

Jones rubbed his square chin and stared at Lynch intently for a moment. "If any of this gets out we can both kiss our asses goodbye."

"You don't have to worry about me. My lips are as tight as a virgin's snatch."

"Famous last words," said Jones, wiping his mouth nervously.

Two hours later Lynch got into his car and drove off the base.

CHAPTER FOUR

Sandra wondered how Howard would be as a sex partner. She found him a little strange and indecisive, compared to her people, but she liked him anyway. In fact, maybe that was why she liked him so much. She was happy that she met him. It would be nice to have someone to *really* talk to, someone who understood. She had made a decision, before meeting Howard that no matter what happened, she would not spend the first night with him. She was given a quick lesson in human morals and didn't want Howard to think too little of her; she would hold out as long as possible. She got up to start her day.

Howard awoke with his love muscle in a little more amorous condition than usual. He was disappointed that he did not make love to Sandra, but he was willing to wait; what choice did he have. With the news of Earth's destruction imminent, he could use all the pleasure and diversion he could get. Anything to ease the pain in his mind of the holocaust that was coming was welcome. Sandra was sweet and sincere, and she needed him. *At least my life can serve some noble purpose, even if it's in this God forsaken place,* he concluded, ironically.

Just then, Sandra's voice came floating at him. It was her voice and face on their version of a picture-phone. He jumped up to say hello, then realizing he had no clothes on, turned his back and ran out to put his pants on. He heard her laughing as he scrambled around in confusion. He came back to the picture-phone flushed with embarrassment. He wasn't quite certain which was worse, his nudity or his fumbling around. At any rate, Sandra was enjoying the show immensely.

"Did you see anything?" he asked, trying to regain his composure.

"Why should I tell, that would only ruin the fun."

"Well at least I know you have a sense of humor," he said smiling. "Am I going to see you today?"

"You see me now and I've seen more of you than I expected already." She paused for effect. "I'm teasing, I'll be over in a little while. I'll give you enough time to—pull yourself together." She laughed.

"God, it's nice to hear laughter again," he said aloud, "even if it is at my expense."

He was all smiles when she appeared at the door. She looked so pretty and fresh. He walked to her tentatively, not quite certain how she would respond. He bent forward and kissed her on the cheek. She smiled and he hugged her warmly and she hugged him back. She felt so good in his arms; it made him think about how this had been missing between him and Maureen for the last few years. He yearned for that feeling again.

"Do you want to know where we're going today?" she whispered.

He felt like a school kid. He let her go and just looked at her for a moment. "Where are we going?" he asked sweetly.

"To my special place," she said glowing. Sandra took Howard by the hand and led him out of the apartment and down the corridor. They walked for a while. They did not pass many other people on their way. They seemed to be going to a very remote part of the city. Then they turned through a passageway toward the outer perimeter of the city. He could see the natural sunlight growing stronger as they got closer. Finally, they came to what looked like a terrarium for people. It was a beautiful garden, with flowers, birds and insects flying around. The smell and colors filled Howard's senses. He felt intoxicated. He just stood there for a moment taking it all in.

Just then, what appeared to be a butterfly, sailed by them. He could not suppress the feelings of euphoria that welled up in him. She shared his emotion as though it passed directly from him, through their clasped hands and into her. It occurred to Howard that he had not experienced these natural things this way even when at home. He had been around natural settings all his life, but for some reason they had never filled his senses the way this did. He wondered why.

They walked a little saying nothing. He wanted to say something to her but no words came. Their hands seemed to form a permanent link between them. He turned to say something, but when he saw her look, he grabbed her and pulled her close. Their kiss was slow and passionate. They sat down on a bench and held each other for a while without speaking. Then Sandra got up, and looked down at Howard. "Come with me," she said, extending her hand. He almost felt like a child being taken for a walk. He followed gladly.

They arrived at her apartment. Howard's heart was pounding. She turned on some music and offered him a drink of some sort, but it was not their liquefied food. "What is this?" he asked, trying not to sound like he was afraid to drink it, but just curious.

"You might call it a love potion," she said with coquettish look. "But we use it as your people use alcohol in these situations, to relax with."

"How do you know so much about my people?"

"When our ship went down to capture an earthling, it first went to one of your libraries and we read all the books, or more precisely recorded the information from those books."

"But how did you learn all this information, I mean personally?"

"We are taught to use our brains very close to the maximum. Our 'schools,' if you can truly call them that, are nothing like yours. We learn in an extremely rapid fashion. We do it both visually and auditorily. It's quite pleasant, actually."

As she spoke Howard drank. Although the subject matter she discussed was of a non-erotic nature, Howard was getting turned on. She looked at him and easily interpreted the silly look on his face. She began to walk slowly toward her bedroom; as she got to the doorway, she gave him a come hither look over her right shoulder.

"I guess women are all the same, all over the universe," he said, laughing to himself as he quickly followed her.

Her body was as flawless and well proportioned as he had imagined. He was in heaven. He wondered if it were engineered into their genes or if it had just been that long since he had seen the nude body of a twenty-four-year-old woman. After they made love, they lay there holding each other. "Can they see us?" he asked.

"Impossible," she said, laughing lightly.

"Why is it impossible?"

"It is prohibited by law."

"Just like that, they can't cheat or anything?"

"What does cheat mean? I do not understand this word."

"I bet Rondo does," he said under his breath.

"What did you say?" she asked.

"Nothing you would care to know about," he said, holding her close. They made love again. Howard lay there watching as Sandra got up to go to the bathroom.

He thought about Maureen and whether or not she would understand. The chances of seeing her again were almost nonexistent. How long before she would be with another man? Would the world last that long? Sandra came back to bed and they both went to sleep.

As they awoke, a little fury creature came toward them on the bed. Howard was startled by it although it looked like a walking fluff ball.

"Woowoo," Sandra sighed, "where have you been hiding? Did this strange earthling scare you?" She laughed.

Howard gave Sandra a look. "What is that?" he asked, knitting his brow.

"Woowoo is my 'comfort creature,' oh yes you don't have them on Earth."

"Well, we have pets. The more common kind like dogs and cats, have less fur and more body."

"Are they engineered and bred to be of comfort to their owner?" she asked.

"No, they just happen to be that way; that is why we choose them as pets."
She laughed. "How quaint."

"Well it may be quaint," he said, trying to affect a slight pout, "but it is the way it is on Earth. We have not perfected gene engineering as you have."

"Too bad, you must be missing a great deal. Do you have any creatures like Fred?"

"What's a Fred?"

Just then, something resembling a chimpanzee strode into the room. "Howard, meet Fred." Howard almost felt himself obliged to reach out and shake its hand; it appeared so natural standing there.

"Another 'comfort creature?'"

"Oh no, Fred is my 'habit creature.' Go ahead, ask him for something."

"Does he bite?" Sandra looked at him. "Only joking," said Howard, eyeing Fred, as though he were not sure. "Only kidding, Fred," he added, smiling. Fred smiled back like a very naive and trusting child. "Did I hurt his feelings?"

"Oh no, he hasn't any, except positive ones. Woowoo, you stroke," she said, demonstrating. "And Fred, you compliment. Nice job, Fred." Fred smiled even broader.

"Any other surprises? Is your cook a female gorilla?"

"I don't have a cook. Why don't you come into the living room and relax?"

He sat down in a comfortable chair. A few moments later Fred walked in carrying a tray of refreshments.

"Thanks, Fred, you're quite a guy!" said Howard, flashing an exaggerated smile. Fred beamed. Howard shook his head as the fur clad "butler" turned toward the kitchen.

"Lean back and relax," suggested Sandra, coming up from behind. "Maybe this will help," she said, turning on what appeared to be a lamp.

The light had a very soothing effect on him. He could not quite understand the sensation that came over him as he felt the warmth of the light engulf his senses.

Sandra smiled as she watched the predictable response. "You like my 'love light' I see."

"Love light," he said, looking directly into it. His eyes did not hurt at all. He wondered why. The sensation became even stronger. "Do you ever make love in the 'love light?'" he asked. She laughed without answering.

He stayed and they had dinner together. "You had better go back to your place now," she said, holding him. "It is not that I don't want to have you stay. It is just that I don't want those in charge to think that I am growing too attached to you. I could lose my objectivity. My people have little tolerance for sentiment. They understand it; it's just considered—not useful, in most situations. I just don't want to ruin our chances of being together in the future. We can help each other. But we must first do what is required of us. I will see you soon. Please kiss me and leave."

There was more than just the physical pleasure of her body that attracted Howard to Sandra. He saw in her some hope for the future. Hope for the old way. She had a zeal for life and a fragile fear of the unknown that was most human-like. She was a rebel. She wanted to live her way. The fact that she was willing to buck the system impressed him a great deal.

"There is something about you that reminds me of home," he said, looking into her eyes.

"There is something about you that doesn't," she responded, smiling.

"We will work this out somehow. I promise."

He kissed her again.

"You must go now," she said, holding him.

"I can't if you don't let go." They laughed. He looked at her again, then turned and left.

"What have you found out?" Rondo asked Number 2.

"More of the same, I'm afraid. These Earth creatures seem to be intent on causing their own destruction, even without our help. The situation is actually worse than we originally thought. They are constantly sending out transmissions as though they either are already in contact with other civilizations or, as Howard claims, are constantly seeking contact. This makes the situation even more urgent. First, we must assume that they have tracked the probe to our planet. Secondly, we must find out the true purpose of their transmissions, and third, and most importantly, if they are already in contact with other civilizations."

"Yes, we must know if we are in danger. And, if they have contacted others, which ones? Can we defend ourselves against these others or must we flee? The hardships will be great, unless we stop their communications in time, if it is not already too late. It would be an easy enough matter to destroy their primitive world, but we must first get the information we seek. Any aliens that may be in contact with Earth may have finessed these simpletons into telling them where there are other friendly worlds, so that the alien predator's prize may be that much greater.

"We must send another ship down to Earth. Perhaps we can use their only moon for cover. From that vantage point we can monitor their transmissions, find out what has transpired up till now and calculate the most elegant way to be done with these infernal trouble makers."

"Very well, I will contact the Supreme Warrior General, Titus, right now. She hit the communication button.

"This is Supreme Warrior General Titus at your service," came the response as visual and audio contact was made.

"General," said Rondo, "we are now ready to proceed with the resolution of the problem of the alien probe. You will ready your ship, including all personnel necessary for such a delicate mission. You must carefully calculate the best form of destruction. Before execution, though, we need to seek out and determine information that will allow us to know which other planets, if any, know of our existence and location, through contact with the earthlings. Our very existence may be at stake.

"I understand."

"Furthermore, you must bear in mind that such methods as vaporizing their planet may be dangerous to their entire solar system. There is always the risk of creating an imbalance in the system, if their planet were suddenly gone! Perhaps a method of destroying the earthlings, without disturbing the other innocent creatures on the planet, would be both practical and humane."

"I understand."

"And no execution of any final plan shall take place until I have personally given the order."

"Yes, Rondo, I comprehend your intentions and shall carry out your instructions to the letter."

"I am certain that you will, General."

The trip to Earth took two weeks at hyper speed. They used the moon as a convenient jumping off point. They would orbit around this satellite of earth and try to avoid detection while conducting their operations. Only one ship was used in this operation. It carried everything necessary for its assignment. The ship itself was spherical and had a diameter of one hundred yards. Most of the ship's personnel maintained its functions. The others were on board to conduct experiments as to the physical nature of the Earth and its inhabitants. Also on board was a small team of 'investigators.'

The general gazed at the blue and white sphere of Earth beneath him and wondered what these creatures might be doing and if they had any inkling of what the future held for their race.

Herb looked at the general and just smiled. The general smiled back. Herb was the general's habit creature and was not capable of comprehending the thoughts passing through the general's mind. The general, for his part, was not capable of true emotion, as humans experience it. That attribute was not deemed necessary to the general's makeup.

The ship's crew busied themselves with their mission. Meanwhile, 238,000 miles away on Earth, the human race went about its business without being the slightest bit aware of its inevitable fate. Or was it?

CHAPTER FIVE

Chief Lynch made the trip back to Arlington in two hours flat. It took him all that time to get the thing straight in his head. *So the military really does believe in UFOs, well I'll be damned. I wonder if I could arrest one of those suckers for speeding or something, or do aliens have diplomatic immunity? He laughed to himself. Now, how do I explain this to everyone who's interested, without making an ass out of myself? I guess I just make up a bullshit story and say that I've reached a dead end. Anyway, who's going to know the difference? I mean, no one is going to blame me if Cooper just happens to show up in a flying saucer one day. No one can possibly expect me to believe in flying saucers, even if they do exist. But what the hell am I going to tell Maureen? Do I say: Maureen, your eleven-year-old son is right, Howard was taken away by little green men in a flying saucer? Not likely. I'll just have to tell her the same bullshit story that I tell everyone else. Besides, I don't know for certain what did happen to Cooper. All the evidence we have up to now is circumstantial at best. If flying saucers do exist, that doesn't mean one actually snatched him…does it?.*

I'll just tell everyone that the two-ton lump sitting in my office is a meteorite. What I won't tell them is that it started out as a car when it entered the atmosphere, and that it was originally a fifty-seven Chevy driven by greasers from another planet. What the hell, it does make for a great conversation piece.

Three Weeks Later

Colonel Jones sat behind his desk with an intent look on his face, reviewing the paperwork on the UFO sightings. "That son-of-a-bitch better keep his mouth shut or he'll disappear, and it won't be Martians either! That damn Lynch is a pain in my butt, always was. I hate cops anyway, always nosing around."

Jones leaned back in his chair. "I wonder if this guy really did get snatched. Jesssusss Christ, what a story that would be! I can see the headlines now: Editor of Local Newspaper Kidnapped by Little Green Men. I wonder what those buggers really look like. Little green men! Hey do 'little green men' have pistachio nuts?"

Jones started laughing as his phone began to ring. As he lifted the receiver he looked up at the clock, it was half-past-six. His wife Helen was on the phone. "Bob, General Maddox just called. I guess he thought you'd be home by now. He asked me to call you. He said that you should come home immediately and call him from here. It sounded urgent. What do you think it's about?"

"Well, I guess I'll know when I call him. Won't I?"

She let the sarcasm pass, as she usually did. "Should I have dinner waiting for you?"

"Yes. I'm leaving right now," he said, hanging up.

Major General John Maddox was in charge of the operation that monitored the UFO activity throughout the United States. When Jack called, it was important. He was not one to take lightly. What Jones did not know was that the other nine officers, that shared his responsibility around the country, were also being contacted. They all reported directly to Maddox, and Maddox to the chairman of the Joint Chiefs of Staff, on all matters relating to the UFO issue.

Maddox wasn't a bad guy, once you got to know him. And if you got to know him, it was usually by "hoisting a few" at the officers' club. The guy could drink you under the table, close his eyes for five minutes, wake up and walk away as though he hadn't had one all night. In order to earn his respect and friendship you had to attempt, at least, to keep up with him. He didn't want any "pussys" under his direct command.

Jones pulled into his driveway and entered the front door. He took off his jacket and began to climb the stairs leading to his bedroom. Helen hearing the car came out of the kitchen to greet him and caught him at the base of the stairs. "Your dinner's ready."

"I'll be right down," he said curtly, without losing a stride.

"I'll keep it warm."

He entered the bedroom and dialed the phone. "General Maddox, please—Yes I'll hold."

"General, yes I just got home. Helen told me it was important—I see—

That urgent. I'm packing now, sir."

Jones hung up, threw a couple of suitcases on the bed and began to pack. Just then, Helen entered the room.

"What's going on?"

"I have to leave immediately. There's a plane waiting for me right now. Do me a favor and call for a driver for me, please."

"What about your dinner?"

"No time."

She looked at him. He glared back. "Okay, I'll call."

She was standing and waiting for him as he got to the bottom of the stairs. "Your driver is here. How long will you be gone?"

"I don't know. I'll call you as soon as I can."

She opened the front door for him. He kissed her lightly as he went by. She stood there watching as the driver helped him with the suitcases. She was still by the open door as they drove off into the cold drizzle of the evening, Jones never looking back.

A plane was sitting on the runway waiting for the colonel to arrive. Also waiting was Jones' assistant. The rain had increased its intensity and the driver held a black umbrella over the colonel's head.

Captain Jeffrey Smyth's tall, thin figure came out of the darkness as he helped the colonel with his bags. "I didn't know you were invited," said Jones smiling.

"General Maddox's people called me about an hour ago."

"How thoughtful of Jack. Looks like this is more serious than I thought. Your gear on board?"

"Yes, sir."

"Good. Let's go then."

The two sat side by side with Smyth at the window and Jones on the aisle. It was becoming difficult to see out of the rain-streaked window. Smyth peered silently out into the chilled night as the driver stood holding his umbrella and watching as the twin prop airship disappeared into the bleak evening sky.

They sat in a large room with semicircular rows of permanent desks facing a small stage with a rostrum. It looked like a university lecture room with the lecturer's platform larger than expected. Colonel Jones, his nine counterparts and their assistants filled the first two rows. They all anxiously awaited the start of the session.

It was three minutes shy of eight hundred hours as a small group entered the room. To the surprise of most of the attendees, they emptied the platform and quickly left themselves. Then, after what seemed like an interminable pause, came the deliberate and determined stride of General John Maddox. He stopped at center stage and faced the men. After looking each officer in the eye he said: "Gentlemen and ladies, the party is over! This cushy assignment, which you have enjoyed for the past four years, will, from this moment forward, cease to exist as you know it. This planet is in trouble. Which means our country is in trouble. Which means our military is in trouble. And we, ladies and gentlemen, shall have a great share in the responsibility of getting all of us out of this trouble. And we are lucky, lucky indeed that we even know of the impending disaster that is facing us."

All eyes were glued to the square shouldered six-foot frame of the general. With his one hundred and eighty-five pounds of muscle and bone, moving in rapid animation in front of them, no one dared blink an eye. He was not the two hundred and five-pound running back who broke records at the Point thirty-five years before, but General Jack, as he was loving referred to, still packed quite a wallop in more ways than one.

Maddox never joked about certain subjects and all these men were familiar with his personality and character. He made certain that they knew when he spoke he meant business.

"As you are probably aware," he continued, "certain parties from the scientific community, for some dubious reasons, have been seeking contact with other life forms in the universe. Well, ladies and gentlemen—I believe that they have succeeded!"

His uncharacteristically emotional remarks unnerved the men. "In our endeavor to contact these alien intelligences our government has been sending out and receiving radio waves on many frequencies. It was just by sheer luck that we were listening in on a particular frequency when we picked up this message. The form of the message was similar to the way computers communicate with each other. In other words, it was an emulation of a digital signal. It took our cryptographers, with the aid of their computers, exactly five days to decipher the code, and therefore the message. It was ironic that it took so long. The code was simple, in fact, deceptively so. They spent most of their time trying to crack the proverbial peanut, with a sledgehammer.

"When we finally did decipher the message it simply said: 'Our ship is in position. We await further orders for the destruction of the inhabitants of planet Earth.'"

The following silence was deafening, as the attendants tried to absorb what had just been said. There were murmurs, tentative laughs, and the sounds of bodies shuffling in their seats. Then the general raised his hands for silence, and the audience became hushed again.

"Yes, I know exactly what you must be thinking right now. Some of you are thinking it's a joke—well it's not! Some of you are thinking that parties unfriendly to our nation are trying to unnerve us—not true! Or, perhaps you can speculate that this is all just a hoax—wrong again! We checked the exact location the message came from and have confirmed the existence of an alien spacecraft near the vicinity of the moon!

"To sum up, people, we feel that these, who or whatever they are, are highly logical, consummately cool, and deadly serious. And why have all of you been called here? WE NEED YOUR HELP!"

Bob Jones sat upright in his chair and stared straight ahead. Others thought they would shit their pants. The rest just stared into space, dumbfounded. With all they heard they still could not believe it was true. But the thing that made it hit home the hardest was the fact that it came directly from the general.

"Before you say anything, I suggest that you take a ten-minute break. No, longer please. I want this information to sink in, but not too far."

The men and women returned from their break in approximately the same state as they left. Maddox was waiting for them. "Gentlemen and ladies, I don't expect you to solve this problem today, but I'm sure I don't have to spell it out for you either. We are running out of time."

From the expression on the faces of the officers in the audience, Maddox had made his point. They felt somehow that they might have been responsible in some way for the situation. Maybe they should have taken this business more seriously. Was it this sighting or that one? Or was it all part of some master plot or operation that had been going on for who knows how long? They had a difficult time pulling themselves together to reconcile what was happening. How the hell were they going to help now? Wasn't it too late? They were lucky that they could find the bathroom, in their condition and manage not to piss all over themselves, no less come up with some magical solution.

"How can we help?" came the question from the audience. It seemed to snap most of them out of their stupor.

The answer came shooting back. "You had better go over all the information ever collected and come up with answers fast. You will all have access to the computer files that have been amassed up until this time. All information will be coordinated through my office. The remainder of our time together will be spent planning possible strategies. Computer specialists will be on hand to discuss how information can best be extracted and correlated.

"We did not call you people here just to massage the data that we already have or to scare the crap out of you. I'm looking for the subtleties. Most of you have been personally tracking this stuff for quite a while and you all, hopefully, have an extra sense for the details of the sightings that have been reported thus far." Maddox was silent while he looked at the men and women.

Jones looked like he was in shock. He couldn't believe that this was actually happening. Could that little discussion he had had with Lynch been meaningful? Lynch said that he really believed that the newspaper guy could have been snatched. Could it all be part of the same scenario? It was Jones' only real lead and he knew it!

CHAPTER SIX

He was average height, average weight, handsome but not too handsome and very sure of himself, at least from appearances. Perhaps he seemed too confident. No one in this world knew everything. Anyone that confident was either a phony, someone really unusual or not human. His name was M22 and he was all three. He was in fact a spy from another planet, the Hidden Planet to be exact. He was average height and weight so he would not stand out; he was good looking because good-looking people are more apt to get their way.

It was a bright sunny Monday morning as he strode down the main street of Arlington, Texas, directly into the offices of Cooper's newspaper, *The Daily Pride*. As he entered, he nearly was run over by Kevin Briggs.

"Excuse me," said Kevin as he passed, "is anyone helping you?"

"Not yet," replied the stranger. His cockiness was evident, though somehow not offensive.

"If you have a seat I'll be right with you."

"Thank you," he said smiling. He looked around the office. *Originally built in 1888 and restored in 1939*, read the old sign on the wall. *This structure is almost as old as I am*, thought M22. He looked like he was in his middle thirties. His features were pleasant but unassuming; one might say that he was good looking, without describing him as very handsome. He looked like most people's idea of the "boy next door," sort of a male version of Doris Day. Those from his planet were all made to look as appropriate as possible for their particular occupation. He was pleasant looking so that one would feel comfortable spending time with him, but not someone that you would feel was unusual. M22 was actually 175 at his last birthday.

Briggs returned. "Hi, I'm Kevin Briggs, the acting Editor-in-Chief..."

"*Acting* Editor-in-Chief," interrupted M22 with a wry look. "What happened to the original one?"

"He's on an indefinite leave of absence, why do you ask?" returned Briggs, trying to measure the fellow.

"Just curious. Actually, I'm looking for a job. Do you have the power to hire?"

The stranger's manner is direct and disarming, thought Briggs. "What kind of job did you have in mind?"

"Reporter," he said flatly.

Hum, with Howard gone we can definitely use someone to fill in, thought Briggs. "Can't pay much. And can't promise that the position will stay available to you when the boss returns," he said.

"When might that be?" asked M22, laughing to himself.

"Your guess is as good as mine."

"Better probably," said M22 to himself.

"What's that?"

"Better tell me where to start," said M22, ignoring the question.

"How about starting with your name?"

"Marshall, Marshall Brown."

"What experience do you have, Marshall Brown?" returned Briggs, not knowing exactly why he said his name like that.

"I was an English major in college, then I studied journalism in night school."

"Where was that?"

"Los Angeles, I got my degree from UCLA. I was a proofreader and a copy editor for a small magazine. I'm sure you never heard of it," he said, before being asked.

"Why did you leave?"

"They went out of business."

"Not your doing, I hope—just joking. What brings you to Arlington?"

"Pot luck. I wanted a change and figured I could get better experience quicker in a small town. Just stuck a pin in a map and...."

"And—we were the lucky ones." He laughed. "I'll give you a shot. If you work out you can stay. At least until Howard comes back, then he can decide what to do with you."

"Perfect," said M22 with a knowing smile.

"What do your friends call you?"

"Marty's okay."

"Do you have a place to stay, Marty?"

"Actually, I was hoping that you would be able to recommend one."

"I was just going out anyway; I can drop you off at Mrs. Harvey's place. She takes boarders. You can get yourself set up there and I'll pick you up in the morning on my way in to work."

"That sounds wonderful."

They drove down to Millicent Harvey's place. M22 enjoyed his first ride in an automobile. He took in all the sights and sounds along the route. To him it was so much chaos: men, women and children walking and riding in automobiles in all directions. *Was there a purpose to all this?* he wondered.

Briggs pulled up to the curb. "This is it, 128 Maple Street. Just tell Mrs. Harvey that I recommended you. It will be all right. Oh, did we forget your luggage or is that little bag all you have."

"No, it's in my car. I can get it all tomorrow."

"Fine then, I'll see you in the morning. Quarter to eight."

"Yes," said M22, leaving the car and walking toward the house.

Maple Street looked like a street in anytown USA. M22 walked up the flagstone walk to this big white colonial that looked like it was straight out of an Andy Hardy movie. M22 had no trouble settling in for the night. His kind did not require sleep, so he borrowed some books from the old lady's bookshelf and retired to his room for the night. He read as much as he could all night, anxious to glean as much extra knowledge as possible about these earthlings.

M22 was told that breakfast was served between 7:00 and 7:30 a.m. or he could have juice, coffee and donuts or just fend for himself. He was sitting at the dining table at 7:00 a.m. sharp.

"Good morning, Mr. Brown," commanded Mrs. Harvey.

"Good morning, Mrs. Harvey," returned M22 politely as possible.

"Sleep well, Mr. Brown?" queried Mrs. Harvey.

"Just fine, thank you, Mrs. Harvey," replied M22. "Very comfortable bed," he added.

"I noticed that you had the light on till very late, Mr. Brown, perhaps all night even, I thought that you said you slept well. Do you always sleep with the light on, Mr. Brown? You know, electricity costs a great deal these days, rates are sky high, at least around here, I don't know if that's the case where you come from. By the way, where do you come from, Mr. Brown?"

"Please call me Marty," he requested.

"Okay, Marty, but you will please continue to call me Mrs. Harvey, if you don't mind."

"Yes, Mrs. Harvey."

Mrs. Harvey almost smiled, but then caught herself. "You never answered me about the light being on all night," she said, waiting for his reply.

"I'm sorry," he said, "I must have dozed off while reading. I promise to be more careful from now on."

"I'm sure you will," she said, agreeing, "or else I may be forced to raise your rent, and I wouldn't want to do that. Now how do you like your eggs, Marty?"

"Any way you make them is fine with me," replied M22.

"Well how do they usually have their eggs where you come from, by the way, where did you say you came from?"

"I didn't, Mrs. Harvey. I come from very far away...California."

"That is pretty far away, but not that far."

"It's far as a state of mind is concerned, Mrs. Harvey, and scrambled is fine for the eggs."

It was 7:53 a.m. with the sun shining brightly as Briggs pulled up. "Sorry—waiting long?"

"Eight minutes," said M22 nonchalantly.

Briggs smiled and shook his head. Briggs was wearing sunglasses but the glare still bothered his eyes. As they drove off, he noticed M22 wasn't wearing any, but he wasn't squinting. "Did you leave your sun glasses with your bags? Doesn't the sun bother your eyes?"

"No," he said shaking his head then turning to Briggs and smiling. What Briggs didn't notice was that M22's cornea was actually getting darker to adjust to the change in the light's intensity.

"How were the accommodations? Did you sleep well?

"Adequately."

"Well that's good, I guess."

M22 was actually quite offended by the dirt, the smells and the unclean food. He was all right because he had brought his stabilizer pills with him. It would have seemed strange if he had not eaten with the rest of the guests. The last thing he wanted to do was to arouse suspicion. He also brought a breathing device, which he used to clean the dust particles from his lungs.

. "What did you think of Mrs. Harvey?"

"A delight, she's quite a charming young—old lady," said M22 smiling.

Briggs looked at him sideways. "Well I see you have a fine sense of humor to go along with your other qualities. I guess she is a spry old biddy at that."

70

Time was short and M22 knew that he had to complete his mission as soon as possible. His people's existence might depend on his success. But how did someone who was an alien find out the kind of information that he sought? Even with a look-a-like body and a perfect reproduction of voice and manners he still had to find out answers to questions that he should, as a earthling, already know or not have the right or privilege to know in the first place. He believed that Arlington was a good place to start. With the disappearance of Cooper fresh on everyone's minds and the report of a "UFO," a topic even brought up at dinner, he believed the discussion of these subjects would not arouse suspicion. Besides, a reporter was supposed to be nosy, that was what they were paid for, wasn't it? That was why he chose this avenue to obtain his information. Maybe he could make Howard Cooper's disappearance his first assignment. Did it not always help to have a truly disinterested third party look at things with fresh eyes?

"By the way, Mr. Briggs—"

"Please call me Kevin. We're not formal around here."

"Kevin. I happened to hear during conversation at dinner last night, that Howard Cooper left town unexpectedly or disappeared."

Briggs looked at him. "You don't waste any time do you?"

"I sure don't. That's what a good reporter is supposed to do isn't it? Keep his eyes and ears open?"

"I can't argue with you there," he said flatly.

"And I can understand your sensitivity about it."

"I bet you can," said Briggs, a little uneasy, "I bet you can."

They pulled up in front of the newspaper office and walked inside. "New reporter," said Briggs to the pressman. The pressman wiped the ink from his hands and came over to shake. "You can use this desk and PC," Briggs said, finally.

"That will be fine."

Briggs turned to leave.

"Aren't you forgetting something?"

"What?" asked Briggs, cocking his head to one side.

M22's eyes seemed to twinkle and were accompanied by his ever-present smile. "My assignment!"

"Can I open my mail first?"

"Sure. But I can make it easy for you."

"How is that?"

"I would like your permission to follow up on the Howard Cooper

71

disappearance."

"I don't think so."

"Is someone already on the story?"

"No, but there's no point in pursuing it."

"Aren't people concerned?"

"Certainly," said Briggs, remembering Lynch's warning.

"Then, why not?"

"It's very simple," said Briggs, becoming uncomfortable. "If we, who know him and this part of the country so well, can't find him, what makes you think that you could make a dent in the situation?"

"Well that's just it. Maybe you all know him too well. You all are too close to it. Maybe someone needs to look at this thing with fresh eyes."

Briggs found it difficult to argue with the man's logic, *but what about Lynch*, he thought.

"There are no more maybes. It's just no and that's final!"

"Is someone hiding something?"

Briggs just stared at him. *Christ, this guy is pissing me off. But if I fire him, he is just the type that would go around causing trouble,* he concluded. "Boy! You sure have nerve for a new guy."

"Reporters need nerve, don't they?"

"Yeah, but you're beginning to get on mine. Tell you what, since you're so hot to trot with this thing, it's yours. But, I cannot tell you anything about the case. Any leads that you need you'll have to develop yourself."

"It does not make sense, but if I have no other choice I'll take it. Just tell me where to start."

"Chief Lynch." *It will probably end there, too,* he thought, *but at least I'll get him out of my hair for a while, and I can keep tabs on him.*

"Great!"

"Wait a minute. Before you go, there are a couple of ground rules for you to observe. If you don't, this assignment is off and you're history—"

"What are they?"

"You are to keep me informed as to any new information that you come across—"

"How do I know what's new?"

"Just keep me informed! Next, when you speak to Chief Lynch make certain that it is clear that it was your idea to do this and that I didn't tell you anything."

"What's going on?"

"Deal or not?"

"Deal!"

Briggs turned to leave, then stopped and turned back again when M22 spoke. "Why would you want to find Cooper anyway, if his return can cost you your job?" he said, thinking, *ha! I have you now.*

"First of all, I want to find Mr. Cooper because he is my friend and there are people concerned about him and it won't hurt our circulation none. As far as my job is concerned, I'm just filling in, he owns the paper not me." Briggs turned and started to walk away. "Well what are you waiting for?" he said without turning back. "If you're going, get the hell out of here!"

"Hi, my name is Marshall Brown, and I would like to speak to Chief Lynch."

The officer at the front desk eyed the stranger up and down. "And what do you want to see the chief about?"

"I'm a new reporter for *The Daily Pride* and I'm here to speak to Chief Lynch on an important matter."

"So what is the important matter that you have come to discuss?"

"I was told to speak to Chief Lynch."

"Well the chief is busy now. I guess you will have to talk to me."

"I've already spoken to you. Now I need to talk to Chief Lynch."

"What are you some kind of smart ass?"

"No, sir. I just need to speak to Chief Lynch."

"Hum," said the sergeant, not sure what he was dealing with. "Please have a seat." He pushed the intercom button. "Chief, there's some guy out here. Never saw him before. He says that he is a new reporter for *The Daily Pride* and he insists that he will only speak to you. I told him that you were busy."

"Get his name and send him in!"

"Yes, Chief."

"Excuse me, what's your name?"

"Marshall Brown."

"Okay, go ahead in, the chief will see you. Wait a minute. You're not carrying, are you?"

"Carrying what?"

"A gun!"

"No. Why would I carry a gun?"

"Well, you won't mind if I pat you down then."

"As long as it doesn't hurt or take too long."

The sergeant looked at him hard.

M22 flashed his usual innocent smile. The officer frisked him. "Okay, you're clean. Go ahead."

M22 walked to the chief's door, opened it and walked inside. "Hi, I'm Marshall Brown—"

"Don't you knock when you enter someone's office?"

"Sorry, the sergeant told me to go right in. I'm a new reporter with the Daily—"

"Know that. What can I do for you?"

"I'm doing investigative reporting and I need whatever information that you can give me on the disappearance of Howard Cooper."

"Who sent you here?"

"It was my idea to do this story. Mr. Briggs, at the paper, wouldn't give me any information. He said it was a police matter and if I wanted to do the story I would have to talk to you about it."

"Well, he got that right at least. So why the interest?"

"That's funny. Briggs asked me the same question."

"So, what's the answer?"

"You see, I'm new in town and I'm staying over at Mrs. Harvey's on Maple Street, and I heard people talking about it at dinner and my reporter's nose told me that it would be an interesting story to start with, especially since I'm working for the paper that Mr. Cooper owns and edits."

Lynch eyed him up and down, trying to figure out if he was for real. He couldn't really make up his mind. But he figured he had nothing to lose. "Mr. Cooper just disappeared. It was about three weeks ago; he went out for some ice cream to have after dinner and he never came back."

"Is that all you know?"

"That's it."

M22 was silent. For no apparent reason, he began to look around the room. He stopped as his glance fell on the lump of metal on the hand truck. "What's that?"

"Meteorite."

M22 walked over to the lump and rubbed his hand across it. "Are you sure?"

Lynch hesitated. "Hey, that's what they told me. Why, what do you think it is?" he asked, trying to bait the stranger.

"It's no meteorite. First it's too smooth and second, it's too dense—too much iron, probably."

"I guess I got gypped then, huh? They said it was a genuine meteorite," he said, playing dumb.

M22 knew Lynch was lying, not only because it was a bad lie, but because he was taught to read a person's aura (the energy field around a person's body). An edge of an aura is normally smooth, but when it's not, it means the person is lying.

"What is it really?" asked M22.

"Beats the hell out of me. Look, I'm real busy, so if that's all you wanted— I really have to get back to work. Besides, why the hell are you so interested in this lump of whatever it is?"

"Just curious, reporter's curiosity," he explained. "Thank you for your time."

A few moments after M22 left the office, the phone on Lynch's desk rang. It was Colonel Jones.

M22 decided to head back to the newspaper office. Something was bothering both Briggs and Lynch. And it wasn't too hard to guess what it was. That lump sitting in Lynch's office was, from its size and apparent density, probably Cooper's auto. It was elementary for M22 to figure this out. M22 was able to push the lump just enough to get its approximate weight. Estimating the size of the lump and knowing the specific gravity of iron allowed him to calculate that it weighed about the same as a car. So, M22 figured that Lynch must have guessed that Cooper was kidnapped, since he had his melted down car, but for some reason, this subject was not to be discussed. One thing seemed certain, the humans did not have a strong grip on the situation.

M22 entered the newspaper office looking for Briggs. But he was gone. He picked up some back issues of *The Daily Pride* and began reading. Just then, the phone rang. Frank, the pressman picked it up. M22 continued his reading. Frank listened, said something back and hung up. Then Frank came around toward where M22 was sitting.

"Oh, Marshall, that was for you. I didn't know that you were here. You must have just come in. Huh?"

"Yes, I came in a couple of minutes ago."

"It was Chief Lynch. He said that it was important. I didn't know that you were here."

"It is all right. What did he say?"

"He said that when you arrive, you should wait here. He said that he was sending one of his men over to bring you back to the station. He said that he has some new information for you, and that you would understand."

"Thank you, Frank," said M22, flashing his million-dollar smile.

"Anytime, young man. Anytime!"

"First he will not talk to me, now he is sending a car. I wonder what happened between then and now?" he said to himself. "I wonder if they are suspicious. Well, even if they are, I will play along. This way I may get closer to the source of information. I am sure they will not be able to hold me, if I need to leave. Anyway, it is better than a dead end." He sat back down and resumed his reading.

The sergeant from the station house entered the office. He was a decent size, six-one, two hundred pounds. He was hoping that M22 would resist— just a little. "Mr. Brown," he said, gloating, "I have been asked by Chief Lynch to give you a ride back to the station house."

"Thank you. I appreciate the ride." His tone was just saccharine enough to annoy but not enough to be accused.

They rode in silence for most of the trip. "Mr. Brown, if you don't mind my asking, where are you from?"

"Los Angeles."

"Hum. Been in town long?"

"No. Just got in yesterday."

"Plan on staying long?"

"That depends."

"May I ask on what?"

"It depends on how long my job lasts here." M22 was pleased with himself for making what he believed was a clever statement that would also serve to end this annoying conversation.

"Huh," grunted the sergeant, keeping the rest of his thoughts to himself.

As instructed, he ushered his passenger into Lynch's office. M22 felt like the fly, being invited into the spider's parlor. Lynch just sat there looking like the cat that swallowed the canary.

"Why did you call me back?" asked M22 with anticipation.

"Well, you said that you wanted to know more about Howard Cooper's disappearance. I just spoke to a Colonel Jones, from the air force. He says that he has some additional information for you. In fact his people are on their way right now to escort you to the base, where Colonel Jones will be happy to discuss the matter with you, personally."

"I will be delighted to talk to Colonel Jones," he said, flashing his trademark smile. *It seems we are getting closer to the source, but why would they want to escort me,* he wondered. *I might be in trouble but I must take the risk,* he reasoned.

Lynch had to hold this guy for at least an hour and a half. He was not to let him get away at any cost. At the same time, M22 was not to know that he was, in fact, a prisoner. The sergeant was posted outside with orders not to let this guy get away, but he was not to be killed, no matter what. It would be better to let him get away than to kill him, even if he were an alien. Besides, he might be just a nosy innocent. At any rate, avoiding any hassle would be the best route of all.

"How about some lunch?" asked Lynch. "I know it's early, but by the time the food gets here it should be close to noon."

"Fine, where do we go?"

"I'll just have it sent in. My treat. I'll put it on the expense account," he said, winking. "We'll call it official business. The Howard Cooper case." He smiled at M22, trying not to seem too patronizing.

They ate their lunch and talked. Lynch was getting edgy. *When the hell is this guy gonna get here*? he wondered. "So what do you think of our little town, Mr. Brown?"

"I have not seen much of it yet, but what I have seen looks very nice."

Lynch thought he was going to throw up. This guy was so polite it was sickening. Who was shitting who anyway? "Where did you say you were from?"

"Los Angle—"

"—Oh yes, LA. You did tell me."

They heard some noise outside Lynch's office, then a knock on the door. "Thank God!" said Lynch. Then he smiled, catching himself. M22 was unmoved. "Come in!"

The young officer opened the door and marched in. He stood right next to M22 facing the chief. "I'm Lieutenant Walsh. Colonel Jones sent me, sir." Walsh was stout, well built and had a face like a bulldog. He looked more like a hit man than a soldier. He had the look of someone who would get the job done at any cost. Jones was trying to reduce the risk of anything going wrong. He knew Walsh would rather die than fail. Both Lynch and M22 noticed the sidearm strapped to his waist.

Lynch rose. "This is Mr. Brown—he's all yours—I mean," he switched his glance to M22. "The lieutenant will take you to see Colonel Jones, Mr. Brown." Relief showed on Lynch's face as he smiled.

"Thank you for lunch," said M22 as they left the office.

Lynch just nodded. He pressed the intercom and held the handset to his mouth without speaking, until they passed through the doorway. "Greenburg! Make sure they sign off on Brown before they leave. But please, try not to make it look too obvious."

Standing at the doorway leading outside was an armed MP. Sergeant Greenburg grabbed Walsh's arm as he and M22 came by. "Lieutenant, I just need you for a second."

"What is it?"

"It will only take a second. Over here." He signaled M22 to stay where he was as he gently took Walsh by the arm and went into a nearby office. "I need you to sign off on the prisoner—or whatever you want to call him."

"Is this necessary?"

Greenburg looked him in the eye. "That's the way the chief wants it."

"—Fine. If that's the way he wants it." He signed the paper and left.

"What was that all about?" asked M22 innocently.

"Nothing, he just wanted to tell me something funny about someone we both know," he lied.

"Do you always wear a sidearm when escorting people to the colonel?" he asked.

"These are tense times," lied Walsh, "what with the strange disappearance of Mr. Cooper and all."

There was another armed MP in the car sitting next to the driver. M22 sat in the back with the lieutenant. A fool would realize that this was no informal discussion. But it was too risky to send the lieutenant alone. One extra man or two would be a giveaway in either case. So, the colonel decided to have enough muscle to overpower the stranger if that became necessary.

"It looks like I will be well protected on this trip!" said M22.

The MPs stiffened a little. "You never know when the Indians might attack," laughed one of the MPs attempting to lighten the mood.

M22 spent most of the rest of the trip gazing out the window. *There is no purpose,* he thought, *in speaking any more than he had to.* Why increase the risk of giving himself away when there was no upside. They may suspect him, but they couldn't know for certain. At least not yet. The lieutenant probably possessed no information that would be of value, so M22 decided that he would respond only when spoken to. Walsh did most likely know who would have the information M22 sought, but that was tricky territory and one had to tread lightly.

He found the countryside interesting, although it was barren. He saw some prairie dogs, passed some farmhouses, and spotted large birds circling above, obviously looking for prey. He even saw the prey, as the jackrabbits and other small mammals scurried about. Occasionally a car would pass going in the opposite direction. He wondered if his people, before they became "hidden," lived in such a place. He marveled at the mirage that the hot sun would create on the long, straight stretch of highway before them. He was curious, but would not ask the others how such a phenomenon came about.

M22 and the lieutenant smiled at each other occasionally, but managed to do without any verbal intercourse during the trip. Both had nothing to gain by conversation.

They passed a sign that read: *STAY OUT, GOVERNMENT PROPERTY.* A few minutes later they came to a guard post. They were waved right through. Up ahead were the barracks and beyond that the main building where Colonel Jones had his office. M22 took in the surroundings with an eye for what this earthling military camp had to offer. *Not very impressive,* he thought, *rather primitive, actually. When the time comes, resistance should be minimal,* was his cursory conclusion.

The car stopped in front of a nondescript building and Walsh and the MPs got out with M22. As they entered, they stopped at the desk and Colonel Jones was informed of M22's arrival. "Send them right up," ordered the colonel.

As Walsh escorted M22 into Jones' office, it was easy to read the relief on his face as the responsibility for this important guest was transferred to the colonel.

"Mr. Brown, my name is Colonel Robert Jones," he said while extending his hand, which M22 shook. "Can I get you anything after your trip?"

M22 didn't really need any creature comforts, but he made believe he did. "What did you have in mind?"

"Oh, a beverage or use of the bathroom."

"Both, please."

"What would you like to drink?"

"Black coffee would be fine—" He paused.

"Oh, the men's room is right outside and to the right."

Walsh stood there in limbo. "That will be all, Lieutenant. Thank you." Walsh saluted and left.

"Sergeant," Jones said into the intercom, "our guest, Mr. Brown, is using the men's room; make certain he doesn't get lost. And after he's back in my office, please fix that cup of black coffee for him."

"Yes, sir."

M22, as all spies from his planet, were equipped with built-in voice transmitters and audio receivers. The transmitter was built into his lip and the receiver into his outer ear. The antennae ran from his head into his extremities and all were virtually undetectable. It was best to transmit and receive while alone. While the transmitter could pick up the lowest whisper and the wearer could hear a message that was inaudible to most bystanders, without the limbs extended, the signal was usually weak and unreliable. Since it was a human activity, standing up to stretch was probably the most convenient way for M22 to send a message while on Earth; the Hidden People, after their body replacement, did not require stretching as a normal function.

M22 stood spread-eagle and tried to establish contact with General Titus' ship. He used a simple signal on a pre-established frequency. Once contact was confirmed, they would speak briefly. "M22 reporting one hundred eleven Earth miles south, southeast of last point. Orders?"

"Negative," came the response.

"End of transmission."

M22 was required to fix his position every time he moved from one general location to another. He then urinated, flushed and left the men's room.

"I heard that you were interested in Howard Cooper," said Jones upon M22's return.

"Yes."

"What do know about his disappearance?"

"Not much yet. I had hoped that you could enlighten me, that's why I'm here."

The sergeant came in with the coffee. "Yes, of course. Is the coffee okay?" asked Jones.

M22 tasted it. "Fine."

"We use a special blend, I'm sure you'll enjoy it. I'd have another myself, but it makes me piss too much," he said, flashing his down-home smile.

M22 smiled back and took another sip.

"Never had a guest not finish my coffee."

M22 drank some more.

"Now, about Mr. Cooper's sudden disappearance," said Jones, "it seems that Chief Lynch had this strange notion. Look, this has to be off the record— not for publication."

"Certainly."

"For my own part, there's really nothing to hide, but I just don't want to embarrass the chief. You know how it is with these small-town officials—it's important for them to keep up their image."

"Sure."

"More coffee?"

"No, this is fine." M22 drank some more.

"You see, Lynch had this strange notion, something about—UFOs—stuff like that. You know anything about UFOs, Mr. Brown?"

"Only what I read in the papers," he said with a blank look.

Jones looked at him with an intensive stare. M22 drained his coffee cup. Jones leaned back and smiled himself. "You newspaper guys sure have some sense of humor."

"May I ask you some questions, Colonel Jones?"

"That's what we're here for."

"You mentioned UFOs; has the military ever actually communicated with beings from other planets?"

"That's quite a bold question, Mr. Brown, but as long as you asked it, the answer is no, not to my knowledge, and I am in a position to know."

M22 blinked his eyes, then shook his head.

"Anything wrong, Mr. Brown?"

"I don't think so, why would there be?"

"No reason."

"So there has never been any communication between us earthlings and creatures from any other planet?"

"Well, except for the movies and supposed encounters that some civilians have claimed, there has been no official or military contact, at least not by this government. Why do you ask, Mr. Brown?"

"Background information for the Cooper disappearance investigation. Remember, that's why I came."

"Oh yes, certainly."

"I—don't know. I—feel—a little—strange," said M22, putting his head in his hands.

"Excuse me for a moment," said Jones, leaving the office. He closed the door behind him.

M22 now had the information he needed, and he just had to get some time alone to transmit the information, but the apparent drug in his coffee was having the expected effect and he needed time to recover.

"Sergeant!" he shouted. "Get the MPs." Four burly MPs came around the corner. "Wait here," he told them.

Jones peeked into the office. M22 looked like he was sleeping. "Okay, guys, but remember, be very gentle and don't underestimate him. He may be stronger than he looks.

"No problem," smirked the sergeant in charge.

The MPs rushed in, handcuffed his arms and legs and carried him to a secured section of the infirmary.

Once in the infirmary the doctors checked his vital signs and put him on intravenous, to keep him under.

Jones turned to Major Jackson, the base psychiatrist. "How much sedative did you put in that drink I gave him?"

"Enough to knock out Big Foot. But he's fine, I didn't want to kill the guy either."

Major Paul Jackson was from Mississippi. He could not decide between psychiatry and flying, so he did both. He was short, about five feet, seven inches, with a slightly stocky build. His wife would have preferred that he were in private practice, but Paul loved the uniform.

"When do you want to talk to him, Bob?"

"Let's wait for the tests, then I have to clear it with Maddox. I don't know if I'll get to talk to him at all by myself. If he's for real, you can bet he won't be around here for long. The big boys are going to have a go at him. But I guess I can still be a hero."

They came by the room where M22 was being held. Two of the burly MPs were standing guard. "Everything all right, men?"

"Yes, sir, he's sleepin' like a baby," responded the sergeant.

Jones opened the door just enough to stick his head inside. M22 was lying on his back, eyes closed, looking very peaceful. Jones closed the door. "Sleeping like a tot!" he said to Jackson, while slapping one of the guards on the shoulder as a sign of satisfaction. "Come to my office, Paul, we'll have drink."

"You're buyin', I'm drinkin'."

M22 was being kept under sedation; they were taking no chances with this most valuable prisoner.

They were sipping their Jack Daniels and shooting the breeze when the phone rang. Jones picked it up, expectantly. It was the lab. "Did you find anything?" Jackson looked at Jones for a reaction. Jones put down his drink.

His eyes were wide. "I'll be right there." He hung up, and rose from behind his desk.

"For Christ's sake, Bob, what the hell is going on?" asked Jackson.

"They wouldn't give me the details on the phone. But one thing we know for sure—it ain't human!"

They walked quickly toward the lab, their feet clattering loudly on the carpetless floor. Jones' heart beat like a snare drum as many alarming thoughts rushed through his mind. "Could this be true?" he asked, looking at Major Jackson.

"Who's to say. There has been speculation about extraterrestrial humanoids for a long time. Most things that are new seem strange, until we get used to them."

Jackson's objectivity was due mostly to his lack of knowledge of the imminent danger of the situation. And Jones, for his part, certainly wasn't about to tell him or anyone else outside the circle, about the threat from the aliens. This discovery of an extraterrestrial in their midst only served as confirmation that this incredible revelation, of an alien invasion, was true beyond any doubt. But how was Jackson to know the weight of the question Jones was really asking.

As they approached the lab, they could see the doctor peering into a microscope. They entered the room with a flourish. The bright lights of the lab made each individual's figure appear stark. The doctor turned to see who entered and then gazed back into the eyepiece of the microscope.

"So how do you know that he's not human, doctor?" asked Jones, reserving any formality.

"If I did not take these samples myself, I would not believe what I am seeing," said Dr. Jenkins without raising her head.

"What is it?" insisted Jones.

"Come look for yourself."

Jones bent over and looked into the eyepiece. He played with the fine adjustment. "What am I looking at?"

"It's cells from the skin scraping that I took from—whatever it is that's lying in that bed. How does it look to you?"

"Fine. Very uniform. Perfectly healthy. Doesn't look strange at all."

"Very uniform," repeated Jenkins. Jackson controlled himself from butting in. "Now look at this slide." Jones lifted his head as the doctor removed the first specimen and replaced it with another. "This scraping I took from myself."

Jones looked. "See how irregular this one is. These are normal human skin cells."

"Let me see the first one again," asked Jones.

Jenkins switched again. Jones looked again. "I see the difference. These are perfectly uniform."

"Precisely! It's not human. It's incredibly good stuff. But definitely, NOT HUMAN!"

Those last words rang in Jones' ears as though he were riding the clapper of a ten-ton bell.

"That's not all," continued Jenkins. "The blood proved even more interesting." Jones looked dazed. Jackson maintained his silence. "Perfect in every way except too perfect, or so it appears. I know this area pretty well. Now, I have to run more tests to corroborate my findings and I don't have the proper equipment here, but—"

"For God's sake, Jenkins, what are you driving at?"

"I'm sorry. Anyway, the blood sample looks human except for extra antibodies. Now I can't prove anything conclusively from these initial tests alone, but my educated guess is that this blood would probably give whomever has it in his veins, immunity to all known diseases. Now remember, this is only a hypothesis. There are still many tests to be done."

"That will be quite sufficient, Jenkins."

"But, Colonel, we must pursue this. This is one for the medical journals. It could revolutionize medicine."

"Now that's fine, Jenkins, but not right now. Much more urgent matters must be taken care of now. And remember—this is top secret!"

"I understand that," said Jenkins, eyeing him warily.

Jackson finally chimed in: "Anything else that we should know about this humanoid?"

"Well, there is something that could potentially be important. I extracted some muscle tissue, along with blood and skin scrapings, and if what I think I see is correct, this guy is probably *as strong as ten men!*"

"Good work, Captain Jenkins," said Major Jackson.

Jones turned and left with Jenkins in tow.

CHAPTER SEVEN

"She wants to live with him," said Rondo concerned. "Is it her gene engineering or her indoctrination that failed?"

"I do not know," answered Number 2, "but I am aware that Sandra is unnaturally afraid of having her 'body replacement.' I could easily check the problem out and get the answer as swiftly as you need it. It is always a burden when these anomalies occur and I am certain that it would be useful to find and correct the problem. It is amazing to me that we still have problems with our individual development systems after all this time. I guess we are not perfect after all," she said, attempting humor.

Rondo's serious expression did not change, though. "Do not take any action that will interfere with her current relationship with the alien, Cooper. Let her have her way for now. Her anomalous behavior and their relationship may prove helpful in the future. And for now, it is not harming anything. I am sure this diversion will keep our guest content for the time being. And, although the chances are quite slim, we just might require his services in the near future, if a hitch should develop in our plans. We will let them have their fun. But do not indicate that they will be permitted to continue in this fashion indefinitely. Make them believe that they are in a temporary situation that can change at any time. This should have the affect of their believing that their time together is more precious and keep them from thinking too much about any long-term arrangements. Let us just think of them as two more content and joyful souls on the Hidden Planet."

Sandra rushed to Howard's apartment flushed and excited. "Howard, Howard, have you heard?"

"Heard what?"

"The wonderful news! This is even more wonderful. I get to tell you myself. We can continue to see each other. Even live together, if we want."

"I'm glad," he responded half-heartedly.

"So why do you seem so sad?"

"I'm sorry," he said without changing expression.

"What is it?"

"I guess you're right. I should be happy. Now we can cry on each other's shoulder. You about your 'body replacement' and me for losing my family and my world."

"Why are you so cynical today? I thought this would make you happy. And you are ruining it for me."

"I'm sorry. I already told you that. But I just feel so helpless. I guess you could say that there is a good side," he said with sarcasm. "I have the unique privilege of being both the last of my kind and having the opportunity to get a blow by blow account of my planet's destruction. Oh yes, I can also claim for the benefit of my progeny, if there are any, that humankind did not, as we feared, destroy itself. We and our world were destroyed *for us*. But wait, on second thought, we are responsible for attracting the amorous attention of *your* so-called Hidden People. So I guess we are, at least indirectly, responsible for our own destruction, after all."

"Would you like me to leave?" she asked upset.

"No, I've gotten it all out—I think?" he said, contritely.

"Are all humans as brooding as you?"

"Not really, I guess there are some, though. I'm a newspaperman. That automatically makes me susceptible to being a crusader. And crusaders often brood, when things are not going well."

"So why don't you forget about things that you have no power to control? What about us? We are here together now! We can both get a body replacement, and live on my planet. Will you do it if I do?"

"Whatever for? You said you feared this thing more than death."

"But then we could live together for a very long time."

"Women!" he said under his breath.

"What did you say?"

"Nothing, don't you think that we should try out our relationship for a while before I trade my vitals and private parts for what amounts to a living pacemaker and a rubber dick?"

She covered her mouth and laughed. "You're funny. All right, maybe I am getting a little ahead of myself. But I am still happy that we can be together."

"So am I. They say if you can still laugh at yourself, things probably aren't as bad as you think."

"I love you," she said, pulling him close to her. "And you are even better than a 'comfort creature.'"

"Gee, thanks."

Sandra smiled warmly at him. "And we are going to help each other, I promise."

"How?"

"I do not know yet. But if I can find a way to save your people and your planet, will you make a pact with me that we will both have the body replacement and live together till the end of time?"

Cooper knitted his brow in thought. "Wouldn't that be ironic? You save the world on the condition that I cannot return to it. What choice do I have?" He shrugged his shoulders and smiled. "Where I come from," he said, "this is called 'making an offer that I can't refuse.'"

She smiled also.

"So what can you do? You're not even part of the government here?"

"As you said, when I pretended not to hear you, I'm a woman."

They stood in front of Rondo like two lost children. He turned and stared outside through the transparent wall onto the harsh landscape below.

"Why have you come?" he asked without facing them.

Sandra began to speak, but Howard grasped her arm and gently bade her to wait. She stood there anxious to speak her piece. Rondo felt the pressure of her gaze. He knew she was resolved, and would not be dismissed easily. He turned to face them.

"We are here to try to save a world from useless destruction and a man from useless agony," she finally answered.

Rondo smiled benignly. "Please understand, I hold no malice for Cooper or his world," he said, glancing briefly at Howard. "But it is impossible for me to act otherwise. You cannot know, because you are too young. And Cooper, you and your people are naive to the dangers that exist. We are not a heartless people, but even those who hold kindness dear have the right to defend themselves and their society." He paused before continuing. "About two centuries ago," he began, "after our people had experienced two millennia of peace, prosperity and advancement, there came to the part of the galaxy that we inhabited, a terrible horde. And we were careless then, very careless. If we were not, these cunning barbarians would not have found our planet and had us at their mercy. While we were not as foolish as the earthlings, advertising their whereabouts as though they were looking to be rescued, we were not as cautious as we should have been and paid dearly for our laxity. As it turned out, we allowed a chance meeting to almost lead to our annihilation.

"We were on a routine space flight and came upon aliens calling themselves Alvons. We had had similar chance meetings from time to time, but without incident. Most of the others that we came upon were not as advanced as we are. What the Alvons may have lacked in sophistication they more than made up for in zeal. They possessed an aggressive single-mindedness that was awesome.

"They asked for help and while our people were visiting their ship, they ingratiated themselves with us. They begged for our help and we consented to take them in tow to our planet where they could secure repairs for their disabled ship. While their ship was being repaired, they made small talk and gained our confidence as friendly creatures. They exhibited a curious nature and inquired into every imaginable aspect of our existence. We accepted their inquisitiveness as natural, when meeting people from an unknown culture. Their stay, though, became longer than expected and your adage about fish and guests starting to become bad after too long was very appropriate in this case.

"When they began to inquire about our defense systems, in a casual manner of course, we knew it was time for them to be on their way. They said things like 'we have had difficulty in defending against this kind of attack or that kind of strike.' They seemed to be telling us all about themselves. This lowered our defenses in a number of ways, that we later found, were predictable to them. We were embarrassed not to speak a little more freely than we had been. They were masters at their nefarious trade. Since we could not very well tell them any of our secrets, we could at least give them our assessment of their weak defenses. Of course we could not tell them anything of significance, but the way they phrased their questions enabled them to ascertain the information they needed to crack our defenses when that horrible day came."

By this time, Rondo and his two guests were sitting at the conference table. Sandra's sweet face held a far away look, while Howard's expression alternated from fascination to introspection to pain and back again.

Rondo continued. "They left as amiably as they came and we wished them well in their future endeavors, obviously unaware that they were in fact endeavoring to destroy us," he lamented. "I remember thinking as they left what a model they made of the gracious visitor, almost to the point of envy.

I made the biggest fool of myself that I could possibly make. I can still recall how we conversed in a casual manner discussing our recently departed guests and how interesting and pleasant their visit was, even if a little too long. We also spoke of how open, sincere and honest these strangers seemed and how pleased we would be to have them visit us again in the near future. Oh, but that it was to be that we would have our wish!

"In the weeks that followed we went about our affairs in the usual manner. About three weeks to the day of our visitor's leaving our early warning station sent a signal indicating that a warship, other than our own, was in the vicinity of our planet. Our ships scrambled to meet the potential offender. The alien ship turned out to be from the planet of Sheldon, a nation friendly to us. The commander of their ship asked for permission to land on our planet. This was quickly granted. Something was obviously wrong and strange in their nation. I myself was well acquainted with the Sheldonas, having personally dealt with their leader for many years. The commander was quite agitated and nervous, which was quite out of character for these proud and righteous people.

"He said: 'Our people have been attacked by a fierce tribe and as we speak they are at the mercy of these savages.'

"I asked him if we could offer any assistance.

"He replied: 'There is nothing you or your people can do, but to protect yourselves from experiencing the same fate.'

"I told the commander that he needn't worry, for our defenses were fail-safe.

"'So were ours,' he persisted, 'but these fiends are insidious.'

"Then he began to relate a story that made my hair stand on end and my skin crawl. My face, I was later told, took on the quality of a white stone mask, and I had to sit down, for my knees began to buckle beneath me.

"The Sheldonas, the commander told us, came upon a distressed ship. The people they assisted were able to gain the Sheldonas' confidence. So, they towed the ship to their planet for repairs. What transpired sounded identical to our experience with the Alvons, right down to the Alvons' 'candid' discussion of their planet's defenses.

"'Oh,' I said to the commander 'but this cannot be! I cannot accept the idea that we will be rendered defenseless as you were.'

"But the truth was unavoidable. We calculated the amount of time it took the Alvons to comprehend and break the defenses of the Sheldonas and assumed we would have the about the same amount of time to save ourselves.

It seemed that we had about two weeks to prepare for the onslaught.

"We immediately prepared our defense and evacuation plans. You cannot imagine the distress these circumstances caused us. It was only fortunate that we were capable of sustaining our society away from our planet. Otherwise our people, as well as our planet would have been lost.

"The decision was made that all but the defense force would leave. There were two reasons for this. One was on the off chance that we could beat off the barbarian's assault and could all return to our home. And the second was that even if we could not defeat them, the battle would create a diversion so that the civilians could get away.

"The Alvons came with a vengeance and our beautiful planet was but a fond memory soon after our hasty departure.

"Our people got away with a minimum of possessions. They were fortunate to have been able to take their habit and comfort creatures along. From the radio messages that we monitored from the open channel, we were told of great destruction that took place due to the frustration of our disappointed would-be captures. Prayers are said that they will never locate us again. The brave defenders have our eternal gratitude for their ultimate sacrifice."

Rondo got up, walked to the glass wall, and just looked out for a while in silence. He raised his right hand, pointing outside to what lay within his view. "This is what we traded for our beautiful planet—and we were lucky to even find this place and build our new home."

Then he faced his guests with a frightening look. His features appeared to be etched in stone, and his eyes pierced their souls. As he spoke, the voice that passed between his lips seemed to enter the room from another realm. "There may exist in this part of the universe a more terrible horde than those vile and barbaric Alvons. And if so, my senses maintain the constant vigil and my continuous prayers the hope that I may never find out."

The silence in the room became palpable. Then Rondo looked at them both again, but this time gently. "Do you understand our position a little better now?"

Sandra wept and Howard held her. Howard looked at Rondo as though the latter were inanimate. Rondo's expression remained unchanged. Howard glanced again at Rondo briefly, as he took Sandra's hand and slowly left the room.

CHAPTER EIGHT

M22 lay in his cell, as two heavily armed guards stood watch outside. He wondered how long the wait would be until the big brass came by. He got up slowly and waited a moment or two until he felt that he had his equilibrium back. He walked to the door and looked out through bars of the small opening near the top. He held the bars in his hands just to gage their strength against his. The bars won the contest, he was strong, but not that strong. He looked briefly at the guards stationed nearby then turned and headed toward his bunk.

"They got me good, these ignorant earthlings," he said ironically under his breath.

It was a dark and drizzling cold rain as General Maddox's helicopter landed in the cleared parking lot at the rear of the main building. Colonel Jones was waiting for him. He stooped low to avoid the spinning blades as he approached the ship, his hand out to greet his superior officer.

"I'm sure happy to see you, General; this could be the big break that we've been looking for."

"I hope for your sake it's not a hoax, Colonel. We have little enough time as it is without wasting it on boogie men."

Maddox walked right past Jones. Jones in his excitement almost forgot the whirling blades above his head as he started after his boss, barely missing a puddle in his pursuit.

"I can assure you, General, that this guy is the real thing. I looked at the tissue samples myself," said Jones, over the noise of the helicopter. "Now, I'm not a doctor or anything, but what I saw under that microscope was not human. I can assure you of that, General. Believe me, the last thing I would do is waste your time, especially with the situation as it is."

Maddox just sort of grunted back, which made Jones just a little nervous as he began to second guess himself, just enough to make his palms sweat, or was it the rain?

"You sure it wasn't some plastic surgery that the guy got that you were looking at or some other such thing?"

"I can assure you, General, it wasn't just the skin samples that tipped us off. We have strange blood samples, muscle tissue, the guy is strong as an ox, much stronger than a human, the doctor claims. It says spy to me, wouldn't you agree, General?"

"We'll see," grunted Maddox.

They reached the entrance and the dry warmth of the building as Maddox and his entourage filed in one at a time with Jones looking anxious at his side.

Jones stood directly in front of the general.

"I thought that the best way to handle this would be to bring you to the cell where he is being detained, this way it will reduce the chance of a break out."

"Fine, fine. Let's get on with it."

As they approached M22's cell, two armed guards joined them. The two at the door saluted as they reached the door. One of the guards unlocked the cell door as the second stood with his weapon at the ready.

"I've given strict orders that he is not to be killed, even in self defense."

"Well, if he is what you say, I can only agree with that order completely. But if he's not—your ass is in the meat grinder!"

Jones looked uneasy as he nonchalantly wiped his sweaty palms on his pants legs.

They entered the cell. M22 was now lying on his back with his hands and feet manacled to bars embedded into the cell wall. He smiled as Maddox and the colonel approached. The room was a drab gray and bare, except for the bed and its occupant. The two guards resumed their posts at the door. The general approached cautiously without appearing to be threatening.

"How do you do? My name is General Maddox," he said while making an embarrassed face. "What is your name?"

M22 just looked up without speaking.

Maddox put his hand to his chin and rubbed it in thought. "You do speak our language, don't you?"

There was another pause. "I can assure you, General, that he does speak—"

"I'm capable of having my own discussion without any assistance, Colonel."

"Yes, sir."

"You must be uncomfortable, like that," continued the general.

M22 smiled and nodded.

The room was silent for a moment.

"Please release him," he said firmly.

The guards looked nervously at Jones, who nodded his assent.

"Thank you, Colonel," he said, flashing a little smile.

Jones looked at Maddox with a puzzled expression, hoping his remark was not sarcastic.

As they released him, M22 seemed to lunge toward the general, with no intention other than greeting him. The nervous guard closest to him, misinterpreting his intention, shoved the butt of his rifle into the face of the supposed attacker. M22 went crashing down to the floor. Everyone, including the perpetrator and the victim, were aghast. M22 looked up in amazement, his bottom lip and teeth well smashed. The guard looked confused, not knowing whether to be proud or ashamed of his action. He searched the faces of the others hoping for a confirming look on at least one of them. But their shocked expressions were of little help.

"What the hell did you do?!" yelled the general.

"Ahh—I—thought—"

"Thought! You need brains to think! Which you obviously don't have! Now get the hell out of here!"

"—Yes, sir!" he said, quickly saluting and leaving.

Everyone remained silent, waiting for the general's next move. He bent down and tried to lift M22 into the bed. The others, still partially in shock, just stood there.

"Why are you all standing there gawking? Give me a hand!"

M22, slightly stunned, said nothing. As they laid his head on the pillow, Maddox leaned over him to speak as softly as possible.

"I cannot apologize enough—" Maddox looked up. "Well don't just stand there, get this man—er, this alien a doctor." He looked back at M22. "Are you all right?" he said, shaking his head in frustration. "I can't believe this happened. I really do apologize for this terrible treatment. And I can assure you that we will give you the best care and treatment possible from now on. Try to rest. We can speak later, after the doctor has treated you. Can we get you anything in the meanwhile?" Maddox was hoping more to hear the stranger speak, than he was concerned about the reply.

M22 shook his head, then laid back, closing his eyes.

"All right, let's clear out. We've done enough damage for one morning."

They all followed the general out of the room.

"I want four guards posted at all times. And no one, I mean no one, enters or leaves this room without my express permission," he said, glaring at the colonel.

"Yes, sir—General."

In his room alone, M22 stretched out and touched his sore face. In his ear, he could hear his people trying to contact him from their ship circling the moon.

"M22, please report. Have not heard from you in an Earth day. M22, please report."

"This is M22, no change in status."

"M22, please report."

"This is M22!"

"M22, we are not receiving your signal! Please report."

He felt the inside of his lip with his tongue. "No, not my transmitter! They smashed my transmitter! Without it, I am lost. This is M22, can you hear me?"

"M22, please report...."

CHAPTER NINE

Number 2 announced himself at Rondo's door. "Come in, Number 2."

"Rondo, please put General Titus on your communicator."

Titus popped onto the screen and began to speak. He looked intense and sounded concerned. "We have lost contact with M22. We do not know if he can hear us but he does not respond. We chanced contact after one Earth day of silence. We attempted contact twice more during the following day, with the same lack of response. We require instructions to proceed."

Rondo spoke without hesitation. "We must establish contact. Time is critical. Each day that passes increases the danger of our planet being exposed. Transmit to M22 again, this time tell him to stay wherever he is, or if he has left the last location, to stay close enough to wait for our contact to meet him. Perhaps he can still hear you even if he cannot transmit."

"Please hold on for a moment," interjected Number 2. Rondo turned toward her, somewhat glaring and seeking an explanation.

She answered his look without missing a beat. "Perhaps the general should be told that if M22 cannot be located within a strategically optimum amount of time, then he should proceed with the destruction of the human species in order to minimize our risks going forward."

Rondo nodded his ascent. "General," he continued turning the transmitter back on, "how long until you are ready to proceed with the destruction of the human population?"

"About fifteen days."

"Fine, move forward with those plans, regardless of your success finding M22 or recovering additional information. Time is our enemy. Keep me informed of your progress. I've sent the earthling Cooper down to assist you in your efforts, along with San321, use them as you will."

"Yes, Rondo, signing off."

The sound of the door opening jarred Cooper out of his thoughts. "We must leave now," the guard said.

"Where are we going?" asked Cooper

The guard ignored his question. "Follow me," he commanded.

They left through an air lock into the shuttle vessel that would take them to General Titus' attack ship. The trip in the shuttle was pleasant. Cooper felt like the astronaut Neil Armstrong seeing the Earth from this vantagepoint. How stunning it must have appeared the first time we saw ourselves from the outside. As he peered outside, Sandra's hand went around his waist as her face appeared next to his at the porthole. She was devoted to him and he was struggling with the thought of his wife and family down there on that pretty blue and white planet.

Rondo had decided to send Howard, realizing that it would be the fastest way to make contact with M22 without having another agent captured and most likely abused by the violent earthlings. Since Cooper was worthless as a hostage, he was more than expendable. And of course, he knew his way around. But, naturally his loyalty was in the wrong camp. When Sandra complained about losing him, Rondo realized that she would be the perfect companion. At least he could depend on her loyalty. And, Rondo knew she would never let Howard out of her sight. What a perfect setup!

They reached the mother ship and prepared for their journey to Earth.

The trip took minutes with the Earth getting larger and larger as they approached. Upon entry into the atmosphere they experienced a slight bump, but soon regained their trajectory. Cooper could make out the geography below as the ship made a couple of revolutions before landing.

They landed at night in a clearing a few miles out of Arlington. The doors opened and Howard strolled out of the ship, followed closely by Sandra. Howard watched as the craft rose into the evening sky. When it was gone from sight he dropped to his knees, felt the grass, smelled the cold moist earth and sobbed. Sandra rubbed his head and back, as one comforts a small child.

The night was a little cool for August and they sat side-by-side taking it all in. The insect noises were very strange to Sandra, so was the big sky. Living all her life indoors, except for the terrarium, did not prepare her for this boggling effect on her senses. She gazed open mouthed and for the first time in her life truly experienced transcendence.

Cooper felt an aliveness he decided that he was not ever willing to give up again.

The doorbell at the Cooper's rang.

"Coming," said the female voice from inside.

Maureen sounds happy, thought Howard, somewhat disappointed.

The door swung opened. "Oh!—Oh!—Howard!?"

They stood staring at each other.

"Who were you expecting?" he asked, with a tinge of jealously in his voice. He noticed that she looked somewhat dressed up for just staying home. He also noticed her perfume.

"Well—er—no one! Er—I mean, darling, your home! I just didn't know what happened to you, where you were."

"Well I'm here now," he said, suddenly thinking of Sandra waiting for him outside hiding in the bushes. The combination of feelings was boggling his mind.

"Sweetheart," she said, embracing him, "we didn't know what happened to you. At first, I thought that we would hear from you. Then we thought— we thought maybe, you might—well, you might never come back," her tone turning sullen. "Children, it's Daddy! Daddy's home!" she shouted.

Howard immediately felt a great emotional distance between them.

"Daddy!" yelled John, running. Christine followed, tears in her eyes. Howard also began to cry as he hugged the children. The thought about Sandra outside would not go away.

"They said that we might never see you again. But I never believed it. I knew you would come back," said John.

"Sure you did!" said Christine, sarcastically snapping Howard out of his trance.

"Yes I did, you're just jealous."

"Please," pleaded Howard, "I'm not even home five minutes and you're at each other already."

"Sorry, Daddy," said Christine. "You little brat," she said under her breath.

"Howard, come into the living room. Let me make you a drink," said Maureen.

"That would be wonderful."

As she finished preparing the drink, the doorbell rang. Howard looked up, startled. "Don't tell anyone I'm here!" he said in a strange, serious tone. They all looked at him, seeing the fear in his eyes. They never heard him sound that way before. "Er, I'll explain later." Then he thought it might be Sandra and his face went white.

The doorbell rang again. John went toward the door, but Maureen intercepted him. "Here, bring these drinks into the living room, I'll get the door, and be *quiet*."

John shrugged and took the drinks as Maureen walked to the door, her expression showing concern. Howard noticed and was puzzled. "Don't tell anyone I'm here," he repeated, in somewhat of a whisper.

With her back to him, Howard could not see the ironic smile on Maureen's face. As she reached the door Howard held his breath. She opened it slightly and held it firmly.

Howard tried to hear what she was saying without being too obvious about it. Maureen seemed to be having a hard time getting rid of whomever it was. *What the hell is this all about?* he wondered.

Maureen closed the door and started back into the living room. "Who was that?" he asked.

"Oh, just officer Greenberg, honey."

"Were you expecting him?" he asked, now believing she thought that he was Greenberg when he arrived. "What is he sniffing around for?" added Howard, not allowing her to answer his first question.

"He's not sniffing around," she said, not pleased with his implication.

"Christ! The guy's hardly thirty. Is it you or Chrissie he's keeping an eye on," he said with a note of sarcasm.

"He just was checking to see if we were okay, they do think you're still missing, you realize," replied Maureen.

Howard noticed Christine looking upset.

"I'm sorry," he said, "with all that's been happening, my nerves are shot."

"What *has* been happening?"

"It's the government. They grabbed me when I went out that night. I discovered something and they were there, too. Once I saw it, I was involved, and they couldn't very well let me go free after that. I'm sorry," he added, raising his hands, "but I can't tell you any more, it would also put you in danger." Howard looked uncomfortable as he spoke. He hated lying. "Now I'm working for them. All this time I've been gone, I've been under their indoctrination. They figured that as long as they had me, they might as well put me to work for them. I guess my intelligence work in the army didn't hurt."

"Wow! Dad's a secret agent," said John.

"Shut up, you asshole!"

"Chrissie!" said Howard and Maureen almost in unison. She just made a face. "Well he is."

"So are you!"

"Let's not start," said Howard, looking anxious. He was still worried about Sandra getting restless.

"Relax," said Maureen, smiling, "we have the whole night to talk."

"I'm sorry," he said, looking sincere as possible, "but they won't let me spend the night."

"What!?"

"I was lucky to get here at all. I guess they think if I stay the night, I may weaken."

Christine began to cry. Maureen looked pissed. And John was in heaven.

The doorbell rang again and Howard froze. He wanted to get it but Maureen got to the door at the same time.

"I'll get it," Howard said nervously.

"I thought you didn't want anyone to know that you're here."

"Oh!—Right. Don't open the door until I look through the window to see who it is."

Oh shit! thought Howard, *it's Sandra. I'm dead!*

"I'll get it. It's my guy. I probably took too long." Howard signaled Maureen by moving his head sideways, indicating that she should go back into the other room.

Maureen didn't budge. "Open it," she commanded.

"This is not a good idea," he pleaded.

She stood her ground. He knew she wouldn't budge. He opened the door and tried to hold it, but it was no use. They saw each other. Sandra was looking at Maureen curiously. Maureen just stood glaring.

"Is this the other agent?"

"Well—yes, I didn't say it was a guy agent. Anyway, I have to go now." Then he looked at Sandra. "Please wait outside, Agent Sand—ers," attempting to sound as firm as possible.

"What's the matter? Don't you want to introduce me to your—government friend?"

"Please, Maureen; it's difficult enough as it is."

"I'm sure what's-her-name helps soothe the pain. Couldn't you find anyone younger? What is she, twenty-one? Twenty-two? Why don't you rub my face in it a little?"

"Maureen, that's not the way it is."

"Oh! Well then, how exactly is it? I bet it's good. Real good."

"—Maureen."

"—Let me finish! She had better be damn good. You left me for her, didn't you?!!!"

"Maureen, the children."

"Don't give me that crap! You walk out, without saying a word. Everyone worried to death about you. Then you show up with a kid just barely older than your own daughter, then hand us some wild cock-and-bull story about government agents, and then you have the nerve to caution me about *my* behavior?"

"Oh, God. I can't believe this."

"You can't believe it, after your bullshit story? You can't believe it. Oh, my, they won't let me stay the night," she mimicked in a mocking tone. She was ripping him to pieces. Howard tried to speak, but there was no stopping her. "And as long as you asked, it *was* me that Officer Greenberg came around to look after." She glared at him, shaking her head from side to side, hands on her waist.

"I have to go," he said, obviously shook up. "Let me say goodbye to the children."

He kissed them and hugged them tightly without saying anything. When he came back to the door Maureen was waiting, holding it open for him, her visage like stone.

As he walked through the door, he looked at her expectantly.

"Don't say anything. You disgust me." She snarled. Her look made his heart sink. "And don't bother coming back here again. This isn't your home anymore."

Sweat beaded up on his brow. "One day you will understand, it is not what it looks like," he protested, as she slammed the door in his face.

Howard bowed his head and slowly walked hangdog into the night.

Sandra was waiting for him. She was leaning against a tree with a dreamy look on her face. As he approached, she spoke without looking at him. "Your wife is angry."

"Angry would be an improvement."

"Are you sorry you saw them?"

"I don't know what I am," he said with exasperation, "I'm certainly not happy. I don't think it could have worked out worse," he said, sighing deeply.

"What did you expect?"

"I don't know. I just wanted to see them again—before it was too late. I just wanted them to know that I was alive."

"I am sorry you are so unhappy. We are doing important things. You must understand that."

"Oh, I understand it. I understand it perfectly."

A moth flew toward Sandra's face. She waved it away with her hand and smiled dreamily.

Howard wondered if she could comprehend or care about his situation. He realized that she had no idea about his situation; marriage was not something practiced on her planet. She was as naïve as a child. There was no malice in her actions, just hope. Hope for a better life than she thought she was facing with her body replacement. "Let's go," he finally said, "we've done our damage here."

CHAPTER TEN

M22 lay in his bed in a secured section of the Pentagon building in Arlington, VA. He had received the message transmitted from his spaceship two weeks before, that Howard and Sandra would try to locate him. He wondered when and if they would ever find him. He could have probably escaped but he believed that the violence would have cut off any chance of his contacting any more senior individuals in the government and therefore jeopardized his mission. If he acted civilized, he might be able to secure an audience with someone that could answer the questions for him. He had refused to speak for two weeks, writing notes to the effect that he would only speak to the man in charge. This was frustrating to government people but not threatening. They hoped that as long as M22 was on the planet his people would not destroy it. It also implied that these great, powerful invaders lacked some knowledge or information in order to carry out their objective. Or else, why this pathetic spy? Maddox argued: "We can hold out forever, as long as we have their man, so to speak. They are the ones that are in the hurry, not us." So, he convinced the rest of the brass and particularly the President to take a wait and see approach. Maddox argued that they should wait for the alien to tip his hand before they conceded anything to him. Besides, until he agreed to speak they weren't about to "lower" themselves to communicate on a less than one-to-one basis.

M22 had all the time in the world, now that his people were monitoring the Earth's transmissions. At least that's what he was told. And the Hidden People never made mistakes of logic. Or did they?

Cooper stuck his hand in his pocket and pulled out a huge pile of bills. He started counting it and then just estimated how much he had. *It's quite a lot,* he thought, *at least ten thousand—too bad it's phony.* "Well it may be phony, but it looks as good as any I've ever seen, and spends just as good too," he said aloud. Sandra heard the grumbling and gave him a funny look.

Howard had some money in his pocket when he was kidnapped. His "hosts" replicated his twenty-dollar bill and used it to finance M22 and Howard's expeditions.

"They should have given us travelers' checks," said Howard, attempting to pull Sandra's leg, "this way we could get an instant refund if they're lost or stolen."

Sandra just stared at him. Howard shrugged his shoulders. "It worked in vaudeville."

"What do we do now?" she asked, trying to ignore his silliness.

"We need to find a public phone so we can call a cab service," he said. He put on a hat, which he had grabbed from his house and pulled it low over his eyes.

As Sandra watched he said: "It doesn't pay to be recognized and start a lot of excitement." She smiled at him.

They phoned from a gas station on a road near Howard's house. He tried to be inconspicuous but people kept staring.

"Why are people looking at you so funny?" Sandra asked.

"It's this dumb hat I'm wearing, I guess. Sometimes it's worse when you try not to be noticed. Well anyway, let them stare. As long as they can't identify me, that's all that counts." He gave her a wink. Sandra smiled back. Then he reached out, gave her hand a squeeze, and looked into her eyes. She moved closer to him and they looked like they were about to kiss when the sound of a car horn interrupted their mood.

"Boy that was fast," Howard said.

"Just a little too fast," cooed Sandra.

Howard opened the rear door of the cab for Sandra and he followed her in. The driver looked Mexican, the name on his license read Carlos Rivera. Howard leaned forward and asked the driver if he knew the way.

"Yes, "he said in a Spanish accent, "dee pilots get drunk in town sometimes and I have to drive dem back to dee base."

"Fine," said Howard, "I want to get there as soon as possible but no speeding tickets, please."

The driver stepped on the gas and pulled out into traffic. "But, senor, why are you concerned about my getting a speeding ticket?"

"It will just slow things up, that's all," he lied.

As the cab sped down the long, straight road toward the air force base, Howard sat quietly holding Sandra's hand and daydreaming. He was wondering if this was really happening to him or was just some wild-ass dream. His relationship with Maureen was gone, he would probably never see his children again, and the whole fucking world was about to be blown to smithereens. It all seemed too absurd to even be a dream. It had to be real.

He pondered his life. *Any regrets? Not really*, he thought. He would have done things a little differently, but not much. There was this one girl he really liked, when he was a kid, but he never asked her to marry him. If he were only a little more aggressive. "Oh stop second-guessing yourself," he mumbled. "You did the best you could. Didn't you?"

What am I thinking about this shit for anyway. What am I going to say to Colonel Jones when I get to the base? That's what's important now. I have to deal with the present and the future. The past is done. Just a memory, at best. Or worst.

Colonel Jones, what did you do with that spy that you're holding? Not a likely opener, he thought. *I don't think that we will have any trouble, though. I'm sure Jones will be thrilled to see us, so that we can help with his 'situation,'* he considered.

Howard nodded off and Sandra didn't bother to disturb him. She was too busy watching the scenery: tumbleweed rolling along, the jack rabbits darting about, the cactus standing nobly by, the prairie dogs on their hind legs looking around for predators, lizards scurrying by and a big hawk circling above watching it all from his heavenly perch. The car sped on.

There didn't seem to be any unusual activity going on as the cab passed the guard post and headed for the main building. Howard wouldn't tell Jones why he was there, when the guard stopped their car and he asked for the colonel. But then he did say that it concerned the unexpected visitor that Jones was holding and Jones told Howard that he would be waiting for him in his office.

"I wonder where they're keeping M22," he whispered to Sandra.

"He's very strong you know," she responded. "After the body replacement, you become five times stronger than you were before."

"Which means that if you had had your body replaced you could beat me up."

"Sounds like a good idea anyway."

"Don't try it, I have the air force to protect me now."

They wrestled a little in the back seat, they laughed and he kissed her. It seemed to soothe Howard's nerves.

The cab pulled up to the door. "Do you want me to wait?" asked the driver.

"No," said Howard. I have no idea how long we will be." *If we get out at all*, he thought. "How much?"

"Seexty dollars," said the driver smiling. "We have to charge you for driving boat ways. Tha's why eet's sometimes cheaper to have me wait."

"That's okay, money's not the problem." Howard paid the driver and added ten dollars for a tip.

"Tank you, senor."

Howard waved his hand and turned to enter the building. As he did, a man in uniform stepped up to greet him. The man was short and stocky with a blond crew cut. A wide gap between his upper front teeth predominated when he smiled. "I'm Corporal Pendleton, sir—and ma'am. I'm here to escort you to Colonel Jones."

"Lead the way, Corporal."

They walked up the stairs to the colonel's office. Pendleton knocked.

"Come in," said Jones.

As they entered Jones got up walked out from behind his desk and crossed the floor to greet his guests. Pendelton stood stiffly by.

"Thank you, Corporal. That will be all."

"Sir," responded Pendleton saluting, turning and striding out. Then he softly but firmly closed the door behind him.

"Mr. Cooper," Jones began.

"Howard is fine."

"Okay, Howard. And who is this lovely young lady."

"Colonel Jones, please meet Sandra."

"Is Sandra involved in this in some way?"

"I guess you can say that. She's from the same planet as Marshall Brown, whom you are holding."

"So he *is* an alien spy, and what planet are they from, Mr. Cooper?"

"It doesn't have a name and neither one of us would know it if it did."

"Fair enough," said Jones, staring at Sandra for a moment. "Another one."

The hair on the back of Howard's neck bristled.

"She's not—another ONE. Her name is Sandra!"

"Yes, of course. Sandra, I'm pleased to meet you," said Jones, regaining his manner. He looked at Howard again, as though he were an interpreter or guide and Sandra one of the natives not capable of speaking or comprehending the language. "Are there any other ones with you?"

"No," said Howard, obviously pissed again, but trying to maintain his composure. "Just Sandra—and Marshal Brown of course. Speaking of Marshal Brown, could we see him?"

"No, that's not possible."

"Why is that?"

"He's not here."

"Where is he?"

"I'm afraid I can't tell you that."

"Well then, I guess we cannot tell you anything until we see him."

"I don't have the authority to allow that."

"Do what you need to do to get it. Because if you want our help, we must know that he is all right and be able to speak with him."

"Whose side are you on?" asked Jones testily.

Howard went pale. He didn't realize that it would be this difficult. "Whose side do you think I'm on?"

"I don't know. They set you up with a nice piece of ass and I don't know what else and all you have to do is to betray your country. What—your country. The whole fucking world. Don't you have a family? Don't you give a shit? Boy, she must be pretty good, this one. Or maybe you're not what you say you are. That's it, you're probably one of them in disguise trying to get your partner free."

"Oh bull shit," said Howard. I'm not one of them. I'm one of us. I'm just caught in the middle of this. I've already lost my family and now I have to put up with this crap from you. Look, if I were really one of them, I could rip your head off with no trouble, with my bare hands. Do you know how strong these people are?"

"Oh, people, are they?"

"Don't get technical, you know what I mean. If you were on their planet, how would you like to be called a creature or a being?"

"But I'm not a creature or a being, I'm a person—and they're not! And I'm not on their planet they're on mine!"

They stood there regarding each other for a moment. Jones slowly changed into his best official smile, realizing that this was neither the time nor place for a dick measuring contest. And that perhaps he was overstepping his authority by conducting himself in this manner. He also thought of how he could make amends for his conduct.

Sandra spoke. "Well you know who I am."

Jones was startled slightly, not expecting the young lady to contribute. He stared at her expectantly.

"Things will be at lot easier if you cooperate with us and let us see Marshall. He will not speak with you until we are in his presence."

Jones looked at Sandra, then at Howard, then turned and slowly walked behind his desk. He picked up the phone while still attempting to size up his visitors. He dialed slowly. "General Maddox please, it's urgent."

Jones continued to eye the two warily, at the same time maintaining his best forced smile. "By the way," he said while holding, "is she as strong as five women?"

He put the phone back to his ear. "General, you'll never guess who I have sitting here in my office. That's right, Howard Cooper, the newspaper editor who claims to have been kidnapped by the aliens and another alien, a young woman, this time. Her name is Sandra. They say that they are here to help us, but insist on speaking with our 'guest' before any of them will cooperate."

"Well then, jump on a plane and get your collective asses out here," said Maddox firmly. "And don't lose them or you'll be sweeping out airplane hangers in Alaska."

"Yes, General," he said, making a face into the phone, then caught himself and smiled again. He hung up and looked at his visitors.

"Well you got your wish. I hope you all enjoy the trip."

"Are you coming?" asked Howard curiously.

"I wouldn't miss it for the world. Besides I'm responsible for you two, so please behave yourselves. That is if you don't mind."

"For you, Colonel, anything," said Howard mockingly.

M22 lay in his bed. The door opened slowly. General Maddox and four other military personnel entered, two armed. M22 maintained his position, lying on his back and staring up at the ceiling as the general came into his view. Maddox looked down at him for a moment before speaking.

"You have visitors on their way to see you."

M22's eyes widened.

"They came all the way from your planet to see you. Does that make you happy?"

M22 tried to look pleased without speaking.

"They should be here in a few hours. Would you like to do something to prepare for their arrival?"

M22 shook his head no.

"After they get here maybe we all can sit down and have a nice civilized conversation? Do you think that that would be possible?"

"That would be nice," responded M22 to everyone's surprise.

"We can start speaking now if you wish," said Maddox, excited by M22's newfound speech.

M22 just shook his head.

"Are you certain?" persisted Maddox.

M22 just lay there staring up at him. Maddox looked at him for a moment, then waved his head toward the door and they all left. He lingered a moment hoping for a surprise, but none came. He followed the others out and closed the door tightly behind him.

CHAPTER ELEVEN

"I'm picking up an interesting thought from you," said General Titus, "please elaborate."

Rondo continued for another moment staring at Earth through the portal of his ship. He turned and faced the general squarely. "It is a beautiful planet. What a shame it is inhabited by fools. If that is the thought you read, you are correct. Too bad our telepathy does not work on Earth; if it did, M22 would probably be finished with his task by now. But he says there is so much interference down there that he cannot read any minds clearly. So he has been forced to rely on the more primitive methods of communication."

"If only we had such a beautiful planet and were not forced to live in the barren wasteland as we inhabit," he said.

"Yes, of course, Titus. You use such an interesting word, *forced*. We were not really forced to live there, as you know. But we chose our planet for a particular reason: because it is so undesirable. And that is why we cannot live on Earth. We hide from the barbarians. If we were on such a beautiful planet as Earth, we would fear discovery and possible conquest. It is dangerous enough inhabiting such a desirable planet, but with all their projectiles and radio signals flying all over the universe, trying to attract more attention than they already might have is sheer madness. If barbarians do not yet know them, they will soon enough. The predators must think it is a trick that the earthlings are playing; why else would they do such a foolish thing. And we know we must hide, even if they do not. Our planet may not be beautiful and full of life-giving oxygen like theirs, but at least it's safe."

"Can we eliminate the people and still save the planet?" asked Titus.

"Well," said Rondo, "in fact it's quite ironic. For it seems from our analysis of the planet and its inhabitants that the only way to save the planet is to remove the ones who are destroying it, namely the humans. So we are doing this planet and all its other inhabitants a favor."

"How can this be done?"

"I will ask Einstein to find a way. We need something that kills only humans. He will find a way. You can bet your life on that!"

It stands only five stories high, with two additional floors beneath ground level. But with a circumference of nearly one mile, this monstrous squat structure faced with Indiana limestone is occupied daily by nearly twenty-five thousand people. It accommodates twice the office space of the Empire State Building and covers more than twenty-nine acres of what was once known as Hell's Bottom.

The building, consisting of five separate concentric structures or rings, one within the other connected by passageways, has its own train station, post office, infirmary, police force, radio and television station, heliport and telephone exchange.

This edifice, the inspiration of much fiction, myth and legend, which sits with one of its faces peering out over the Potomac, at the nations capital, houses the joint military command of the United States of America. It is called the Pentagon and other less flattering names from time to time. If it could fly, it would look like quite an impressive space ship.

The rings of buildings are designated A through E from the center out. M22 lay in the second sub-basement of E ring, in the side of the building facing away from the Potomac, in a drab isolated room, in a secured section of corridor. He is watched and monitored twenty-four hours a day. Two heavily armed marines stand guard outside the bolted door and additional men are but moments away.

"Maggie, get Professor Clearview on the phone—immediately! Tell him he must come at once," said General Goodwood, the chairman of the Joint Chiefs of Staff, into his intercom. "And Maggie, tell him that it's a national emergency. No, an international emergency." Goodwood turned toward his window and watched the noonday traffic on the highway flowing by the building. "Could it really be possible?" he wondered aloud. "Are there truly people from another planet threatening Earth? Could the message we intercepted be real? God, if it is, we're not going to need officers and enlisted men to fight this battle, we're going to need diplomats and negotiators and scientists and priests. Our conventional forces are capable of fighting Earth bound foe. We..."

"General," called Maggie, interrupting his monologue. "The professor is not at Yale today. He's right here in Washington."

"Excellent! Track him down and get him here as quickly as possible. Tell him as of now he is on expenses and that the government is prepared to pay for any loss due to his inconvenience, but he must come immediately."

"Yes, sir." She dialed the phone again. "This is the office of the chairman of the Joint Chiefs of Staff calling. I would like to know where Professor Clearview can be found at this moment...He is at lunch. Do you know the restaurant? It's quite important...Thank you."

"General," said Maggie into the intercom. "We found him, he's eating lunch."

"Good. Get Major Farrel on the phone and tell him to take a staff car and two burly marines immediately to get the professor."

Twenty minutes later the staff car arrived at L'Atoil restaurant in downtown DC. As the major and two marines entered all heads immediately turned to look. Farrel asked the maitre d' and the professor was pointed out. They waited politely as Clearview was told that they were there. Farrel was given the signal to come over to the table. As the three of them approached, they saw the professor wiping his mouth with a napkin.

"Yes, gentlemen. How can I help you? Would you like to join me in dessert?" He was about to dig into a delicious-looking Grand Marnier mousse.

"No thank you, Professor," said Farrel, politely.

"You're certain? It's quite good. You don't mind if I have mine, you appear to be in quite a hurry."

"Of course not, sir," replied Farrel, slightly embarrassed. The marines stood there impassively looking straight ahead.

"Now, what is this all about?"

"We were asked to take you to General Goodwood right away, sir."

"Not until I finish my mousse you don't," he said with mock anger. "Must be quite important if he sent all three of you. Did he anticipate that I would put up a struggle?"

The marines looked at each other and smiled. "I'm sure one or two of you would be quite sufficient. Although carrying me out these days might require at least two or three strong men. Especially with all these rich desserts I'm eating lately."

Just then, the waiter brought the bill. "The maitre d' thought that you might be wanting this, sir," he said to Clearview.

"How considerate."

The major grabbed it. "Complements of the general, sir—for the inconvenience."

"Well, the general was always considerate that way."

A moment later they were in the car and on their way to the Pentagon.

From Pennsylvania Avenue to 11th Street, the car turned right onto Ninth toward I-395 South and Arlington. They merged into US Route 1, and the professor could see the Pentagon looming as they crossed the Potomac River heading into Arlington, VA.

As the general's staff car approached the building, Clearview again marveled at the extent of this manmade structure. "It still amazes me every time I see it," he said to no one in particular.

"Yes, Professor," returned Farrel, smiling, "pretty impressive for an Earthbound object, isn't it?"

The car let them out at an entrance near General Goodwood's office. After securing the proper pass, Clearview was escorted up.

"Go right in, Professor," said Maggie, "the general is expecting you."

"I would hope so," he said with a smile, "after he practically kidnapped me to bring me here."

Maggie gave Clearview an uncomfortable look.

"Only teasing, Maggie. And how are you doing these days? Is the good general working you to death as usual?"

"I'm just fine, Professor. And thank you for asking."

She pressed the intercom. "Professor Clearview is here, sir," she said, then pressed the buzzer to let him enter. Clearview strode in with an expectant look in his eyes.

"Sam, good of you to come so soon. I appreciate your understanding."

"What understanding?" he said with a wry look on his face. "Those bruisers of yours looked like they were prepared to carry me out bodily if I didn't consent to come along peacefully."

"I see you haven't lost your sense of humor, Sam."

"I suspect I'm going to need more than a sense of humor to handle what you're probably planning to spring on me."

Hum—you got that right, he thought. He considered the man in front of him: professor of astronomy, astrophysics and biology at Yale University. Author, lecturer and expert on the concept of extraterrestrial life. This man may hold the fate of the human race in his hands, he thought, and it gave

Goodwood a funny feeling. "This may be your first opportunity to speak to an alien, or someone who claims to be one. Well he certainly isn't human; our tests have shown us that. Unless he is some kind of humanoid, someone cooked up in a lab somewhere, he comes from some place else other than this planet. And as an extra-added attraction there's a man who claims to have been kidnapped by these aliens, who's expected here at any moment with his alien girlfriend. I guess you can say that there is no limit on how far this guy will go when he wants *a strange piece of ass*."

"Boy if I had known this, I would have even given up my mousse," said Clearview with a smirk.

"Look, seriously, Sam, what are the odds that these guys are for real?"

"Well let's put it this way. Mathematically speaking, the chances of hitting any given point on the wall with a dart are zero. Yet, the dart must land somewhere. So it's a paradox, because theoretically the area of a point is zero."

"Please, Sam, speak English."

"Well the point is, even in a situation where mathematically the chances are nil, it can still happen. It's what we call—a paradox."

"Therefore?!" the general asked impatiently.

"Therefore—technically speaking—depending how you calculate it—there can be between one hundred and one hundred thousand planets capable of creating and sustaining life as we know it. But what does that really mean? What does it tell us?"

"WHAT?!"

"That it's possible—that's all," said the professor with a hands-open gesture.

"Shit! In other words—you just don't know."

"I suppose you could put it that way. You see, you could have saved my fee."

"Oh, you didn't earn your fee yet, not by a long shot, Sam. Not by a long shot."

"Well then, how do I do that?"

"By telling me if you believe if these—whatever they are—are on the level and to know where they're coming from."

"You don't mean that literally, I hope."

"Damn it, Sam. Are you pulling my leg?"

"Yes, I suppose I am, but just a little. Okay. I can certainly judge by their manner if they seem to be on the level or not. Theoretically, of course. But then, if these guys know their beans, we might be fooled. All I can do is my best."

"God, Sam, you paint such a glum picture."

"Not to worry. We scientists are pessimistic by nature. The odds are always against something great from occurring. So—we learn to be pessimistic for our own sanity and peace of mind."

"Well, my sanity and peace of mind are not doing very well at this moment."

"Not to worry, General, they haven't fooled me yet."

"Finally, some comforting optimism."

Colonel Jones and his guests landed at Langley Air Force base in Virginia. From there, the group took a helicopter to the space ship that never flies.

As the helicopter flew over the Capital, Howard pointed out all the places of interest to Sandra, as Colonel Jones sat with a long face wondering if this information would ever be used against the country at a later date. At first he wanted to stop Howard from conducting the sight seeing tour, but then realized anyone could find out this information without much trouble and just sat there with a long sourpuss.

As they landed, General Maddox and a small entourage were waiting patiently for them. As the three visitors cleared the helicopter blades, Maddox was waiting with his hand outstretched and a big official smile on his face. "What a pleasure it is to have you two here. I just know that we can help each other to resolve this international—er, that is—interplanetary problem."

Howard and Sandra gazed back at Maddox not knowing what to say. They were asked to sit in two-man golf carts for their trip inside this city within the walls. Maddox sat next to Howard, while Jones accompanied Sandra. The latter pair was silent but Maddox had plenty to say.

"It's okay," he said to Howard in a reassuring tone, "we'll just take it a step at a time. First I want you to freshen up because tonight the chairman of the Joint Chiefs of Staff wants to meet and speak with the two of you."

Howard looked at Maddox with resolve. "We must see Mr. Brown first."

"You mean the spy? But the chairman wants to see you two."

"You have your instructions and we have ours."

Maddox, obviously upset by Howard's last remark, hit the brakes and skidded slightly in an attempt to miss crashing into a wall. He gave Howard a strange look, but before he could say anything Howard spoke again.

"They had me up there on their planet. I thought that I would never come back again. I'm not here to betray my country or my world, but nothing can happen until I speak with their agent, Mr. Brown." Howard wasn't sure if he believed what he was saying himself. But at least he thought that he might find a way to settle this problem if he got the opportunity. But first, of course he had to do their bidding or at least appear as though he was. "I hope you drive a car better than you drive one of these," he said, ending on a lighter note.

Maddox was not amused. "How do we know that you're not just another one of them in disguise?"

"Test me if you want. But I guess that won't do you any good. I could be brainwashed of something. But does it really matter? You will just have to monitor my activities as we go along. But I swear I'm just as human as you are. Now, we must see Mr. Brown right now if we can, and then we will speak to the chairman."

They came to a bank of escalators. One of the entourage led the way down one flight. They walked the rest of the way.

"I have to get clearance." Maddox finally said in response to Howard's request to see M22.

"Do as you must, but please bear in mind that this point is non-negotiable."

Maddox gave Howard a vengeful look without replying.

"Here are your rooms," said the general, flashing his official smile again.

Howard leaned over to Sandra and whispered, "Go in your room, I'll be by in a moment." Sandra smiled politely and entered her room.

"I'll wait for your response," Howard said as pleasantly as he could.

"I hope you enjoy your stay," returned the general in a tone Howard could not quite judge.

The call came within the hour, but Howard was not there. They tried Sandra's room and Howard came to the phone. "Yes?"

"Mr. Cooper?"

"Yes—this is Howard Cooper."

"This is Major Murphy calling for General Maddox. Can you be ready in fifteen minutes, sir?"

"Yes."

"Good. The general will be by to pick you up, sir, to take you to see Mr. Brown."

"Fine. Sandra and I will be ready."

"I'll tell the general, sir."

Cooper put down the phone slowly and looked at his companion. After he related the conversation to her, he added: "I hope it's not one of their tricks."

"Would they do such a thing?"

"You don't know. The military is capable of anything. I really don't know how they think. There is an old expression that seems to sum it up: 'there's the right way, the wrong way and the Army way.' But—I guess there's no reason for them to play games," he said, thoughtfully rubbing his chin. "There's too much at stake and they're at a stalemate with M22. They need us right now. And they know it."

"But what will they do with us after we help them?" added Sandra.

"That's the sixty-four-dollar question."

"They did not seem very friendly, especially that Colonel Jones."

"It's not up to Jones," he said. "It would be his superiors who would make a decision like this. But you can rest assured that they are going to play it as safe as possible; that is why they're in the military. They're not where they are for being nice guys. They're here because they get the job done."

"Are they really that bad?"

"Only if you're on the wrong side," he said, shaking his head and flashing an ironic smile.

Sandra responded with a look of concern.

Howard felt bad that he had alarmed her. "We'll work it out," he told her, trying to act confident. "We'll find a way to keep ourselves valuable to them. They need us and they know it!" Howard punctuated his last remark by making an aggressive gesture with his fist.

"We'd better get ready. They'll be here in a few minutes," he said, moving toward the door.

Howard was ready for the knock on his door when it sounded. He opened it slowly and he and Sandra again joined Maddox and his men riding their golf carts to the "nineteenth hole." They again rode to a set of down escalators. Went down and continued their ride on fresh "horses." As they rode down the endless corridors, Sandra was almost dizzy as she watched the infinite stream of floor tiles passing under her cart.

Finally they came to the restricted area and they had to leave their carts and walk. The trip had been passed in virtual silence. Howard spoke first.

"You have this guy locked up pretty tight, don't you?"

116

"What did you expect?" asked Jones.

Maddox glared at him. Jones tired to look contrite. But it was not Jones' usual posture.

"I hope he's being treated well."

"What are you from the Red Cross?" snapped Jones.

"Colonel Jones!" said Maddox.

"Yes, sir," replied the colonel.

The general just shot him another look.

"No, I'm not from the Red Cross, Colonel," offered Howard with a charitable look. "This is for the sake of all of us."

"We'll find out just whose sake you're really concerned about, Mr. Cooper, when the time comes."

"That will be all, Colonel!" demanded Maddox.

"Yes, sir," repeated Jones, moving away from Cooper.

"Actually," added Maddox, "this security is more for our guest's protection, than anything else."

"Guest, aye. Well I'm glad you think of him that way, General. Does that mean he would be free to go whenever he wanted?"

"Well—not really. You see that decision is out of my hands. Only the President has the authority to decide that."

Jones gloated at watching Maddox being backed into a corner, but he tried not letting the general catch him at it.

They approached the room. It was not the same room as M22 occupied before.

"Two armed guards, General?" asked Howard.

"Protection. As I said, he's a very important guest."

"Hmmm," responded Howard. Sandra smiled peculiarly. Major Murphy knocked politely on the door. No answer came. He knocked again, with no response. The major looked back at Maddox, who nodded. The officer opened the door slowly. There was M22 seated comfortably in a chair.

"Would you accompany us please?" said the major.

Howard and Sandra glanced inside the room as M22 rose from his seat and proceeded toward the door. Howard thought the room looked comfortable, which was obviously why they moved him there.

As M22 came out, Howard rushed toward him with Sandra in tow.

"I'm Howard Cooper and this is Sandra, from your planet. We have been sent here by Rondo to speak with you."

M22 smiled and seemed happy to see them. Jones looked as though he was about to interfere but Maddox grabbed his arm before the former could act. Then Maddox addressed Howard: "Why don't we proceed to a conference room so that we can all talk?"

"We need to speak to Mr. Brown alone for a minute."

Maddox gave Howard a suspicious look. "I can't allow that."

"Why not?"

"It's just not permitted. No one may talk to him alone. You said you wanted to speak with him, you said nothing about being alone."

"If you want my cooperation, I have to have yours!"

"It's not my decision."

"It's irrelevant whose decision it is. I'm concerned about the policy, and if that's the policy, then everything stops right now. And you're right back where you started from. Nowhere! Fine, if that's what you want. So, what are you going to do to us now? Torture us? Kill us? The aliens won't allow it, and you know it. We will all die anyway. So do what you want."

"Okay, okay, calm down," said Maddox, throwing Jones a look as if to say *maybe you were right after all* and Jones throwing back one to say, *I told you so.*

Maddox knew that he had little choice. Howard was just being smart about it and playing his cards to his advantage. "I'll have to call for permission."

Howard shrugged his shoulders as if to say, *whatever!*

Maddox went down the corridor and turned into one of the rooms. A moment later he came out. He approached Howard. "Go ahead. Do what you have to do. But make it quick." Maddox looked defeated. Jones was loving every minute of it.

Howard suspected that Maddox had never even called anyone. It was an old salesman's trick to hide the extent of your authority in making concessions in a negotiation and Howard was hip. But it really didn't matter, except perhaps for future reference.

Maddox had decided that it really didn't matter anyway, since none of these three were going anywhere. Maddox was just trying to exert as much control as possible over the situation, to make things move more quickly in the direction he wanted to go.

"We'll find a room on the way," said Howard.

"What's wrong with the room he just came out of?" asked Maddox.

Howard smiled an ironic smile. If he were a cartoon character the word *Bugged!* would be floating above his head connected to him by little circles meaning *guess what I'm thinking?*"

Maddox did not require the super titles. "As you like," he said, "just please do not take any longer than necessary." Jones just watched in silence.

"God, this guy doesn't miss a trick," Maddox said to himself.

They walked a little way down the hall and found a small office that seemed adequate for their purpose. The three walked inside and closed the door, while the armed forces waited outside.

"I just received a message from Rondo," started M22.

"How?" blurted out Howard.

"That is not important. The important thing is that we must play for time."

"Why?" asked Howard.

"I shouldn't tell you that either."

"You had better tell me something. Either I'm involved completely or not at all. This is really bullshit; I'm not trusted by either side. Look, you guys either work with me or forget the whole thing and you can handle it yourself. I want to know what's going on. Or you can all go to hell! And remember that I am the only one who can effectively deal with both sides."

"I can see how effective you are," said M22 ironically. "Rondo warned me that you might be difficult."

"Difficult! My entire world is about to end. My whole planet is about to be wiped out and destroyed! You're goddamned right I'm difficult! And I'm going to get a lot more difficult unless I get some answers. Now—are you going to tell me or not?"

"You may not like what you hear."

"I'm sure I won't. But I have to know, anyway."

M22 just looked at him for a moment without saying anything. Then he spoke slowly. "They will spare your planet—"

Howard began to smile. "I thought you said I wouldn't like it."

"I'm not finished. Do not get too happy too fast. Your people will die— all the people—but only the people. Everything else will survive - all the plants and all the animals. In fact, they said getting rid of the people might be the only way to guarantee the survival of any kind of life on the planet. If it is not already too late."

Howard's face dropped. He looked down at the floor. Sandra stood closer and held his hand. She appeared frightened and upset by Howard's display. She came around to face him, still holding his hand in hers. "You knew your people were doomed. At least the planet will exist and everything else on it. We can come visit it from time to time."

Howard seemed to be ignoring her. But she knew he heard every word. "You mean like visiting a cemetery," he gave out with a mock laugh. "Ha! The funny part is that they're probably right. How simple it is to come to logical conclusions when you're on the outside. We're too close to it. We're too busy worrying about our own insignificant little lives to see what the hell we're doing. And when someone on the inside tries to warn us, we yell CRACKPOT! SAVE THE PLANET—KILL THE PEOPLE! What a great picket sign that would make. I ought to go into business printing the signs; I'd make a million bucks."

"Do not upset yourself," consoled Sandra. Howard smirked and shook his head.

"I am sure it must be very difficult for you," said M22.

"What can be done to save us?" Howard asked.

"We had better get back outside, before they start complaining," said M22.

"Yeah," said Howard, "I'm sure the natives are getting restless."

Professor Clearview sat in Goodwood's office. "When did you say that you expected them, General?"

"General Maddox went down for them awhile ago. I don't know what's taking so long. Maggie—oh that's right she's gone. She left early today. I'll get him myself." He reached for a walky-talky on his desk. He pushed the talk button. "General Maddox please, this is General Goodwood."

"Yes, sir," snapped the answer from the officer on the other end. "This is General Maddox."

"Jack. What's taking so long?"

"It's the damned Texan, sir. He's just being a great big pain in the ass."

"Whatever he's being get his ass in gear and get it up here fast. Professor Clearview charges by the hour!"

"Yes, sir."

Clearview smirked and shook his head. "I just love the way you use humor, General."

Maddox started walking toward the room where Howard was having his conference. As he approached, the door opened and Howard and the others walked out.

"We're ready, General."

"Good. The chairman of the Joint Chiefs is waiting for us in his office."

"I hope we don't disappoint him," said Howard.

M22 tugged at Howard's coat, signaling him not to make waves. This was consistent with M22's orders to get as high as possible, and get the information needed to help the Hidden People to proceed with their plans. This had to bring him closer to the President, he thought.

They were ushered to the anteroom of the chairman's office. On the right of the entrance were filing cabinets that held mostly computer media. To the left was word processing equipment. The major knocked on the door and was told to come in. He opened the door and stood aside to let the others by.

The chairman sat at the end of a rectangular table, the professor on his right. He and the professor rose. "Thank you, gentlemen, and lady, for coming so soon."

The professor laughed to himself; he didn't know if the chairman was being cute or just polite.

Maddox, Jones, Howard, Sandra and M22 were the only other ones at the table. They all sat. Maddox did the introductions.

"General, this is Howard Cooper, the brave patriot who was permitted by the aliens to visit their planet over the past few months. This is his friend, Sandra, from that same planet. I believe they call it the Hidden Planet. And this is Marshall Brown, who is also our guest from that same planet."

Jones rolled his eyeballs and looked toward the ceiling, trying to survive the saccharine sweet introduction. The professor smiled with understanding.

"And this is General Glen Goodwood, chairman of the Joint Chiefs of Staff," Maddox continued.

"And this is Professor Sam Clearview," added the chairman. "The professor has come as a consultant, on loan from Yale, to help keep things in prospective."

They all proceeded to size one another up. The newcomers looked around the office. It was spacious, the most spacious in the building—about the same size as the Secretary of Defense occupied. Everyone who visited was curious to know who had the larger office of the two. Along with the conference table there was a couch and armchairs with a coffee table in front of the couch.

"Why don't we sit by the coffee table. I believe we will be more comfortable there," said the chairman. "I'll have some refreshments sent in," he said, picking up the phone.

As they sat, the chairman turned to the group. We face a grave matter. No one wants war or bloodshed. I believe that these things have been overheard from conversations emanating from the space ship that your people have flown to our planet," he said, looking from M22 to Sandra and then to

Howard. "Please excuse my bluntness, but my understanding is that we, and our planet, are in grave danger." The chairman just sat silently, waiting for a response.

Cooper spoke believing neither M22 nor Sandra was prepared to address the greater issue. "If you don't mind my starting General," he said to Goodwood. "From my understanding these people from the Hidden Planet are of a peaceful nature. They only maintain arms for defensive purposes. We violated their secret place, which is the planet they now inhabit. It is called the Hidden Planet for that reason. They believe that it is necessary to hide from others that inhabit the galaxy that we share. Well, that may come as a surprise, but is it so surprising? We ourselves, who send up signals to the universe, have conquered and destroyed many lands and peoples around our own planet. So please do not look so shocked, gentleman. Naturally, we are of no direct threat to the Hidden People, because our technology is primitive compared to theirs. So, how do we pose a threat? By exposing their planet to others. What others, you might ask. The ones who may be receiving our radio waves and other earthly advertisements that are beaming out right now, as we speak. Will we survive? I doubt it. But the only chance that we might have at all is to convince these logical, moral creatures that we do not know the location of their planet, and if we do, we would not ever reveal it to others. The problem is, of course, if others conquer us we may have no choice but to tell whatever they want to know. To sum it up, what those aliens out there threatening us are saying is: 'Look, you Earth people, if you are foolish enough to jeopardize your existence we are not willing to allow you to take us with you.' That, gentlemen, is our predicament."

Moments passed with no one speaking.

"Go ahead, Professor," said Goodwood, "you're the expert."

"Don't you think that this is quite a severe way of making a point?" asked Clearview. "If I understand you correctly, we are being threatened with complete destruction."

"I could have said that," grumbled Goodwood under his breath.

Hearing his employer, the professor looked at him as if to say, "I'm doing the best I can." The chairman got the message.

M22 spoke. "If you do not know where my planet is, then there should not be any problem. If you do, then there are other things we must discuss."

"Like what?" asked Goodwood.

There was silence.

"Well, if there are other intelligences, as advanced as Mr. Browns, considering our lack of technology, the only damage we could do is tell others where Mr. Brown's planet can be found, as Mr. Cooper said," offered Clearview. "Before anyone says anything remember that we are only valuable to them alive if we have information that they want. Isn't that so, Mr. Brown?"

"I do not get involved with these kinds of considerations. That is for my leader and his advisors to decide. And again it is irrelevant, if you do not know where our planet is."

"What do you think, Mr. Cooper?" asked Goodwood.

"Well like the man—person says, General, if we don't know, what reason could they possibly have to harm us or our planet? I can assure you of one thing, conquest and subjugation of peoples is not part of their repertoire. And neither is wanton destruction," he said.

Goodwood gave Cooper a studied look. "Getting kind of preachy aren't you, Mr. Cooper." Then he brightened again. "Well, it's quite simple then, we just prove that we do not know where their planet is and we're home free. Isn't that right, Professor?"

"Well, I can't answer for the aliens, but as far as proving that we do not know where they are, well you must realize that even if it's true, and it is, I can assure you," he said, looking directly at M22, "it is infinitely easier to prove that something exists than to prove that it doesn't."

Sandra sat with a confused look on her face. M22 looked content. It seemed to him that his job was going to be a lot easier than he had expected.

"Excuse us a second, gentlemen—and lady," said Goodwood, taking the professor aside.

"What is it?" said Clearview.

"Sam, do we really know where their damn planet is or not?"

"No. We lost track of Pioneer 10 when it left our solar system twenty years ago. It must have somehow picked up speed, when it passed Pluto and wandered into their solar system."

"So how do we prove it? Like you said, how do you prove what you don't know?"

"You can't always. We can only tell the truth and hope that they believe it. If they are as smart and wonderful as Mr. Cooper claims, then they should know the truth when they hear it. Or maybe they have some version of a lie detector test."

"And not just destroy our planet, to be on the safe side?" asked Goodwood solemnly.

123

"Exactly, General."

They walked back to the couch and sat down. Goodwood smiled a long, slow, broad smile, scanning the gallery for a moment or so before speaking. "Mr. Brown, what would you consider adequate proof that we have no knowledge of your planet's location?"

"I cannot say. And, I am not the one you must convince. I am just here to gather information."

"And what have you gathered so far?"

"Only that you say that you do not know the location of my planet," he answered cautiously.

"Nothing else?"

"That is all. Therefore, I believe that my mission on your planet is now complete. If you will allow me to return to my ship, I will inform my superiors of the situation."

Colonel Jones began to speak, "General—"

Maddox grabbed his arm and raised his hand to silence him. "General," interjected Maddox, "why don't we have a private session and discuss our alternatives."

"Yes, that's a good idea. If you three would excuse us for a few moments—You can wait in the anteroom."

"Would it be possible for us to have some privacy also?" asked Howard.

"I don't see any harm in that," said Goodwood, pulling Maddox to the side. "We might as well be as nice to these people as we can afford to be."

"Alright, but I just don't trust them."

"Well, I don't trust them either, but we can discuss that further when they're gone. Are we secured? Can we allow them their privacy in my anteroom, without jeopardizing security?"

"As long as there isn't any material that you want to exclude them from in that room."

"Whatever is sensitive is locked up tight, so take care of it, Jack."

Maddox shook his head. "I still don't trust them." Maddox fiddled with the intercom as Goodwood walked back to the others. Maddox leaned hard on the talk button. "Major!"

"Yes, sir."

"Our guests will be using the chairman's anteroom for some privacy. Make certain the area outside is secured."

"Yes, sir."

Maddox turned to Howard and his companions. "Whenever you're ready you may use the chairman's anteroom."

Howard, who was now standing next to Sandra's chair, took her hand and started toward the door. M22 followed. Howard made certain that the door was closed securely behind him. They gathered around the secretary's desk in the anteroom. Except for them, it was empty. Howard sat behind the large desk and motioned the others to gather around. He started fiddling with the intercom. He noticed voices emanating from the box.

"Oh my God," he said to the others, "they must have left the talk button on." He motioned M22 closer. "How's your hearing? If they replace all your body parts, they should be better than mine. Can you hear what they're saying? Tell me verbatim what you hear."

M22 leaned over to listen. "I can hear them."

"Good," said Howard, "let's listen!" Somehow, Howard got the feeling that M22 found this scenario somewhat strange.

Let's try to look at this rationally...

"Who's speaking? Tell me who's speaking."

"That was the professor."

I don't care what you say; I just don't trust a one of them—especially that Cooper guy, at least with the others we know what we're dealing with.

"That's Maddox."

Just give me ten minutes alone with him and I'll beat the truth out of the traitor. I'll get him to talk or kill him trying. He probably deserves it anyway. Fuckin' turncoat!

"That's Jones."

Calm down.

"That's Goodwood."

Let's nuke the fuckin' spaceship and be done with it. I don't believe Cooper for a second—moral—logical—not in their repertoire! Who in the hell does he think he's talking to. That's the biggest bunch of shit I've ever heard. What does he take us for, a bunch of goddamned yokels?

"That's Colonel Jones again."

Well we certainly can't let this Marshall Brown go. Not until this thing is resolved. If we're blown up, he goes with us!

"That's Goodwood, again," said M22, betraying no emotion.

"Jesus Christ!" said Howard.

"Who's he?" asked Sandra.

"Never mind," he said, shaking his head, "you wouldn't believe me anyway. At any rate, we had better get out of here, as quickly as possible."

"How?" asked M22.

"I don't know!" shouted back Howard. "But we'd better use our heads. We'll never break out; they probably got half the damn Pentagon guarding us. We'll have to test the waters and see what our options are." Howard walked up to the door and knocked on it.

"Who is it?" said Goodwood.

"Howard Cooper."

"We haven't finished our discussions; we'll call you when we're done."

"I must talk with you now!"

Howard waited for a reply. Goodwood slowly opened the door while giving Howard an intense look. "What is it, Mr. Cooper? I hope it's good news."

"We overheard your conversation."

"What?!"

"Don't get angry at me. It's not my fault you left the intercom open."

Goodwood's eyes flashed. "Who the hell left the intercom..." he said, walking to his desk. "Jesus Christ! It *is* on. Jack, I can't believe you did this," he said, putting his hands on the sides of his head and shaking them.

"Who is this Jesus Christ?" Sandra whispered to M22.

"I don't know. Someone's name you say when you are angry, I guess."

"Hum," said Sandra.

"Okay," said Goodwood, looking at Howard. "What did you hear, and what about it?"

"You must let M22 go."

"Who?"

"Oh, Marshall Brown, his real name is M22. What's the sense of holding him? The aliens are not going to change their position whether you have him or not. It's just going to make things more difficult. Look, they have us by the balls and there is really nothing we can possibly do about it, except tell them the truth and hope for the best. All we can do is to try to appeal to their better nature and maybe they'll leave us alone. It certainly isn't going to help if we piss them off by holding one of their own hostage."

"Maybe!" remarked Maddox. "What the hell do you mean *maybe* they'll leave us alone?"

Clearview had a satisfied *I told you so* look on his face."

"Wait a minute, Jack," said Goodwood. "Let me handle this. So you're saying that we should just put ourselves at the mercy of these aliens?"

"Well, don't say it that way. How do you know how bad they are?"

126

"Well, you're telling me that they say that we're naive about the benign nature of alien life in the universe. Then you turn around, say that we should trust these aliens, and just allow ourselves to be at their mercy? What are you, nuts or something? What makes you so sure that they're benign? I'm a military man! Not a goddamned politician. I'm not paid to sit on my ass and let a bunch of creatures from God-knows-where do us in without a fight! Whether or not you think that they're all a bunch of Mother Theresa's and Mahatma Ghandi's rolled into one! And even if they do look like us."

"Talk to them at least. See what they have to say."

"I've already spoken to this one. It hasn't gotten us anywhere."

"He's just here to gather information. You have to talk to their leaders."

"Fine. If they want to talk, we'll talk. How do we get in touch with these aliens?"

"I'll take care of that."

"How?"

"What difference does it make?"

"It makes a great deal of difference," said Goodwood angrily. "You could communicate what you heard through the damn intercom. Where's the communicator?" he demanded.

Cooper stood silently defiant.

"I'll get that goddamned communicator," said Maddox, rushing at Cooper. Cooper stepped back but Maddox managed to grab him anyway.

"You fuckin' traitor. Give me that goddamned thing or your dead right here and now," said Maddox, pulling his side arm out of its holster. He lifted the gun and aimed it toward Cooper's head. M22 ran forward and grabbed Maddox's hand. Colonel Jones pulled his sidearm out.

M22 lifted Maddox off the ground like he was a rag doll. Jones began unloading the clip of his automatic into M22. As the first two rounds hit home, Maddox dropped from his grip. The next four put M22 down.

Everyone in the room watched in horror, Sandra fainted to the floor. Howard rushed to M22 to check his vital signs. Thirty seconds passed without a word being spoken. It seemed like an eternity. Howard looked at Jones with blood in his eyes. "Are you going to shoot me next?" he shouted.

Clearview looked like he was in shock.

"How about her?" yelled Howard. "Are you going to kill the girl, too?"

"Medic, get a medic!" yelled Goodwood.

Maddox rushed out of the office screaming for his men. "Major, Major, get a medic quick. A man's been shot."

"One of ours, General?"

"No. That alien. Hurry up, Major."

"Yes, sir."

Goodwood walked over to Howard, who was helping Sandra to the couch. "I don't know what to say."

"I think you said and did enough. Look what you did. You killed someone for nothing."

"It wasn't me, Cooper."

"One of your men then. What difference does it make who actually pulled the trigger."

Jones started toward Howard with blood in his eyes.

"Nothing?" he yelled. "Someone killed him for nothing?" he mimicked. "He attacked a general officer. What did you expect me to do? Stand by and watch a general officer of the United States Air Force being ripped apart by some alien gone wild. He lifted him up like he was a child. He could have killed General Maddox with his bare hands if I didn't intercede. Don't make believe you don't know how strong these creatures are. Would you rather that General Maddox was lying there ripped apart, instead of that alien?"

"I believe you're exaggerating just a bit, Colonel. He was just trying to protect me, that's all. Maybe it would have been me lying there if he hadn't stopped your precious general."

Just then, Maddox reentered the office. They all stood silent for a moment facing each other.

"Now I believe it's you who are exaggerating, Mr. Cooper. The general just wanted to talk to you," said Jones.

"Yeah, with the barrel of his gun."

Maddox made an almost imperceptible move toward Cooper but Howard instinctively backed up.

"*General!*" commanded Goodwood, in his sternest voice.

Maddox backed off. "Yes, sir."

"I'm sure your intentions are proper, but I think we've had enough for one day. We're going to have to deal with these creatures on their terms for now. Mr. Cooper, do what you have to, to make contact with them. I give you my word that there will be no violence, at least from our side. Now, where the hell is that medic?"

CHAPTER TWELVE

At 4:30 a.m., Howard's wrist alarm went off. He rolled over, half-asleep, half-awake, feeling quite disoriented. It took him a few moments to remember where he was. He jumped up when he realized what he had to do this morning. He got a little light headed from jumping up so fast, so he sat back down on his bed and wiped the sleep from his eyes. He sat staring for a moment at nothing in particular, like someone in a daze. Then slowly got up and walked into the bathroom. He shaved, showered and dressed.

At 5:15, there was a knock on his door. When he opened it, Major Walsh was standing outside. They went next door and got Sandra.

As they left the building, they found two black Cadillac stretch limousines parked outside. The major opened the back door of the front car, letting Howard and Sandra in. Maddox was already waiting for them. Walsh went into the second car.

"Where is General Goodwood?" asked Howard.

"He changed his mind about coming. He thought it would be better this way. He didn't want to seem too anxious or appear to kowtow."

"Kowtow! Haven't you people ever heard about manners or protocol?"

"We are in a life and death struggle here, Mr. Cooper. Fuck protocol! Power plays on all these creatures, understand?" Maddox shot a glance at Sandra who seemed somehow out of it.

"That's pretty funny. That's like a mouse trying to intimidate an elephant."

"I heard elephants were afraid of mice," returned Maddox.

"That's only in fairy tales."

"Well if you ask me, this whole damned thing resembles a fairy tale. With you as the chief fairy."

"Oh! Getting personal now, are we?"

"No, Mr. Cooper, I'm on orders to treat you in a courteous manner. We'd better get started, so that we're not late for our meeting with our alien."

The first car pulled out and the second one followed. They traveled on the main highway for a while, then, turned off onto a deserted stretch of road. They pulled into a meadow where a large circle of army trucks stood. All the trucks had special colored lights that shined directly up. The circle they made was fifty yards in diameter, which was determined to be quite adequate for General Titus' shuttle space ship to land safely.

The sun was not quite up. The time was 5:50 a.m. Maddox sat in the car. Howard and Sandra got out to stretch their legs and watch the sun rise. The sun was just sitting at the horizon. As they walked their shoes glistened from the heavy dew covering the grass.

At precisely 6:00 a.m., a space ship whizzed into view. It hovered for a moment overhead before landing exactly dead center in the middle of the circle.

The door of the space ship slid open and the majestic figure of General Titus slowly strode out, his silhouette framed against the rays of a breathtaking orange-yellow sunrise.

Howard, meanwhile, hurried back to the car as the space ship was landing, so as not to mess up any special procedures that Maddox had in mind.

The cars pulled up to where Titus was standing and the driver got out to open the door for Maddox. Maddox, Howard and Sandra all proceeded toward the space ship

Major Walsh waited by the cars.

"General, it is a great honor and pleasure to meet with you, sir. I am General Maddox."

"It is a pleasure to meet you, too.

"And this is Howard Cooper and Sandra, whom you might already know."

"No, I haven't had the pleasure, though I know of them," said Titus. Where is General Goodwood?" he said, turning his head to scan the area.

"He is making arrangements for our meeting."

"Umm," said Titus, "I look forward to our meeting."

Maddox was trying to size up this General from outer space. He still could not get over the fact that they looked so much like humans. Maddox could find no weakness in his carriage, no flaw in his manner. He truly understood how he could have been programmed to look and act exactly the way that he did. He was the perfect model of a commanding General.

"Please come with me, General."

Maddox led Titus back to his car with Howard and Sandra trailing behind. They all got into the first car, while Walsh brought up the rear.

"We brought the two cars, anticipating your entourage," said Maddox.

"That was very thoughtful of you, but as you can see, I can manage on my own."

The small caravan started back with a police car, one in front and one in back, as escorts.

They road for a short while in silence. Then General Titus said, "This is pleasant but don't you find this mode of travel rather slow and bumpy? You have this beautiful space in which you can fly. We, on the other hand, live in a closed environment."

"You are quite correct, General, but it is too expensive and impractical for the majority of the people to fly short distances all the time."

"Expensive? Why, building these roads much cost a great deal more in time and what you call money to build and maintain."

"No doubt, General, but the roads were here long before our flying machines took to the skies. But, hopefully, we will be in that mode in the future."

The last word seemed to hang in the air. *Future!* Would there be one? It seemed to end the conversation for the remainder of the trip.

They reached the Pentagon at 6:35 a.m.

His long, gray cape would have turned every head in the corridors if they had not been empty at this hour. He walked ramrod straight and his face carried a pleasant look, not quite a smile. Titus seemed to enjoy riding in the golf cart. He smiled just slightly more than usual during the short ride.

They arrived at Goodwood's office and went immediately in.

As Titus walked in Goodwood was just inside the door waiting to greet him.

"General Titus, how was your trip down? I apologize for not being able to meet you. And how do you like Washington?"

"Great, I'll take it!"

Goodwood stared intently at him. Everyone else seemed puzzled.

"Just a little alien humor, General," said Titus, smiling broadly, "they told me it couldn't miss."

"Oh, that's very funny, General Titus," said Goodwood, forcing a laugh. "It's nice to know that you have a sense of humor."

"Only when appropriate, General Goodwood, only when appropriate."

Everyone else seemed relieved and a little bewildered.

"Well, shall we sit down? Please sit on the couch," said Goodwood.

They all sat.

"Please ask what you will," said Goodwood, hoping to avoid any superfluous humor.

"What can you tell me about the probe?"

"The probe," said Goodwood, trying to act nonchalant. "You mean the one that your people intercepted?"

"Why, are there many others?"

Goodwood wanted to kick himself for saying that. "Not really, General, we have some others flying around our solar system for scientific purposes. But that's about it."

"Well, I understand that you send these things up all the time in an attempt to contact other life forms like yourselves."

"Not really, General. It takes a great deal of resources to send these probes up and we have other problems to deal with on Earth that require these resources."

"Yes, I've heard about that, too. But getting back to this probe that we intercepted, can you tell me a little more about it from your perspective?"

"Well, it was launched twenty-five years ago, as a means of contacting other forms of life in the universe."

"Did you track it?"

"Only until it left the solar system, by that time the batteries were so weak and the signal so faint that we lost all contact.

"Well, that would be quite convenient if it were true. It would make things a lot easier."

Goodwood and all his guests let out a sigh of relief.

"We must study the power cells on your probe to see whether or not we can determine this conclusively. The problem is, though, even if the batteries did give out, how would we know when? How would we know how long you tracked the probe? It could have given out just before it reached our planet. Do other peoples from other planets know of this probe?"

"We have no way of knowing that. We do not know of other peoples; that's why we sent up the probe."

"What are you saying?"

"Well, General Titus, I'm trying to be precise in my answer. We are not aware of other intelligences in the universe, except yours, now. But, if there are, well, as small and insignificant as our probe is, it could have possibly

132

been tracked. But if it were tracked, we have no knowledge of it."

"I hope for all our sakes that the probe was not tracked, General Goodwood."

"We can certainly agree on that, General."

"And if it were tracked?"

"Then, I guess you can say that we might unintentionally bring harm to your people. But in either case, there would be no reason to harm our planet or us. There would be one, of course, which would be vengeance. I am told that you are not a vengeful people, though. Am I correct, General Titus?"

"You are correct; we are not vengeful. We do what is right. We are what you would call a logical and moral people."

"I'm very pleased to hear that, General. And I want you to know that we try to be moral as well."

"That pleases me, too. Do you know where our scout, M22, is? You may know him as Marshall Brown. I am surprised, frankly, that he is not among you."

Everyone froze. All eyes went to Goodwood. He had discussed this with Maddox and Jones, knowing it might come up. "He left before you came. We thought perhaps he had returned to your space ship."

"No, he has not."

"He had requested to leave. He said his job was finished and he left."

"You just let him go like that?"

"We had no right to hold him. He was just a guest up until then and you were coming to meet with us, so we did not believe that we should hold him against his will."

Goodwood was lying through his teeth and both Howard and Sandra knew it and Titus suspected. Goodwood was betting on their keeping their mouths shut. He really had little choice. He could either lock them up or take his chances. As he saw it, they should see no point in betraying him. *After all,* he thought, *what would they gain by throwing a monkey wrench into the situation?* He was fairly certain Howard would be cool, but the girl was less predictable. Howard had been briefed on the matter and he gave his assurances that he would not betray Goodwood and his country. Goodwood's only hope with the girl was that Howard had enough influence over her to keep her quiet. The truth was though, that Howard was naturally obliged to go along with the plan, or at least pretend to. But Goodwood and his fellows could not know what would actually happen. Certainly if Howard and Sandra were missing it would have raised even greater suspicion, so the balance was struck.

"He has not returned to us and did not tell us that he had left here," said Titus about M22.

"Maybe he is still doing some scouting for you? Naturally, we would not be too pleased with that, but what could we do about it? He told us that he was returning directly to your ship when he left."

"I guess we will have to solve this mystery together then, General Goodwood."

"I would like to move further in our discussions, General Titus."

"I'm afraid until M22 is found there can be no further discussions."

"But what if he's off some place; we can't let this get in the way of these talks. It's too important to both our peoples. I'm sure you and your people have better things to do than hang around our planet. Besides, who knows where he might be? He could be anywhere. He could have drowned at sea for all we know. Or fallen off a cliff somewhere or is out celebrating and having a good time for himself at the end of his assignment. Maybe he is just letting off some steam. Maybe he found some of the women around here attractive...."

"Enough, General! Our people are disciplined and do not participate in any of the things that you described. We are specifically bred for our work, programmed, I believe you call it. So M22 would report straight back to us if he were truly free. So we shall see, General Goodwood, we shall see. These things have a funny way of clearing themselves up one way or another."

No one spoke; all eyes were on Goodwood and Titus. They all wondered who would speak first. And as these things go, the least likely person spoke.

"Isn't it wonderful to be on a planet where you can see the sky and breathe the air outside, General Titus?" asked Sandra.

Maddox wanted to give her a dirty look so badly it hurt, but he was afraid Titus would catch him, so he just had to grin and bear it.

Goodwood was happy that the girl lightened the conversation up a bit. He hoped that Titus would jump on the bandwagon and lighten up a little himself.

"Yes, it is a wonderful planet, Sandra, but that is not the issue that we are discussing," said Titus evenly.

"M22 may be out there right now enjoying the beauty of this planet, while we are sitting here concerned about his situation," continued Sandra.

It's amazing, thought Maddox, *this innocent little fool may be, if even in a small way, helping to save our onions and she probably doesn't even realize it.* Goodwood couldn't help feeling grateful.

impeccabHoward looked at her but was trying not to make it seem too obvious. Who could have more credibility than one of their own?

Goodwood jumped on the bandwagon. "That is quite possible, General Titus. I would have not thought of that myself, but the young lady is making quite a good point. I'm sure she knows your own people better than we do."

"Of course it is possible," replied Titus. Diplomatically he was in a difficult position. He didn't want to discredit or embarrass one of his own people but he didn't want to lose the advantage either. He wished that she had told him this in private. But the deed was done. And that was that. He had to make the most of the situation. "We will just have to wait and see if he turns up. If he is out there enjoying himself as Sandra says, I'm certain he will not be there for long. Our people act more responsibly than that. He will return soon." Titus knew well that trained spies would never act in such an irresponsible manner as Sandra so naively suggested. And he was not the only one who knew it. Sandra had saved their asses, but only for the moment.

"What will you do now, General Titus?" asked Howard.

"I must go back to my ship."

"Now?" asked Goodwood.

"There is no point in continuing our discussions, with M22 gone. Until we know his fate the purpose of this meeting is groundless."

"General, Sandra and I will return with you," said Howard.

Goodwood and Maddox both knitted their eyebrows at Howard. But he was getting out whether they liked it or not.

"I'd prefer if you stayed on, Mr. Cooper, we have things to discuss," said Goodwood.

"Well, you cannot keep me here," said Sandra, "if I do not want to stay." Titus looked at Goodwood.

"I'm not going to keep anyone against their will. You are all guests here."

"Good," said Howard, "I would like to leave with the general then as well."

"But you're from Earth, you're one of us, and we have things to discuss," said Goodwood as firmly as possible, without seeming harsh.

"I made a commitment to return to the ship with General Titus."

Maddox was getting pissed. And Goodwood was afraid of what he would tell them when they were alone. In reality, Howard didn't want any part of either side. At this moment, he felt he needed time to think. Somehow, he would have to escape.

"Shall we go, General?" said Howard.

"General?!" said Titus to Goodwood.

Goodwood stood for a moment, seething inside. He had no choice and he knew it. Maddox stood, grinding his teeth. "General Maddox," he said finally, "please show our guests back to their ship."

"Yes, sir," said Maddox, displeased that his boss was knuckling under.

Howard and Sandra got their stuff and the three were on their way back to the space ship. They rode in the limo with Maddox and the driver.

"Could you pull over to the side of the road?" asked Howard as they passed a deserted stretch.

"Are you kidding?" said Maddox.

"No, I have a very weak bladder."

"We'll be at the ship soon."

"But we're stuck in traffic and I have to go, now. What difference does it make to you?"

"None, I guess," said Maddox, thinking he was losing Cooper anyway, so what difference did it make, except that the man annoyed him.

General Titus and Sandra didn't know what to make of it.

The car pulled over to the side. Howard got out and went into the bushes. After five minutes, Maddox sent the driver out to look for Cooper.

"There's no sign of him, sir," said the driver, returning to the car.

"I don't believe this," said Maddox, shaking his head and laughing to himself.

Sandra looked stunned. Titus stared straight ahead without speaking.

"What should I do, sir?" asked the driver.

"General, your call," said Maddox. "He was yours anyway."

"There's nothing I can do now, General Maddox."

"Okay. Continue on, Corporal," he said to the driver.

The limo sped toward the ship as Howard made good his escape.

CHAPTER THIRTEEN

Howard had to get out of the area as soon as possible to cover as much distance as he could before nightfall. He hiked until he found a road and then walked up the road trying to hitch a ride. He got a couple of rides and went far enough for him to feel that his trail would be more difficult to follow. He was bumming his last ride of the night before finding a motel. He still had plenty of cash left over from when he arrived.

A car coming down the road stopped to pick him up. It was a white Lincoln Continental. He was surprised when he got to the car and looked in. It was a woman, a very attractive woman. It seemed too good to be true. She smiled a pleasant, comfortable smile. Howard estimated her age to be thirty-five. And from what he could see, she had a knockout figure.

"How far yer goin'?" she asked.

All the way, he felt like saying, but thought better of it. "As far as you're willing to take me."

"I can take you far," she said with a seductive smile.

He got in and she drove off.

"Aren't you afraid to pick up strange men?" he asked ironically.

"What you really mean is," she said, smiling confidently, "why am I not afraid? Well, I'm certainly not stupid. And I'm nobody's fool. You just don't look that dangerous, that's all. I mean, you don't look like a killer or anything like that."

"Well that's a relief, anyway," said Howard, smiling to himself.

"I guess I'm also a little bit of a risk taker. Yer know, I go by my gut. I like the excitement, I guess. Don't get me wrong, I'm not about to pick up every *gavone* that I see standing there with his fly open and his tongue hanging out."

"He'd have to have a pretty long tongue for that," he said. They both laughed.

"Anyway, I've always been a pretty good judge of character, and I haven't guessed wrong yet."

"Well, there's always a first time, and don't forget those who screw up once may not be around to talk about it," he said, teasing. "By the way, I'm from Texas. What's a *gavon?*"

"That means *chooch,* yer know, like a jerk or a creep."

"Yeah, I guess we have a few of those in Texas, too, we just call them something different."

"Texas huh? I hear everything's bigger in Texas. Is that true—Tex?"

"Ho—Harry, my name is Harry Cotter."

"Well is it true, Harry?—By the way my name is Jacqueline, Jacqueline Stewart, but everyone calls me Jackie."

"Is what true?"

"Things being bigger in Texas," she said, with a twinkle in her deep brown eyes.

"If I play my cards right, you might find out," he said. They laughed again.

"I like you, Harry. You seem genuine. Yer know, not a phony. I like that. If there's one thing I hate, it's a phony. Like someone who appears to be something they ain't."

"Well, I'm from Texas, there's no question about that. However, I've traveled quite a bit. If I told you how far you wouldn't believe me."

"Try me."

"What if told you that I visited another planet."

"I'd ask you what you're smokin'."

"Well I have. And they looked just like us. And, they are able to talk just like us. In fact, you couldn't tell difference."

"Well maybe you couldn't, but I could certainly tell a Martian when I see one."

"Really? How do know you that I'm not one."

"You tryin' to spook me, Harry?"

"No. I'm human. But I did visit another planet."

"In your dreams, Tex. In your dreams. So, you've been out of this world. Have you ever been around the world?"

"No, but if you're the travel agent, I'm game," he said. She gave him a naughty look.

"So what do you do for a living, Tex? And how come you're out hitching a ride? You in trouble or something?"

"Actually, I have these aliens after me and I'm trying to lose myself as well as I can. What about you?"

"Hey, that's cool. I like a guy with a little mystery. And myself, I'm heading for Atlanta. I sell hardware. Bathroom fixtures and stuff."

"Bathroom fixtures. I would have thought you'd be in something a little more glamorous like clothes or perfume or jewelry."

"Well I wear that stuff. But I sell hardware. I just fell into it. A girlfriend of mine offered me this job in her father's place. I was out of work and I was looking for something. My boss tried to get cute with me and I told him to fuck off, so he fired me. I wouldn't have minded so much if the guy was good looking at least, but he was a real slob. Yer know the kind I mean?"

"Sure."

"Anyway, my girlfriend told me that I should sue for sexual harassment, but I didn't agree. Look, if some chick sticks her ass out and shoves her cleavage in her boss' face to get ahead, that's okay. But if a guy comes on to some broad because he is hot for a piece of ass, that's considered sexual harassment. I think it's all bullshit. If a guy comes on to yer and you don't like it, you should tell him to fuck off. That's your right. No one should have to take shit from anybody. Don't you agree, Tex?"

"Absolutely, Jackie. I'm with you all the way on that one."

"Are you puttin' me on? Don't put me on, 'cause I don't like it. I'll throw your ass right out of this car if you start yanking my chain. I'll toss you out so fast your head will spin."

"Yes, ma'am."

"Just don't get cute with me, Tex."

"You're the boss."

"Anyway, I was telling you about me and my girlfriend, my girlfriend Cynthia. I was about twenty-five then—and I ain't telling you how long ago that was either."

"I wouldn't dream of asking. But I'm sure it couldn't have been very long at all."

"You're sweet, Tex. Anyway, I liked the place and got along fine with her father, who was pretty old at the time. My girlfriend was a change of life, baby…"

Howard watched her as she spoke. She was wearing a short black leather skirt. She had black stockings on and a garter belt. She kept on shifting around as she spoke and her skirt was edging up over the top of her stockings. He could see the pale white skin of her thigh. Her blouse was a silky material and it clung to her breasts. She wore a bra that showed the shape of her nipples through the material. Howard was getting very aroused. He was getting hard and he wondered if she noticed. He wondered if she was just talk.

"So," she continued, "I worked there for a few years and everything was fine. My friend had an older brother who also worked there. He used to bother me from time to time but I was always able to fight him off, as long as the old man was around. I used to threaten to tell his father. He was afraid of the old guy. And besides he was married and everything, with three kids.

"Then my luck ran out. The old man died. And the brother came on to me with a vengeance. He really wanted to get in my pants in the worst way. I just told him no. He said he understood, but he didn't like it."

Howard watched her chest heave as she got into the story. She would pull down her skirt from time to time, but as she got more involved in the story telling, she would lose track of her skirt. It would rise again above the line of her stockings revealing the bottom of her garter belt and the milky white flesh on the inside of her upper thighs. He realized even more how her white skin contrasted so sensuously with her jet-black hair. He was finding it difficult to control himself. He moved in his chair in a vain attempt to control his erection. "I can imagine why he had the hots for you," he said, smiling wanly.

She looked at Howard and quickly fixed her skirt, giving him a devilish smile. "Anyway, Dominic, who was my friend's brother, probably figured since he was now the boss I might give in 'cause I was afraid of losing my job. Not that the guy didn't have other women, he thought he was hot shit or somethin'. If I was his wife I'd have killed him. So I told him if he bothers me again or tries to fire me I'd tell his wife on him. Also, I'd tell her to take him to the cleaners, after she throws him out, of course. I said that's what I did to my first husband and that I had a great Jewish lawyer that would take good care of his wife, in more ways than one. Boy—that really pissed him off. However, he never bothered me after that. Actually, he knew I was pretty good at my job and I don't think he wanted me around too much after our little talk, so he offered me a job in sales where I'd be on the road most of the time. I like to travel. I'm good with people, especially men. I got plenty of balls, for a woman. That's what they tell me. So, here I am, making eighty grand a year and driving a Continental. And Dominic didn't make out so badly either; I'm the top producer in the whole damn company. So thinkin' with your cock sometimes works out after all," she said, laughing.

Howard knew what his cock was thinking and he had to weigh that against his feelings for Sandra. As far as he was concerned, Sandra was a million miles away by now. Or was she?

140

What Howard did not know was that Sandra refused to go with General Titus. When they got to the space ship Sandra offered to stay on with General Maddox to help find Howard, but she made Maddox promise that she could come and go as she pleased. Maddox was thrilled. This meant that the only way the aliens could find out about M22 was if they found Howard before Maddox did.

As far as Maddox was concerned Sandra was a fool to be used and he was using her to the limit. She played right into his hands. They gave her a special gadget for communicating with them. What she didn't know was that she was also carrying a signaling beacon in the small leather case that held the communications device. They figured if she got lucky and found Howard before they did or if somehow the aliens found him and told her about it, they could trail her and maybe pick up Howard before the aliens did. They didn't know what would happen if the aliens found out about M22. They were desperate.

It was getting dark and Howard offered to buy Jackie some dinner. "Well, Tex, think if you buy me a meal you'll get lucky?"

"I already got lucky riding with you this far," he said, flashing a broad smile. He also thought he might be a little safer being with a woman. They would expect him to be traveling alone.

"I knew I liked you all along," she said.

They traveled on a little farther. "That looks like a decent place there, coming up on the right."

It had the look of a big log cabin. There were already quite a few cars in the lot. It was about a quarter to eight. Jackie pulled the Continental into one of the bigger spots and they got out.

"Why don't I go inside and check the place out first," suggested Howard.

"That's okay, I'm sure it's all right. They locked the car and walked toward the restaurant.

It looked like a decent place. Howard liked the sawdust on the floor. Jackie seemed to like the commotion.

"Kind of noisy," he said.

"I like it that way. I'm not here to sleep, I'm here to eat."

"I hope the saw dust isn't here to soak up the blood."

She laughed. He looked around. A waitress came up to them.

"Two?"

"Yeah. Got a booth?"

She looked around and then back to them. "None left. You'll have to sit at a table. That all right?"

"Sure," said Howard.

They sat down and the waitress gave them menus. "My name is Helen. What are yer drinkin'?"

Howard motioned to Jacqueline. "Rum and coke," she said. "Bacardi."

The waitress turned to Howard.

"Do you have Lone Star beer?"

"Yeah, I think we do."

"Great."

"I'll be right back."

The waitress left. In a couple of minutes, she returned with the drinks. "The specials today are fried filet of sole, beef stew, and chicken in the basket. That's my favorite," she whispered, winking. "But the burgers are great, too. So are the onion rings. Enjoy your drinks, folks, I'll be back in a little while."

Howard smiled at her as she left.

"You're used to this stuff, huh?"

"What stuff?" asked Howard.

"These real friendly waitresses."

"Why, don't they have friendly waitresses in New York?"

"Not usually. They seem to be always rushing you in and rushing you out."

"That bad huh?"

"At least it seems that way."

They heard a loud bang and everyone turned toward the bar. Some man of a fairly large size seemed to be picking himself off the floor and giving an unhappy look to a very intense-looking man of medium height and stocky build. What was most intense about the man seated was his eyes.

I bet he doesn't lose many staring contests, thought Howard.

The man, who was on the floor, passed close by Howard and Jackie on his way out. He looked pissed. He kept on glancing back at the bar where the other man was sitting. The other man continued to return his stare. The defeated man left the place banging the door behind him. A moment later, the din rose again from the customers and all was forgotten.

The waitress returned. "What was that all about?" she asked Howard.

"I don't know. But the guy that left didn't look very happy. I sure hope he doesn't have a gun or something in the car."

Jackie gave Howard a strange look. "Maybe I should go back to New York where it's safe," she said, smiling uneasily.

"Well," said Howard. "So what's the specialty of the house?"

"Prime ribs, we're famous for them," said Helen. "Didn't I tell you?"

"No, ma'am. How are they?"

"Great, if you're a meat eater." She laughed.

"Sounds good to me," said Jackie, "I'm starved."

"Why not," agreed Howard. "And some of those onion rings. They had better be good now," he said, teasing.

"If you don't like 'em, I'll pay for them myself."

"No problem," said Helen. "I'm sure we'll love 'em. How do you want your meat cooked?"

"Medium rare," said Howard.

"Medium for me," said Jackie, smiling.

They finished their onion rings and were well into their steaks when the man with the intense eyes got up from his stool and started walking toward the door. As he passed Howard's table, he took notice of Jackie. He continued to the door and left the restaurant. The woman that was sitting with him at the bar got up and left by another exit. A few moments later, the man came back and went toward the bar. When he noticed that the woman was missing, he called the bartender over and asked where she went. The bartender shook his head and shrugged his shoulders. The man looked frustrated. He began looking around the room and his eyes fell again on Jackie. Howard was sipping his beer and watching the proceedings with interest. The man then got up and started walking toward Howard's table.

"Hi," he said, sizing up Howard.

Howard looked real uncomfortable. Jackie was waiting to see what would happen next.

"You didn't happen to see where that lady sitting down at the end of the bar went to, did yer?"

"Actually, I saw her going out the back way," replied Howard, trying to be helpful.

Jackie knew that was a mistake and so did Howard, but too late.

"How long have you been watching her?" he asked Howard. The man was obviously aggravated over the loss of the girl and was looking for someone to take it out on. Besides, he figured he might just wind up with Howard's woman as a bonus.

Howard just looked at him for a second. Jackie was telling herself, "oh shit!"

"I wasn't watching her. I just happened to turn toward the bar and noticed her going out that way. Just tryin' to be helpful, that's all."

He eyeballed Howard for a moment. "Seems to me a man with such a pretty lady to keep him company, shouldn't be lookin' at other women, especially women that are with someone else. Isn't that so?" he said, staring at Jackie.

"My name is Jackie."

"Well hello, Jackie, nice to meet you."

Jackie did not respond.

"How would you like to keep me company, Jackie?"

"Sorry, I'm already with someone."

"Well, we can fight for you, like they used to do in the old days. You look like a woman worth fighting for."

"I'm not looking for any trouble," said Howard. *I'm trying to save the world and I'll wind up dead by this nut from the bar over a woman that I just met and hardly know,* he thought.

"I'm getting out of here," said Jackie, jumping up from her chair.

Howard was silent. Actually, he was relieved. Her leaving would probably solve his problem, he realized.

"Where you going?" asked the man. "You haven't even had a chance to get to know me."

Jackie continued to walk. Right by the door she turned. "Thanks for supper, Tex. Maybe some other time—"

Howard just looked at her and nodded his head silently.

The man started after Jackie. Howard didn't know what to do. He got up and walked slowly after them.

When he got outside, he saw the man trying to talk to Jackie. She was trying to get into her car and he was trying to calm her down. Howard stood outside the door and waited to see what would happen next.

The man reached for Jackie and she landed a swift kick to his groin. The man doubled up; Jackie jumped into her car and drove away.

Howard went inside, satisfied that she was safe. He wanted to pay his check and get the hell out of there as quickly as possible.

The check was on his table when he got there. He looked at it quickly, threw down enough phony money to cover it, with a generous tip, and turned to leave.

As he started toward the door, the man with the intense eyes entered the restaurant.

He looked to Howard like a man who had willingly experienced things that most others took great pains to avoid.

He blocked Howard's way. "Where you going?" he said to Howard.

"I'm leaving. I finished my meal and I'm leaving."

"Don't go so fast. At least I can have a man's company since the women don't seem too friendly tonight."

"I have to go."

"What are you driving?"

Howard looked at him.

"What kind of car?" asked the man.

"I don't have a car, " Howard admitted. He didn't think it would be prudent to lie to this man and be found out. He seemed quite dangerous.

"How'd you get here?"

"That woman gave me a lift."

The man smiled at Howard. "No wonder you let her go so easily. Looks like neither one of us is going to get laid tonight, huh?"

"I guess not," said Howard, relaxing slightly.

"Come on, I'll buy you a beer. Maybe we'll both get lucky, yet."

Howard realized he had little choice.

They walked to the bar and ordered their drinks. "My name is Napoleon Baker, but my friends call me Frank. My middle name is Francis, but if you tell anybody, I'll kill yer."

Howard got the feeling that this guy didn't have many friends to tell it to anyway. "I wouldn't think of it, Frank. Howard Cooper," he said, sticking out his hand.

"You handled yourself well, Howie. No sense getting killed over some woman you hardly know."

Howie? he thought to himself, shaking his head.

"What kind of work do you do, Howie?"

"I'm in the newspaper business. What about you?"

"Live around here?"

"No, I'm a long way from home."

"You doing a story?"

"Not really."

Cooper wanted to tell him the true story, but he didn't dare. Yet, he found himself wanting to. "A great many changes have taken place in my life over the last couple of months."

"It must be something dramatic."

"Dramatic is an understatement."

"Problem with the wife, family, that kind of thing?"

He was making the man work but neither of them seemed to mind.

"Yes, but that's the least of it."

"What is it, gambling? Drugs? Did you kill someone or is someone trying to kill you?"

"No, but it's even worse than that."

"What can be worst than that?" The man sipped his drink and waited for Howard's reply. Before Howard could speak, he added, "You're a mass murderer or you kidnapped the Pope?" He laughed.

"Not quite. But how do I know I can trust you?"

"What do I give a shit? As long as you don't rape little girls or beat up old ladies, it doesn't make any difference to me. I sell burglar alarms and I believe in helping people who are oppressed by others. As long as you don't get in my way, what you do is your business."

"Oh, so you're a crusader. That's very admirable."

"That's right!" he said, getting visibly excited. A lot of people do a lot of talking, but I am the one who can get results. I'm a born leader. And if I were in charge, there would not be the rape and crime and muggings that you see today. The criminals would be dealt with, quickly and justly. I know how to get things done!"

"Then maybe you can help me after all. Would you be willing to give up your life for an idea, an ideal?"

"Yes. Absolutely! What better way is there to die? If I were to go to my death for a cause I'd be willing to die as the peerless warrior."

"What is the peerless warrior?" asked Howard.

"He is perfection. He cannot be defeated in battle. He is the fighting man's version of the Immaculate Conception. He strikes down evil doers and protects the weak and innocent. It would be the greatest challenge of my life to become the peerless warrior."

"I believe that I can offer you that opportunity," said Howard. "You see yourself one day being on the top. There is nothing wrong with that as long as you are benign. But never forget that you will have to be willing to make the ultimate sacrifice. Once you're committed you can never back down, for anyone or anything."

"I never do anyway. Willingness to go all the way, no matter what, is what makes me a winner. And I am that person. The ultimate winner. I never back down to any man."

"You're my guy. Are you in?" asked Howard.

"What is it that I'm supposed to be in?"

"You must swear not to tell anyone."

"I swear," said Frank.

"Not that anyone would believe you anyway."

"Out with it, Howie, before I lose my temper."

"Well, to put it in a nutshell. I was kidnapped by aliens from outer space and now they are threatening to destroy the world."

Baker looked at him. "I'll kick your ass if you're fuckin' with me."

"I swear I'm not," said Howard, frightened. "I can't prove it this second, but I will. I promise you, I will."

"This sounds like bullshit."

"No, it's not bullshit. I need a champion and you need a challenge. It's the first step to becoming the peerless warrior."

"Champion? I'm no one's champion. Especially not yours."

"You're right. You don't represent me. I'm just a symbol. I represent mankind. And, we're mankind's last hope for survival. I'm just your guide. I doubt if I can do it without your help."

"Okay. I'll go along for a while. But if I find out that you're putting me on, you're dead meat."

"Fair enough."

"No one, especially a guy like you would ever have the balls to try to dupe me into something as outrageous as this; unless it was either true or you're completely fucked up in the head. But somehow, I believe you. I don't know why, but I believe you. Maybe I'm becoming crazy, too."

"There's a good reason why you believe me. Because I'm telling the truth. And you're a very intuitive person."

"Alright. Don't get patronizing. What do I have to do?"

"What you have to do is come with me. We have to figure out how to save the world."

"Is someone after you?"

"Yes, lots of people. The aliens want me to find out what I know about the disappearance of their spy and the military want me, so that the aliens don't find out that they murdered their spy."

"How'd they kill him?" asked Baker.

"They shot him, six times. We were in the office of the chairman of the

Joint Chiefs and this two-star general threatened me. The alien, who has the strength of five humans, tries to come to my defense and this colonel shoots him dead."

"Why did he try to come to your defense? You're not on their side are you?"

"Of course not. Why the hell would I be on their side? I was just trying to help our military keep their perspective and not blow the whole deal."

"They didn't brainwash you, did they?"

"There would be no reason to do that. Their people look just like us and speak just like us. They could use one of their own; they wouldn't need me for that. And besides, if that were the case I wouldn't be hanging around here having a beer. I ran away because I need time to think of a way to find a solution to this situation. To keep our planet from being destroyed by these aliens. By the way, they are not malicious creatures. They're just afraid, since our probe landed on their planet, that we will tell others where their planet is, and they fear that more than anything. They believe that there are a lot of bad, intelligent creatures out there."

"There are a lot of bad, intelligent creatures around here," said Frank with a far away look in his eye.

"Exactly my sentiments."

"But what about my job?"

"Job? If this thing doesn't get resolved we'll all be dead. So how can you worry about your job?"

"If you're putting me on you'll be dead!"

"So take a leave of absence, or vacation days or sick days until you decide if I'm putting you on. We'll live on my money. I'll pay all expenses."

"How much money do you have?"

"Enough. As long as we don't go overboard."

"I'll need a day to straighten things out," said Frank.

"We don't have the time. Besides, if you don't do it now you may change your mind or have it changed for you."

"No one changes my mind. Okay I'll take care of what I have to do in the morning. I'll drop you at a motel and pick you up there before noon." He looked at Howard and shook his heard. "I don't believe that this is happening."

Howard looked at him for a moment. "That's what I used to say."

Baker woke up; it was 9:00 a.m. He shaved, showered, dressed and got himself some breakfast. His girlfriend had already left for work. He dressed and packed his bag. He didn't want to tell her what was going on until he was ready to leave. He thought that it would be easier to tell her just before he left.

He picked up the phone and dialed her office. "Hon, it's me."

"What the matter?" she asked.

"Nothing."

"I get the feeling that something's wrong."

"Look," he said, "I have to go away for a while."

"You see, I knew something was wrong. What did you do, meet another woman?"

"No! No, nothing like that. It's difficult to explain."

"Try me."

"I just have to go away, that's all. This guy offered me some kind of job. It's special work and I don't know how long it will take."

"When did this happen?"

"I met him in a bar last night."

"You met a guy in a bar who offered you some kind of job that you can't even explain and you're leaving me and your current *real* job? What are you—nuts?!"

"You'll just have to trust me."

"And there's no woman involved."

"I swear to God."

"Well if there isn't, it'll be the first time."

"It's a chance to do something important."

"Something important?" she repeated. "So why didn't you tell me before?"

"I thought it would be easier this way."

"Go to hell!"

"Don't be that way."

"Fuck you!"

"It's not about another woman, I told you."

"Drop dead!" she said, hanging up the phone.

Frank held the receiver in front of his face. "SHIT! Howie baby—*this better be worth it!*"

CHAPTER FOURTEEN

It was 2:00 p.m. of the same day that Frank Baker left his job and girlfriend and started on his quest with Howard Cooper. A car arrived at the Pentagon. The two men inside were announced to General Goodwood and sent ahead. They were issued passes by the guard, and then sat waiting for their escort. The driver gave the appearance of being the other man's bodyguard. He was of average height with burly limbs and stocky build. The other one, who gave the appearance of being in charge, was about six-two with a wiry frame.

The escort came and they followed him to Goodwood's office. When they came to the general's anteroom, they were told to go right in.

Goodwood got up from behind his desk and extended his hand. The tall one reached out and shook it.

"I'm Julius Bond and this is my associate, Carmine Foli."

"Mr. Bond and Mr. Foli, it's a pleasure to meet you both," said Goodwood, sitting back down.

"Gentlemen, I appreciate that you can come on such short notice."

"That's no problem at all, General, but of course you understand it will be reflected in my fee."

Goodwood looked at them for a moment reminding himself about their reputation and the urgency and delicacy of the matter. "I understand," he replied. "Now let me get right to the point, gentleman, I need to capture a man. I want him taken alive, which shouldn't be difficult. He's not the dangerous type. But of course, I cannot make any guarantees as to how he will react. You just never know if someone decides to become violent. But you are professionals, that's why I engaged you. Kill him only as a last resort. But, under no circumstances are you to let him get away. There will be a significant bonus if you bring him back alive."

"Why do you want him? What's this guy done?" asked Bond.

"I'm afraid that I cannot discuss that in detail. Will that be a problem?"

"No, just curious. But I must ask why you are paying me very high rates when you can just as well use your own people."

"Insurance, Mr. Bond. The job must get done at any cost."

"How will your people know who we are?"

"They will be told that you and your associates will be around and that they should give you full cooperation. But my people will not take any orders from you or your people. You will get cooperation and nothing more. You'll just have to work around the situation as best you can. I will issue special passwords to you so that my men will know that your people are the good guys, so to speak."

"Good guys?" asked Bond. "If we're the good guys, who are the bad guys?"

"Let's just say, they can be dangerous, very dangerous. You'll have to be ready for anything. These others will also try to capture this man, whose name is Howard Cooper. But we must get him first. And remember, if it looks like they will capture him, kill him, it is most important of all that they do not get him."

"Well, I knew there would be danger somewhere in this scenario," said Bond.

"Surely, gentlemen, you didn't think that I would be paying your exorbitant fees for nothing. Did you?"

"I'm beginning to think that we're charging too little."

"I really don't believe that that could be possible, not on this planet anyway," said Goodwood.

"Can you tell us any more about our adversaries?"

"These people are mysterious. They are extremely strong." Foli looked at Bond and smiled. Bond smiled back. "And they may possess some very powerful weapons and strange powers."

"We have a few surprises of our own, aye, Foli?" The burly man smiled again, this time at no one in particular. "Are they Asian?"

"They will most likely appear to be Caucasian and their means of travel may be extremely sophisticated."

"Ah, Russians probably huh? They're tough and sophisticated, when it comes to crime anyway. I guess we're going to earn our money this time, huh Foli?" Foli maintained the same expression.

"There are two other things that you need to know before you go. One is that the reason this man is important to us is that he has information that we do not want our opponents to learn. But he could also be useful to us in other ways. He knows the opposition better than anyone. He was kidnapped and lived among them for a while. The last thing is that there is a girl. Well a young woman actually, that Cooper is romantically involved with. Or so, they would have us believe. She is in fact one of them. She seems to be genuinely interested in this Howard Cooper. She also wants to find him. We have a homing device planted on her and she can be quite useful if we handle the situation properly. She must accompany you in the search."

"That's absurd!" said Bond.

"Nothing's absurd compared to this whole situation."

"But she might be in touch with her people."

"You'll just have to watch her closely. You don't have to tell her anything. And she could be helpful. But nothing is to happen to her. I realize accidents can happen. But I'm paying you people to make certain that they don't."

"I don't know," said Bond.

"If you want the assignment, you have no choice."

Bond looked at Foli who shrugged. "Okay. We're in. But if she becomes a real pain in the ass you will get her back with our bill attached."

"Fair enough. One other thing. You will be getting a phone number that you can call night and day, seven days a week. Just in case you require our help. Don't be shy. I'm not looking for heroes; I'm looking for results. And please keep me informed. That means I expect a call from you at least twice a day."

"You got it, General."

"Good day, gentlemen, and remember time is our enemy. Major Walsh will take care of you from here on, until you leave."

Walsh was waiting outside the office as they left. Foli looked around one last time before exiting the general's office. One might think that he was casing the place, or trying to get a sense of it. As they walked down the hall Bond turned to talk to the major.

"Is this young lady that we're supposed to babysit good looking at least?" asked Bond.

"I would have to say so."

"Well, I guess we should be thankful for small favors, then."

"She'll be well taken care of, Major, I'll personally make sure of that," said Foli, uttering his first words and smiling broadly.

The mother ship loomed larger and larger through the porthole of General Titus' shuttle vessel. At length what was the mother ship became a wall of black gleaming metal. The hydraulic couplers whooshed as the connecting airtight seals of the two spacecraft became one. A moment later, all was quiet.

The general marched into the mother ship. Rondo was waiting for him in a small conference room.

They mentally saluted each other as Titus entered the room. "Bad news!"

"What is it?" asked Rondo.

"M22 is missing."

"What happened?"

"They may have killed him. Or they are holding him somewhere. Maybe for insurance. But he is probably dead.

I doubt if they would chance angering us by holding him against his will."

"We must find out," insisted Rondo. "We must know. It could make our decision easier. It could diminish our moral burden. We must dispatch this matter as soon as possible. Every day away from our planet, we run the risk of exposure and conquest. We must make haste."

"How far along are we with Einstein's bio-chemical weapon?"

"It is preceding more slowly than hoped," admitted Rondo. "One must always be careful when working with these types of agents. The results could be devastating if our people were contaminated before the final substance is perfected and stabilized. Once the final molecule exists, only the species it is meant for would be at risk when in contact. So progress at this point must come with caution."

"What will we do until it's ready?"

"One thing is to find out what happened to M22."

Titus looked pensive. "We seem to have two choices. We can try to force the military into admitting what they did or we can find Cooper and force him to tell. I did not tell you but Cooper escaped as he was returning with us. Also, Sandra refused to come back without him. She can turn out to be a problem for us. I question her loyalty."

"Perhaps she can help lead us to Cooper. Capturing him seems to be our only viable alternative. Forcing the military is too risky. It could create complications. We want their demise to be quick, clean and neat. We want to avoid any invasion or the need to destroy the whole planet and its innocent creatures. The planet and its nonhuman inhabitants have suffered quite enough at the hands of those cultured barbarians who call themselves humans."

"So we must capture our old friend, Howard Cooper," remarked Titus.

"Precisely, General, precisely!"

"I'll send a party down immediately."

"But he must not be killed. Better we lose him. He cannot do us any harm alive, but his dying would be a loss. And if we lose Cooper, we lose Sandra. Our people are too precious to give up without good cause. Hopefully, by the time you complete your task ours will also be done. Their planet is beautiful like our old planet and I wish we had a home like it but for now, we must get back to protect our own. Perhaps one day we could claim it for ourselves but that is only a dream. Now we must deal with realities."

They followed US Route 81 down to Knoxville, Tennessee. As Napoleon (Frank) Baker drove, he wondered how he ever got himself into such a ridiculous situation. He began to boil as he saw himself being made a fool of by this supposed patron. They saw the sign welcoming them to the town.

"So what's supposed to happen here?"

"Don't worry, Frank; you'll get plenty of action. We have to plan our attack. We're here just to have enough time to figure out what we want to do before the shit hits the fan. I figured this town is small enough not to attract anyone out to find us, but big enough that we won't stick out like sore thumbs."

"Sore thumbs. I got something else that's sore," said Frank, grabbing himself. "And only some heavy duty snatch can help with my problem." Howard noticed, to his disappointment, that Frank wasn't smiling.

"You're going to have to help yourself in that area. But please, don't attract any more attention than necessary. I doubt if they are announcing any of this stuff on TV or the radio. But I'm sure the local police must be hip. At least they might tell them I'm an escaped spy or something. So if you have to get laid, please do it quietly."

The car was still moving, and Frank was supposed to be driving, but he turned his head completely to the right and stared intently at Howard for a moment before speaking. "Don't ever tell me what to do! Don't even think about it. I'm nobody's boy. And if *I*—want to fuck every housewife in this shit hole of a town—*I'll do it!* And if anyone has a problem with that—they'll know where to find me. Got it? Howie!" he yelled in his ear.

154

"Sure. I got it. Please turn around. If we get killed, it's not going to do anyone any good. I hear you, Frank. I hear you loud and clear. Please turn around."

Frank slowly turned his head back without commenting.

"I'm not trying to tell you what to do," Howard continued. "It's just that there are a lot of important things happening. I just want to make sure that we accomplish what we need to accomplish. That's all. I'm not trying to run your life or tell you what to do. I just want to make sure that we can do what we have to. This is heavy-duty stuff we're talking about. I'm not trying to butt into your personal life. But if we attract too much attention, the local police might get involved and the whole damn thing can be down the drain before we even get started."

"Don't worry, Howie," said Frank, chuckling, "I can get laid quietly, too."

"That's good," said Howard. He sat there holding his chin and thinking. *How the fuck did I ever get involved with this guy. What a goddamn lunatic. Thank God Sandra's not with me. He'd probably have his hand up her skirt by now. Then I would either have to kill him or, more likely, I'd wind up dead. Well it's too late now. Peerless Warrior...Jesus Christ! Who's going to save me from my own warrior? I feel like Dr. Frankenstein,* he thought.

"Let's stop here," said Frank. "This looks like a nice place. Besides you're payin', right, Howie?"

"Right, Frankie."

Frank smiled as he eased the car into the parking spot. "What's the matter, you don't like when I call you Howie? Howie!"

"The only people that called me Howie were my mother and my aunts and uncles."

"So think of me as family—Howie!"

Cooper shook his head as Frank laughed out loud.

They checked in, then went downstairs to the bar.

It was six o'clock. It was an average-sized place with pictures of sports figures on the walls. Neither man seemed very interested. There was a sign advertising a sports trivia contest later that night, with a free bottle of booze as the prize.

"Let's get a table," said Howard.

They sat down in a corner. The place was still fairly empty with three locals at the bar. Two guys sitting together and a fortyish-looking woman who watched everyone who was coming and going. She spotted the two crusaders and followed them with her eyes until they found their seats.

Howard hoped that Frank would keep it in his pants long enough for them to discuss what they needed to talk about. The waitress came right over and took their drink orders.

"So what's the big plan, Howie?" said Frank, checking out the lady at the bar.

"These aliens think that we are a danger to them. They think that we can expose the location of their planet to other aliens who they obviously know exist. They are afraid that we tracked our probe, Pioneer10, to them. They know we can't hurt them directly but are afraid what we know will get out sometime in the future."

"Are they right?"

"I don't know. But we have to assume that they are, or at least we can't prove they're not, I mean who knows."

"So what the hell am I supposed to do?"

"Well, one thing is to protect me. I know that the aliens will probably want to grab me and the military will probably want me dead and out of the way or at least in their custody."

"Why?"

Howard pondered if he should tell Frank about M22. *Why not? He certainly doesn't want the Earth destroyed, but that's one more person who can spill the beans. But if he finds out that I held out on him, I'm dead,* thought Howard. *Fuck it! In for a penny in for a pound.*

"I'll tell you this, but only if you swear on your honor that if you are captured by the aliens that you will die before telling them."

"I'll take plenty of them with me before I *buy it*, I guarantee you that."

"Say it, I need you to say it. It's that important."

"You mean you want me to swear an oath? You got it. I swear I won't spill the beans about whatever you know, on my life. Didn't think I would do it—did yer?"

"To be honest I wasn't quite sure, but I thought you would. I'm sure with someone like you honor is important."

"What a yer mean, *someone like me?*"

"I mean someone who aspires to become a peerless warrior."

"Good answer," returned Frank, eyeing Cooper warily.

"I was there when the military killed the alien, so they want to get me before the aliens do, so I won't tell."

"Would you?"

"Of course not! Why the hell do you think I'm here? I'm here to figure out what I should do. Why do you think that I risked my life by escaping? I was safe with the aliens. I could have stayed with them if that was what I wanted. So, talk to me, Frank. You seem like someone who would want to rule the world, if he could. Start thinking like a ruler. Your planet is in imminent danger."

Howard started wondering if he should have told Frank after all. What if Frank decided to take matters into his own hands and kill Howard himself, or turns him in?

Howard downed his drink in one gulp.

Frank sat there staring straight into space. Howard was happy that he wasn't staring at him. *Those eyes could drill a hole in lead*, he thought. Finally, Frank turned toward Howard with a strange smile on his face.

"Don't worry, Howie; if anyone tries to bother you, they'll have to deal with me first."

Howard thought that those words should have given him comfort, but somehow they didn't. *Right now this guy is on my side, but what if that changes? What am I going to owe him if he puts out for me? This is one guy whose debt I wouldn't want to be in. But what other kind of guy would be crazy enough to go along with this and be able to handle it, too? Life's a two-edged sword*, he thought. *I just hope I have time to duck on the backstroke.*

"Do you think these aliens would try an all out attack?" asked Frank.

"I don't know how they are planning to destroy us, but whatever they do we wouldn't have much of a chance with our primitive weapons—compared to theirs," said Howard.

"But if, say, they hit us hard even with atomic type weapons, there would have to be some survivors, wouldn't there?"

"I guess."

"And the military's not going to be much good since most of the primary targets will be military. It's just logic. If you were aliens trying to destroy and maybe take over a planet wouldn't you strike at the military targets first? Once you knock out the military, the rest should be a piece of cake. And the civilians are going to need a leader. There are certain to be guerrilla forces operating and they are going to need leaders—leaders like me!"

Frank seemed to be living his own dream in his mind.

"Well, that's all very possible, Frank. But what if they just blow up the goddamn planet and there is nothing left but rocks and dust and water vapor floating around in space?"

"I doubt that."

"Why?"

"Who knows what effect that would have on the solar system. It could throw the whole balance off. I'm sure if these guys are as sophisticated as you suggest they would attain their goal in a more subtle way."

"You got me, Frank. I hope we never have to find out. Right, Frank?"

Frank didn't answer. His mind was elsewhere.

"You're going to try to prevent this from happening. Right Frank?"

A smile began to spread across his face, as he looked right through Howard.

Howard was starting to feel a little sick.

"What are you thinking about, Frank?" he prodded.

"Don't worry Howie everything is under control. I won't let anything happen to you," Frank said, coming back to life.

Frank was again looking at the woman sitting at the bar. By this time, a few others had wandered in and the woman at the bar was talking to a man dressed in a business suit. Frank got up and started walking in their general direction.

Howard thought—*no trouble please!* "Where yer going, Frank?" he asked.

Frank just turned slightly and gave Howard a look. Howard lightly shrugged his shoulders. Frank got to the bar and called the bartender over. The bartender pointed outside and Frank went in that direction. A few moments later, he returned with a frustrated look on his face.

"That bitch," he said.

Howard hesitated to ask him whom he was talking about.

"Fuckin' women, they're all alike. They never believe you, even when you're telling the truth." He turned to Howard. "That bitch I was living with, she told me to fuck off again. Yesterday she was kissing my ass. Now she tells me to fuck off. She ain't good enough to suck my cock. That piece o' shit. I ain't calling her again. She'll beg for me. And she can suck me off. That's all she's good for."

What Frank or Howard didn't know was that Frank's girlfriend had already spoken to the authorities. The military was hot on Howard's trail from the beginning and the call Frank made was the tip off. Bond and Foli had been dispatched to do their thing and capture the fugitive and his bodyguard.

Foli, Bond and Sandra flew into the local airport where a car was waiting for them. They wanted to locate the two and feel things out before making their move.

Foli always drove, and Sandra sat next to him with Bond in the back. There was no status implied by the arrangement it just seemed the most practical setup for them. The two were equal partners and they employed whatever strategy they thought would be appropriate at the moment. Both of them had quite respectable backgrounds.

Foli had won a football scholarship to Notre Dame, and was an A student to boot. From there, he went to Yale where he studied law and graduated cum laude. He practiced criminal law for eight years but wanted a change. He met Bond, when his firm retained the latter in a couple of cases and they became friendly. Foli found the private investigation business interesting. He always enjoyed the investigative part of the work best. He envied Bond for his situation. Bond was impressed with Foli's unusual combination of brains and brawn. When Bond found out that Foli also possessed a black belt in Tai Kwan Do, a Korean version of Karate, he proposed a merger. There were more adventurous assignments out there that commanded triple the fee Bond was earning on his own, but to take them on, he needed a partner to watch his back. Foli, he thought, was the man for the job.

Bond was no slouch himself. After graduating from college, he joined the Green Berets and took two tours in Vietnam. When he got out, he joined the Chicago police force and quickly rose through the ranks. He made Captain at forty-one. At that point, the politics got to him and he quit to go out on his own. He started his own private investigation business, met Foli and the rest was history.

They had complete respect for each other but Bond gave the orders whenever they were in the midst of a conflict. Seniority and experience ruled. When it came to working together, they both took as much of a non-ego-based approach a possible. Whoever was best at a certain part of the job did it.

This assignment was a little unusual, even for them. They weren't quite sure what they were getting themselves into. If the military weren't involved, they would have said no, without having access to more information about everyone involved. But how could they turn down the chairman of the Joint Chiefs of Staff of the United States. So here they were.

They entered Knoxville via US 81, the same way the boys did. They knew the hotel they were looking for but by this time the hour was late.

It was 11:00 p.m. when Foli and Bond wandered into the cocktail lounge. Sandra waited in the car so as not to be spotted by Howard. They walked up to the bar, ordered a couple of beers and slowly looked around. They saw no one resembling Howard or Frank, so they called the bartender over to ask about their two friends. The bartender said that they had left a couple of hours before. They each took another sip of their beers and left.

They checked with the clerk at the desk but he resisted telling them anything. They showed the clerk the ID that General Goodwood had provided and he was happy to cooperate. The clerk said that they were registered, but were not in now, so they decided to wait. They told him that they wanted the room next door if possible. They got it, went back to get Sandra, and told her to wait there until they came for her.

At midnight, Bond told the desk clerk to call him if Howard or his friend showed up. Then they went up to the room. They knocked on the door lightly and let themselves in with the key. Sandra was sitting in a chair staring into space.

"How are you doing?" asked Bond.

"I'm fine. Have you found them?"

"No, but they'll return. We just have to wait."

Bond lay in the bed fully dressed and Foli sat in the chair next to the phone. For a while no one spoke. "What will you do with them when they return?" asked Sandra.

"Just bring them back with us," answered Bond.

"What if they resist or try to escape?"

"Then we'll follow them."

"What if they resist?" she persisted.

"We'll do what we have to," answered Bond, producing a stun gun.

"What is that?" asked Sandra

"A stun gun. It immobilizes the individual so that he can be taken into custody with the minimum amount of injuries incurred."

"That seems humane," said Sandra. "You know," she continued, "Howard is the only one who can save your planet."

"No. Why is that?"

"Because he was chosen to represent your human race. He has been to my planet. He has spoken to my leaders. If something happens to him, your world is doomed."

"That's interesting." said Bond, and Foli's ears perked up.

"You don't believe me. Do you?"

"We are being paid to do a particular job. We are being paid very well to do that particular job. And maybe you're right. But I doubt if the people who are paying us want to have our planet destroyed either."

"They killed one of my people and they are trying to cover it up."

"I'll have to go along with those retaining me for now, until things are proven otherwise. You're not going to interfere with our assignment, are you?"

"I'm here to help you. Why else would they send me with you?"

"Hum," said Foli.

At about 1:30 a.m., Howard and Frank entered the lobby.

The phone in Bond's room rang. Foli picked it up.

"Yeah—Both of them?—Great! Thanks."

He turned to Bond. They're on their way up.

Bond started to rise.

Sandra rose slowly from her chair, then bolted through the door.

Bond grabbed Foli by the arm. "Hang back," he said. "It could get messy if we do it this way, the less dead bodies the better. That new friend of Cooper's won't come along without a fight. His girlfriend warned us that he never backs down. That would create too many unpredictable scenarios. We want to do this as right as possible. Also, it's better that we get her off our hands. We can maneuver faster without her. Besides, we can track her. We'll take them when the time's right."

Sandra caught Howard and Frank at the elevator.

"They're waiting for you!" yelled Sandra. "Run as fast as you can."

"Who's waiting for us?"

"They were sent by the military to catch you. Hurry!"

They pressed the button for the lobby and the doors closed.

"Who is this?" asked Frank.

"My girlfriend. My—alien girlfriend."

"No shit!" said Frank, laughing.

The elevator landed on the main floor and the doors opened.

"What is this all about?"

"Trust me," said Howard. "If the girl says we're in danger, we're in danger. So let's get the hell out of here."

"How do you know she's not working with them?"

"She's an alien. Why would she work with the military? And she loves me." Sandra smiled at Howard. She liked hearing him say that.

The night man rang Bond's room again.

"Those two are leaving," he said. "This time they have a girl with them."

161

"I know," said Bond, hanging up.

"What are we going to do?" asked Foli.

"Let them think that they are getting away, so their guard is down. Maybe we can get them alive."

"You don't buy that crap the girl said, do you?"

"No. I'll kill them if I have to. But not the girl, we can't kill the girl."

"Right," said Foli.

"Why should we run away from these punks?" asked Frank as they left the hotel.

"Because we don't know what we're up against. Let's get out of here and we can figure it out."

"I never thought I'd be taking orders from someone like you."

"What the hell does that mean?"

"Never mind," said Sandra.

"Who is she really?"

"She's my alien girlfriend, I told you."

"A little young isn't she?"

"What can I say," answered Howard, shrugging, and trying his best not to smirk.

"What a great line," said Frank. "My alien girlfriend. I love it. How's her alien pussy?"

Sandra looked at Howard. Howard looked uncomfortable. They continued walking.

They got into the car. Howard put Sandra in the back. He sat in the front next to Frank.

"I believe that they will kill you if they have to," added Sandra.

"That's nice to know," said Howard.

"Not if they die first," added Frank with a sneer.

"Let's try to keep everyone alive. That's what this damn thing is about in the first place."

"Then what the hell did you get me here for?" asked Frank.

"To help keep us alive long enough to save the situation and the planet."

As Howard looked out the window, he noticed that they were leaving the outskirts of town.

"Where are we going to hide now?" asked Frank.

"We'll try to find a small motel somewhere, but we had better first take some turn-offs to throw them off our trail."

"How come they ain't right behind us," asked Frank.

"Good point," said Howard.

"Maybe it's a setup. Maybe this bitch is working for them—"

"No!" said Howard. "She's an alien. I met her up on their planet. This is no shit. She is completely loyal to me. Besides, she's not even with those guys."

"I only came along because I wouldn't leave without you," she said to Howard, taking his hand.

Frank was getting edgy so Howard took his hand away.

"Fucking asshole," said Frank. "I lose my girlfriend and his shows up out of nowhere, from outer space no less."

Howard was beginning to get uncomfortable again.

They drove for a few hours and Frank started getting tired.

"You want me to drive?" asked Howard.

"No, we'll stop."

Up ahead on the right was the old neon sign that read: **acancy**. They didn't know if all three lights were out or just the "V." Frank pulled off the road to find out.

They walked into the office. It was closed. Frank tapped on the door, waited a moment, and then started to turn around. Just then, the light went on. An old man in a bathrobe was coming toward the door.

"Want a room?" he said as he opened the front door.

"Two," said Howard, smiling.

"Your daughter?" asked the old man.

Howard didn't answer.

"Never mind," said the old man. "Today anything goes. Come on in."

They walked in, signed the register and Howard paid for the rooms.

Frank looked annoyed. He didn't like being the odd man out. But he was tired, so he went right to sleep.

Howard and Sandra went into their room.

"Who is he?" she asked Howard, when they were alone.

"Just someone I met."

"He scares me."

"Me, too."

"So why is he with you?"

"I thought I might need protection."

"Who's going to protect you from him?"

"God."

"What does that mean?"

"It means that we're in God's hands. It means whatever will happen, will happen. You can just do so much and the rest is up to God. If he wants us to survive, we will. If not, then nothing we do will matter anyway."

"Who is God?" asked Sandra.

She sounded like a little girl to Howard.

"No one can answer that question," he said. "If you're religious you believe that God created the universe and everything in it in six days. If not then you think that people invented God because we needed someone like that to worship."

"We have a god like that. But our priests pray for us. What do you believe?" she asked.

"It's a good question. I believe in God, but not exactly the way others do. I believe in God, but I don't think he necessarily created every individual thing. I believe he set the wheels in motion, set the overall design, and then let it play itself out. I don't think that he watches everything we do."

"Then why did you say that the rest was up to God?"

"You got me there. I guess what I mean is that I would like to think that he is watching over us to protect us from evil and harm. But I really don't believe that it is true. I do believe that there is a pattern in the universe. And that we can affect what happens to us by the way we think about things—Don't get me started on that. It's late.

They celebrated their reunion by making love. Then they slept soundly in each other's arms.

In the morning there seemed to be quite a commotion in the motel parking lot. The aliens along with Bond and Foli seemed to catch up with Howard during the same evening. They all waited till dawn, thinking that it would be a lot easier to deal with the situation in the light of day. Frank spotted them and thought that they were part of the same team. But Bond and Foli didn't realize who the aliens were. the Hidden People did not care either way.

Frank called Howard's room and told him that they were being watched. Howard and Sandra got ready. Howard unlocked his door and Frank quickly ran out of his door and into Howard's room carrying a satchel.

"What do we do?" asked Howard.

"We can run for it or we can fight it out," said Frank, patting his satchel.

"Great! Us dying isn't going to help anyone. We'd better try and run, if possible. Otherwise do what you have to."

As they looked out the window, they saw four men, two from one car and

164

two from another crossing toward the motel room. As the men spotted each other Foli and Bond aimed their guns at the others, the aliens levitated themselves and rose about twenty feet into the air. The gravity was weaker on Earth than on the Hidden Planet, so they rose even higher than they had expected.

Foli and Bond started firing at them as they made a mad dash back toward their car.

As the aliens came floating back down to Earth, Bond and Foli started driving and firing at the same time.

Noticing the action and spotting their opportunity, Howard, Frank and Sandra ran to their car to make their getaway.

The aliens hit the ground and ran to their car.

Frank drove the opposite way as Foli and Bond.

The aliens started after Frank and Howard.

Bond and Foli realizing that were out in left field turned around to join the party.

"Your people fly?" Frank asked Sandra.

"Levitate actually."

"Levitate, fly, same crap."

"Same crap," said Sandra, mimicking Frank and laughing lightly like one just learning the language.

Frank gave her a little look. Howard held his head.

"Girls!" said Howard, smiling inanely in Frank's direction.

They entered a long stretch of open highway. Frank, Howard and Sandra led with the aliens following and Bond and Foli bringing up the rear and coming up fast.

As Bond and Foli came into view, the aliens fired their laser pistol, *whoosh*, and burned a hole in Bond's outside mirror.

"Holy shit!" said Bond. "These guys have some fancy weapons; Goodwood wasn't kidding."

Whoosh!

The other outside mirror had a clean hole burned into the middle.

"I don't think they're trying to kill us," said Foli, "those shots were no accidents. Perfect bulls eyes in the middle of each mirror. I believe we've been warned."

"Want to turn around?' asked Bond.

"I didn't join this firm to run from danger. Let's risk it until it gets real close. Maybe they're on orders not to kill us. We have to risk it."

"It looks like we have to try and terminate our friend Cooper, as ordered," added Bond. "We certainly aren't going to be able to grab him and get away. Not with these guys and their weapons. I'm sure we haven't even seen any of their heavy stuff yet."

"Yeah," said Foli, "but they haven't seen ours either."

"What did you have in mind?"

"A grenade."

"How you gonna reach their car?"

"Rifle," said Foli as the distance between them and their opponents diminished.

Whoosh! Another perfect hole blew through their windshield and the center of the rearview mirror between them.

"Either these guys are real sharpshooters or we're real lucky, either way we had better do something quickly."

"Are you close enough to fire the grenade?" asked Bond, nervously.

"If we were firing at the aliens."

"I wouldn't do that. That might really piss them off. I want my bonus, but it's no good to us unless we're alive to spend it."

They continued to gain.

Whoosh! Foli's hair was parted down the middle. It looked like a combine had harvested the row of hair in the middle of his head from front to back.

"Holy shit! Do these guys have a sense of humor?"

"Let me see," said Bond, trying to control himself from laughing. "Holy shit," he said, laughing uncontrollably.

Their car got closer.

"Are they in range now?" asked Bond.

Whoosh!—Whoosh!

Foli looked at Bond and went into hysterics.

"What the hell happened?" asked Bond, trying to see himself in the mirror.

"Don't look!" yelled Foli, tears flowing down his face from his uncontrollable laughing. "Remember Robert Deniro in *Taxi Driver*?" he said, nearly choking on his own words.

"What the hell is this? Holy shit!" said Bond, seeing himself in the mirror.

"You got a mohawk!" said Foli, still laughing hysterically.

"I'll mohawk you if you don't shoot that damn grenade."

"Just a little closer," he said, calming down.

Whoosh!

"Fuck!" The rifle was shot right out of Foli's hand.

"Let's get the hell out of here," he said to Bond.

"They're way out of our league."

Whoosh! Whoosh!

Their car started bumping.

"They shot the goddamned tires out," said Bond.

"Why the hell didn't they just do that in the first place?" asked Foli.

"They wanted to make their point first."

"Yeah! And I think it's on the top of both our heads."

"It wouldn't be much worse than we look like now anyway," added Bond.

"It might even be a slight improvement."

They pulled over to the side of the road and just sat there for a moment. Then they looked at each other and started laughing again.

"What the hell do we look like," said Bond.

"We? You got a mohawk," said Foli, pointing at Bond's head.

"At least there's a name for what I have," returned Bond. "What the hell do you call that thing you got? Dueling crewcuts?"

They both shook their heads in unison.

CHAPTER FIFTEEN

President Henry Barnes sat in his oval office pondering the events that had brought the United States and the world to this current juncture. Across from him sat his national security advisor, Pamela Wayne.

"Is this really the end, Pamela? There must be a way of turning things around. What irony, one of our least aggressive acts has brought us to this end. We send up a space probe with greetings of friendship and welcome to the universe and we wind up in hot soup."

"That's what comes of letting the scientists get their way. Those eggheads always think they know better. Spreading their idealist crap all over the place. It's a war zone out there and we should have treated it as such. Always assume the worst, that's my motto. Be very careful about giving the other fellow the benefit of the doubt. That's why we're in this damn mess. We just went along with these do-gooders and look where we wound up, behind the eight ball, that's where."

"So, how do we get ourselves out of this mess, Pamela? If you can solve this one you'll be in the history books. So how would you solve the problem, Pamela?"

"Well, we can't out gun them, so we have to outsmart them. Not directly though, I'm sure they're not stupid. We just have to be smarter than they are. And we have the advantage."

"How's that?"

"They probably expect us to be straight. It's the element of surprise. The one thing a spy has over everyone else."

"Sounds great," said the President, "except for two things. The plan itself and getting them to listen to us. What if they never talk to us again? What if they just go ahead and blow up the place, without even saying: hello—goodbye?"

"You have a very valid point there. But that's why I'm here, to figure out the answers to those questions. Their weakness, we have to find their weakness. Their soft spot, everyone has one. The reason why they will let us survive. The thing that will turn the trick."

"Okay, Pamela. What is it?"

"We'll have to meet them. If we meet them, we may be able to feel them out. Maybe we can read them. Find out where they're coming from."

"How do we get the meeting?" asked the President.

"What about that guy who was kidnapped. That Cooper fellow. What about him?"

"He got away. They're out looking for him now. In fact, I should call General Goodwood to find out what's happening. I should have heard from him by now."

The intercom buzzed.

"Yes, Margaret."

"It's Mr. Olson, sir."

"Tell him to come in."

The President's chief of staff entered.

"Mr. President, the Russians have been trying to get in touch with you."

"Why?"

"The President of the Russian Federation wants to speak to you on the phone, in private. It sounds important."

"What is it about?"

"They wouldn't say."

"Fine. Set it up."

"Just what I need now," said the President, looking at Pamela and shaking his head.

"It's okay, Mr. President, maybe the hiatus will allow time for solutions to form in our minds."

"I hope so."

"Sid, arrange it," he said to Olson. "You'll have to leave me, Pamela, I'll call you just as soon as I'm finished."

Moments later the phone conference was set up with the President and his counterpart from the Russian Federation.

"Henry."

"Uri."

"I have received some startling news from my people."

"What is that, Uri?"

"They say that a space ship of unknown origin is circling the moon—as we speak. A team of our astronauts spotted it while conducting experiments in space. As we studied the moon from that vantage point, we spotted an object that could not be explained. We guessed that it was a space ship or a satellite circling the moon. We wondered if it were one of yours, Henry?"

"No, Uri, I'm afraid it's not."

"Whose is it then?"

"Aliens, I'm afraid. They are aliens."

"Aliens! You're joking me."

"I'm afraid not, Uri, I wish I were."

"Are they friendly at least?"

"It depends on what you mean by friendly. They're pleasant enough when you meet them. They are civilized. In fact, they look just like us. But, I am told—Are you sitting down?"

"Yes."

"They have a problem with us—"

"What kind of problem?" he interrupted.

"They say we put their planet in danger, so they must destroy us."

"Oh, is that all? I thought it was something serious."

"I'm not joking, Uri. God knows I wish I were."

"I wish you were, too. So what are you doing about it?"

"We're trying to negotiate with them."

"Why were we not made aware? It's our lives and our planet, too."

"There wasn't time. I didn't want to start a worldwide panic."

"Panic! I don't know what to say. This is unbelievable. I guess you've had time to get used to the idea. I do see your point about the panic, though. I probably would have done the same. But—now that we do know, we insist on being directly involved."

"You can be involved if you wish, but we must show a united front. We will discuss alternatives with you and seek your advice, but we will have to be the ones to make the final decisions. If you try to interfere, I'm afraid that the results could be disastrous for everyone. If our positions were reversed, I would respect your privacy in the situation. It is just the way it happened to turn out. Our roles could have very well been reversed."

"As long as we are involved, we respectfully request that we be part of the decision-making process from now on. Our lives and those of our people are at stake as well as yours."

"Yes, of course. But you will have to operate from Washington or over the phone. It is your choice."

"We will fly in as soon as possible, Henry."

"I thought that you would, Uri. Have a safe flight. And please remember, complete secrecy."

"Goodbye, Henry."

"Goodbye, Uri."

The President hung up the phone and called his chief of staff and his national security advisor back into the room.

Pamela Wayne and Sidney Olson stepped pensively into the room.

Dr. Pamela Wayne was tall and thin with a serious demeanor and a fast wit. She had been a professor of political science at Duke University, specializing in East European studies before coming to the attention of President Barnes. Wayne had advised other presidents before Barnes, but once he saw her in action he knew that he would tap her abilities if he ever ran for president.

Sidney Olson was a lawyer and an old friend of the President's. He stood at five feet nine inches, weighed 180 lbs, had an average build and a slight paunch. They had known each other back at Princeton Law School when they were both undergrads. Sid was always there for Barnes throughout his political career, starting as a freshman congressman from Ohio, in the late seventies.

"The Russians know about the aliens. They said that a team of their astronauts spotted it while checking out the moon from space."

There was silence for a moment.

"How do you think that they really found out?" he said to no one in particular.

Wayne looked at the President and rubbed his chin.

"They probably were eavesdropping on us or have a well positioned spy somewhere. They could never have spotted that ship out there. I doubt if those aliens would have a ship that could be spotted that easily. They must have some way of rendering themselves invisible or at least camouflaging the ship. The Russians could have never spotted them."

Olson said: "There must be a leak somewhere."

Wayne and Olson looked at each other, then back to the President.

"Whatever. Tell the proper people about the suspected leak; right now we have more important things to worry about. Who cares about a leak if we all blow up. Sid," he said to his chief of staff, "Pamela and I were discussing how we can make contact with the aliens. We must have a meeting with them—

face to face."

"What about Cooper?"

"Yes I know. But Cooper's on the lam and they tell me that his alien girlfriend is with him. Can't you think of anything else?"

No one answered.

"I guess we might as well play that card until we lose it," said the President. If I don't hear from Goodwood by the time we finish our meeting, I'll call him. Now, what are we going to do with the Russians?"

They pondered for a moment. The President started first. "Naturally I couldn't refuse them. They could cause a worldwide panic. But we can't have them running the show either."

"I believe that you handled the situation properly, Mr. President," said Wayne.

"Sure, in theory it's fine, we get advice and suggestions from them but make our own decisions. But how is it going to work in practice? It could get real hairy if they become disenchanted."

"Then we have to stay on our toes," said Olson.

"Well he's coming to our turf and it's our ball, so he'll just have to play by our rules," agreed the President.

The President's intercom rang.

"Yes, Margaret?"

"It's General Goodwood, sir."

"Put him through. Finally," he said, holding the mouthpiece.

"Yes, General, I'm putting you on the speaker; Pamela Wayne and Sidney Olson are here with me."

"It's not good news, sir," said Goodwood.

"What is it?"

"It appears that Howard Cooper has been captured by the aliens."

"It appears?"

"The two private people that I hired were chasing them and the aliens showed up."

"I thought you hired the best men."

"I did, but they were simply no match for the aliens' weapons and tactics."

"Why didn't you use more men?"

"It wouldn't have mattered. The aliens' weapons are far too superior to ours. If we had thrown a lot of personnel at them, we would have most likely ended up with a blood bath on our side. So I used these two men for stealth rather than brawn. It seems that we may be at their mercy. Besides, we didn't want to fire on them, did we? We didn't want to start a land war."

"No, no. Of course not."

"I was trying to accomplish this with as low a profile as possible."

"Yes, yes. You did right," said the President. "So what do we do now?"

"Our men got stopped before they could reach Cooper and his little group. They were following the aliens, who were following Cooper's car. Cooper had the alien girl and someone he met in a bar, with him. I have to presume that they were caught. The aliens were right on their asses. But I can't say one hundred percent."

"Alright. Assuming the worst, what then?" asked the President.

Olson and Wayne had that *oh shit, it's up to us now* look.

"We have to hope that this Howard Cooper will be loyal. After all, if he wanted to talk to them, he would have done that in the first place, and he certainly would not have escaped. Also, the girl seems to care about Cooper, but she could be just a pawn of the aliens."

"Well I don't know about the girl, but we must try to use this Cooper as a go between. At least he's human," said the President." Hopefully we can talk to him and he can talk to them. What is your next step, General?"

"There is nothing that I can think of right now except to sit and wait. We just don't know how to contact these aliens."

"Pamela, what do you think?"

"We're in deep trouble, sir, if we can't even communicate."

"Sid?"

"I have to think about it."

"Well, you had better talk to the people who first intercepted the aliens' message and find out if we can broadcast on the same channel. Maybe they will hear us and come to talk. I feel like a goddamned sitting duck—and I don't like it. I want some suggestions from someone within the hour, I don't care how you get it." He looked at the two of them in his office to make them know that they were included. "I'll hire a medicine man or a psychic, if you people can't come up with some answers."

"Yes, Mr. President," said Goodwood.

He glared at the two in his office.

"Yes, sir," they said almost simultaneously.

He hung up the phone and waved the two in his office out.

The President sat in his chair looking over his office. The knowledge that he held the fate of the Earth in his hands both stimulated and frightened him all at once. *They have to contact us*, he thought. *Cooper has to come through.*

He wouldn't let them blow us up without having them give us a chance. They must give us a chance to prove that we are worth saving. They can't just think of themselves and their own good. They said that these aliens have morals and are not barbarians. They can't just think of us in terms of how useful we are to them. We have a right to survive. We share the galaxy with them. We are God's creatures too, just like they are. They must see that we have a right to live also. For our own sake, if somehow not for theirs.

That evening Uri Radomir, President of the Russian Federation, and his interpreter, Nicoli Isilov, sat side by side as their jet was passing over Canada into the United States. President Radomir sat in the window seat.

"Look down there, Nicki, those are the Great Lakes; beautiful, isn't it? It's like a woman that you know you may never see again. Somehow, she seems that much more desirable. All this may be gone. Can you believe that, Nicki? They say that we are destroying the Earth. And maybe they're right. Looks like we're never going to get the chance to finish the job, if what I'm told about these aliens is true."

"Do you think if we got another chance we would turn the situation around?" asked Nicoli.

"Maybe a scare like this is what we need. I hope so. I hope we get the chance to straighten things out on our own planet."

Nicoli sat and said nothing. He reflected how he came to this climatic scene in the drama of human kind.

Nicoli Ivor Isilov was born forty-five years ago in Moscow. His mother was an intellectual who taught languages and his father was a high-ranking member of the diplomatic corps. Soon after Nicoli's birth, his parents moved to Washington, DC, where he was brought up. He attended Georgetown University where he majored in Russian Literature and minored in political science. From there, he went on to Moscow University, where he received a master's in Eastern European languages. With his strong background and his father's political connections, he secured a visible position in the Russian government, as a translator. Within ten years, he was translating for the President of the Russian Federation.

In choosing him, President Radomir understood that it was not just translating the language per se, it was the intelligence and ability to comprehend innuendo and subtlety that could make all the difference when translating at this level and of course having a grasp of the idiom.

"Even the simple things of life, things that you see every day, become so important when you are threatened with their loss," said the President, startling Nicoli from his thoughts. "You also wonder why you fought over things that seem so petty now."

"It's only natural," said Nicoli. "After all, we're only human."

"Only human! That expression seems all the more significant in light of the events taking place at this moment. It seems that there are others who are more than human. And, right now, we seem to be at their mercy. It's so easy to get lost in your own importance when you don't have to bother with comparisons. But here it is thrust directly into our faces and we come up wanting."

"Don't judge us so harshly, comrade chairman, these creatures have probably been around a great deal longer than we have."

"Yes, Nicki, you make such a wonderful point, but for the other side."

"How is that?'

"They've lasted that long. Who's to say, with the present condition of the planet and the human race that we would even last long enough to be in the same league with these creatures. Could you imagine what some outside intelligence would think looking at us and seeing the condition of our people and planet? Hunger and starvation in the midst of plenty. Destruction of the planet and its resources by the very people who depend on it. Pollution of the very air we breathe and the water we drink. Elimination of the very things, like the rain forests, that give us the air that we breathe. What would be your judgment of such creatures as we are, if you looked at us with fresh eyes? I doubt if we would appear to be the kind of creatures that they would want to take home to mother, no less save. Save for what? More destruction?"

Just then, the steward came by.

"Wodka!" said Radomir.

The steward nodded and left.

"You have to give us more credit than that, comrade chairman," continued Nicoli, "we've done some rather positive things, too. We've been altruistic, and also created beautiful works of art."

"This is true, but unfortunately it doesn't make up for the destruction we've wreaked on the world, the species we've annihilated."

"I'm sure they will see the good also. If they are that smart, they will see our potential for good, and just maybe they will help us find the secret, the thing that will help turn us around in the right direction. Maybe we just need a little help."

"You could be right, Nicki. Oh here's the wodka." Radomir gave a glass to his companion and filled it. I hope so for all our sakes, that you are right. We have to have something to stick out our chests about. Although it is probably wishful thinking to say to these creatures: we know we're here for some positive reason, we just need a little help to find our purpose in life, beyond self-glorification. Lastrovia."

"Lastrovia!" returned Nicki, as they both downed their drinks.

"Perhaps that's it, comrade chairman."

"I guess deep in our hearts and souls we believe that we have a purpose, after all, even if we cannot articulate it or do not entirely comprehend it. We ask the question to remind ourselves that, in fact, there is a purpose. After all, we need to keep reminding ourselves of that fact. Strange the way the human mind works; it's perfectly logical you know, we just refuse to accept the truth if it doesn't fit our plans. But the mind cannot lie to itself, somehow, in different ways; it keeps sticking our faces in the truth. Our conscious mind is our only defense against the deep, dark truth lurking down inside. But the conscious mind ultimately always fails to protect us. I know it fails because that is what guilt and those other gnawing feelings are about—There I go, ranting and raving, like an senile old man. You won't tell on me, will you, Nicki?"

"Your words are true and also profound. How else can you make the difficult decisions that you face without the depth of understanding that you must possess. I am proud and honored to serve you. I could only brag about your statements, nothing else. I drink to your health, to mother Russia and our planet."

"You're too kind, Nicki, much too kind. Look, Nicki, that looks like Chicago down there. Do the gangsters always wear black hats while the good guys wear white ones?"

"I believe that's only in the westerns, comrade chairman."

"You see, you're not a yes man after all. So that means your kind words were heartfelt."

"Of course, comrade chairman, of course."

"I'm going to tell the President, Nicki, that if we survive this we must work toward fixing this world of ours. If we get a second chance then we must take that as a sign that there will not be any more chances after this one, if we don't do the right things for this world."

Howard sat in his chair as the shuttle glided out of the atmosphere and into cold, dark space. Only he and Sandra were making the trip back to the mother ship. Frank had been left behind in a rather frazzled state. Once the ship stabilized, far enough away from Earth's gravity, Sandra got up from her chair and walked over to Howard. She held his hand and looked into his eyes. He thought about her gentle lovable nature. She was somehow different from her people; she exhibited greater feeling and sensitivity.

"What would you have done if you hadn't met me?" he asked, gently.

"I don't know. But now that I have you, I do not intend to lose you."

"I come from that world down there. And I will do whatever I can to save it."

"So why didn't you stay with them?" she asked.

"Those bastards! Those brutal bastards," he said, the rage rising in him. "I needed time to cool off. I hate them, but they only represent what is wrong with our society and our society is only one part of the world. Maybe they're just doing their job, but I don't like them. I have to do what's right for humanity."

"Where does that leave me?"

"Right here. My marriage is finished. I'm lucky if I ever get a chance to see my kids again."

"I will help you if I can."

He smiled at her warmly.

As the day wore on, the mother ship came into view. As they docked, the suction from the mother ship clamped the shuttle vessel into place with a firm but gentle thud. Those on the shuttle felt a slight vibration followed by an odd momentary silence. The shuttle doors slid silently open to reveal a short passageway into the mother ship. As they entered the spacious vessel, Howard felt the seriousness of the mission the Hidden People had come to execute. They were escorted up the pneumatic elevator to the level where Rondo and General Titus were waiting. Their version of an elevator was what we call a pneumatic tube. They were deposited effortlessly at the destination level of the mother ship. The door slid open and they entered a narrow corridor. They followed their escort and entered the room and found Rondo looking at the moon through one of the portholes. He turned as they entered.

"Howard and Sandra, nice to see you two again," said Rondo evenly. "You both met General Titus down on Earth."

"Hello," said Howard, nodding. Sandra just smiled. And Titus slowly nodded his acknowledgment.

"What are you planning to do with my planet?" asked Howard

impatiently.

"We'll discuss that in a moment. We have a small problem with the loss of our agent, M22. Can you help us with that?"

Sandra looked at Howard. "No," he said simply.

"You don't happen to know anything about this, do you, Sandra?"

She smiled blandly. "No," she replied.

"Well it looks like we have a little problem here. We are missing one of our people and we are not getting any cooperation. Let me assure you," continued Rondo, looking at Howard, "I will not be angry with you because you are trying to protect your own kind. That means if you change your mind and tell me what I want to know I will not punish you in any way for lying. The information is what I am after, how I get it is not important."

He looked at Howard again, this time without saying anything.

"Are you going to torture me, if I don't tell you what you want to know?"

"Absolutely not. We do not do those things here. It is simply not necessary. You will tell me what I want to know voluntarily."

"Are you going to give me drugs or hypnosis?"

"No. We operate in a logical manner. We get what we need by being logical."

"What does that mean exactly?"

"We will just assume the worst and act accordingly. Usually the truth will not bring consequences that are as bad, so we find out what we want to know. Simple isn't it?"

"So what are you assuming?" asked Howard cautiously.

"That he was tortured and killed in the most painful and humiliating manner."

"No! That did not happen," said Howard.

"How do we know? And how do you know?"

"It didn't happen," repeated Howard.

"How do you know something did not happen, unless you know what did happen?"

Howard held his head. "What are you going to do, if I don't answer?"

"Worse than if you do."

"That's so neat."

"Tell him!" blurted out Sandra.

Howard looked at her and shook his head. "Is she working for you?" he asked ironically.

"She does not work for anyone," responded Rondo.

"So why is she helping you?"

"Maybe she thinks she is helping you. And maybe she is right." Howard thought about it for a second. It occurred to him that Sandra didn't say much, but when she spoke, she was usually right on target. *Out of the mouths of babes,* he thought.

"Maybe. And. maybe you're bluffing. Ever play poker? You got the face for it," he said to Rondo.

"I will assume that that is a compliment," said Rondo, knowing that it wasn't.

Howard smiled and raised his eyebrows.

"That is your choice," continued Rondo, "whether you believe me or not. We have little to lose either way."

"That's true," said Howard almost to himself.

"What is it going to be, Mr. Cooper?"

Sandra looked at him. Howard hesitated. He knew he had no choice, but he was afraid just the same. He closed his eyes and grimaced. "If I tell you what I know, will you give me your word that you will tell me your plans for my planet?

"You have my word," replied Rondo.

"They killed him," he blurted out: "At least they shot him. Maybe your kind don't die as easily as we do, but they pumped somewhere around a half a dozen bullets into him. Enough to easily kill a human, but again you folks aren't human, or are you? And even if you started out human, after your body replacement, you're probably super human."

"So they tried to kill him?" asked Rondo.

"If they killed him, they didn't think that they had any choice. He looked like he was going to harm one of the generals. He was only trying to help me. Ironic isn't it? He probably thought that I was going to be killed. He very well may have saved my life. Or at least saved me from serious injury. He probably thought that it was part of his responsibility to protect me."

Rondo looked at Titus, Sandra looked at Rondo and Howard looked at all of them.

"How will this change things?" asked Howard.

"It probably will not. It will just make our position stronger."

"Are you saying that we have no hope?"

"Not much."

"What can we do to save ourselves?" asked Howard with desperation in his voice.

"Do your people know how to pray?" answered Rondo.

The President paced. It was a way for him to work off his tension. He peered out his window at the landing pad where the Russian President's helicopter would shortly be landing. There would be no fanfare or publicity. Everything was to be top secret and low key. No one was to know about the meeting. If the press found out it would be explained away with some story about very sensitive talks that could not be made public.

The phone rang. The President picked it up. He was told that President Radomir was on his way and would be arriving within the next fifteen minutes.

The President reflected: *fifteen minutes. What does one do to prepare himself to discuss the fate of the world in fifteen minutes?* As he sat, he could see in his mind the whole panorama of his life passing by. He tried to make meaning out of it. What was it all for? What was it all about? Why him? Was he fated to be the one to face this crisis? If he succeeded, he would be a hero. But if he failed, everyone might go to their death with his name on their lips. It wasn't worth it, he thought. But the choice wasn't his. He was in the hot seat and there was little or nothing he could do about it. He would face it he thought, like he faced all the other crises in his life: bravely and with dignity. It would be all right. Somehow, it would be all right.

He was startled by the sound of the helicopter blades spinning outside. He was escorted out by two secret service men and arrived just in time to see the door come open and President Radomir and his small entourage come out.

The two Presidents greeted each other with firm handshakes and went into the White House. After the personal amenities were addressed, President Barnes and President Radomir went into the oval office to talk privately. The interpreters were not invited in. The Russian President would speak in English.

Barnes sat in a chair and Radomir sat on the couch. They sipped coffee while they spoke.

"Uri, how was your trip?" asked the President.

"You know—the trip was fine. As we flew here, I viewed the sights just a little differently on this trip than I would normally. I was telling my interpreter, Nicki, that you appreciate things much more when you are in danger of losing them. By seeing what we have, I thought about what we could lose. We are in big trouble, Henry, are we not?"

"Yes we are, Uri. Yes we are."

"So what is your plan?" asked Radomir.

"We have to find a way to contact these aliens so we can try to deal with them. I'm afraid that they are planning our destruction as we speak."

"That bad, Henry?"

"Yes. We must anticipate the worst if we are to survive, don't you agree, Uri?"

"Yes. Here we are sitting around sounding so—philosophical when it is practical things we need to do."

"My people are working on that aspect, Uri. They are sending messages out on the frequency on which we first picked up the message from the aliens."

"So we're in worse shape than I thought."

"I'm afraid so. Somehow I believe that they won't just do this to us without giving us a chance, though."

"What kind of creatures are they?" asked Radomir.

"They seem human, somehow."

"God—I hope not. We've made quite a mess of things ourselves. I hope their nature is more understanding than ours is. I hope these creatures don't have our failings."

"Interesting way to look at it, Uri."

It was the President's intercom that buzzed.

"I can't believe they're disturbing us," said the President almost to himself.

Buzz! Buzz!

"This is unbelievable," he said, getting up.

"Yes!" he said almost harshly into the speaker.

"Mr. President, I apologize for disturbing you but General Goodwood is on the line for you, sir, and he says that it is extremely urgent."

Goodwood, he said to himself. "Put him through."

"Mr. President," said the general, "we may have a break."

"What is it, General?"

"My people captured that guy who was running around with Cooper. His name is Napoleon Baker. What should we do with him, Mr. President?"

"Can he help us get in touch with Cooper?"

"He claims that he is The Peerless Warrior, whatever that means. He says that he can talk to Cooper whenever he wants. He says that he will only discuss it with you, personally."

"Is this guy playing with a full deck?"

"I don't know, Mr. President, but he was with Cooper when he and the girl were captured by the aliens. They apparently saw no reason to take Mr. Baker along for the ride. He insists that he can get in touch with Cooper."

"You'd better bring him around. This might be the break that we've been hoping for."

"Yes, Mr. President."

Within the hour Napoleon "Frank" Baker, was in the President's oval office. President Radomir was invited to stay for the interview. The President sat behind his desk with a secret service man on each side for protection. It was the only way that the head of the Secret Service would consent to allow the interview with Baker to take place, without him being manacled.

Next to Baker sat General Goodwood, and next to Goodwood sat Radomir.

The President was trying to act nonchalant, as though Baker was some nice citizen that did a good deed or something. But it was tough.

"Mr. Baker," the President began, "I am so pleased that you have consented to help us."

"That's quite all right, Mr. President, I'm always glad to help," said Baker, grinning from ear to ear and looking like he was sitting in the catbird seat.

"We are all in grave danger, as I'm sure you're quite aware. We need to get in touch with Howard Cooper as soon as possible. We have to try to reason with these creatures. You will help us won't you?"

"Sure, Mr. President. And you can call me Frank. My friends call me Frank."

"Okay, Frank. And this is President Radomir of the Russian Federation."

" President Radomir," said Frank, nodding his head and smiling again.

"Mr. Baker," said Radomir, smiling. "Looks like we have a hero in the making."

Frank just grinned and shook his head. Then he looked up at the ceiling, then lowered it and shook it back and forth. "So I'd be saving the planet by doing this?"

"Well, it would certainly be a great help, Frank," said the President.

"I'm sure it would be. You wouldn't have me here otherwise. I'm sure you all have better things to do than entertain a nobody like me. So, my information must be quite valuable. Quite valuable!"

"Look here—" began Goodwood, before the President cut him off with a wave of his hand.

"It's okay, General. The man has a right to speak his mind. Let him get it off his chest."

"Yes, General, I have to get it off my chest."

Goodwood frowned.

After a brief silence, the President said: "What is it that you want, Mr— er, Frank."

"Nothing really. I'm a loyal American. I fought in the war. I was in Nam. I just want to be recognized for my part in all this. I quit my job and left my girlfriend to help Howard Cooper. He swore that he was the last hope of the world. I believed him, though it did seem far-fetched at the time. I guess he wasn't putting me on after all."

He laughed with his mouth closed.

"Well, we can't put your picture in the papers, Frank, or have you on the Six o'clock news, because no one is supposed to know about this," said the President. "You realize that it would start a panic if anyone knew."

"Yeah, but once this thing is over and we're safe again, you could look like quite a hero, Mr. President, and you also, President Radomir," said Frank, nodding again at the Russian.

"Yes, I agree," acknowledged the President, patiently waiting for the punch line.

Frank smiled broadly.

"There's no question that you would be recognized also if we can pull this one out," he continued.

"How about the Metal of Freedom?" asked Frank.

"Sure. Why not?" said the President.

Goodwood sighed deeply.

"And the Order of Lenin. Absolutely!" said Radomir with exuberance.

"You guys ain't pullin' my pud are you?"

"I assure you," said the President. "If we get through this in one piece, it would be my pleasure to honor you."

"Okay!" said Frank. "What do you want me to do?"

"You must contact Cooper," said the President. "Tell him that I would like to speak with him."

"Sure, why not," said Frank.

"Wonderful!" said the President. "How can we help you accomplish this?"

"Well," said Frank, scratching the side of his head and smiling, "for starters you can get these guys off my ass."

Goodwood made a face and coughed lightly.

"Anything else?"

"The use of a car."

"That it?"

"That's it."

"How long will it take?" asked the President.

"A couple of days."

"We can't wait that long. We don't know how much time we have left. We can fly you down by helicopter and I will personally guarantee that you will be left to your own devices. No one will do anything unless you asked for it."

"That's fine," said Frank. "What would be the purpose of your discussions with Cooper? If you don't mind my asking."

"We need to meet with the aliens to try to convince them to spare us."

"Great!" shouted Frank. "But only if I'm included on the team that meets with them," he said, folding his arms resolutely.

"That does it!" said Goodwood.

"General," said the President.

"If it can be arranged, it will be."

"Not good enough! I want it ironclad."

"You little punk!" said the general under his breath.

The President scratched his head. He looked directly at Frank. "You can go. But we will not allow you to fuck this up. If you try you will be dealt with in the harshest manner. Do you understand, Mr. Baker?"

"Yes, sir! And I agree with you, Mr. President. I would not handle it any differently myself."

The President let his breath out slowly and audibly.

"Let's go, guys!" said Frank. "You all heard the President, we have no time to lose."

CHAPTER SIXTEEN

General Titus glided swiftly toward Rondo's apartment. His normally serene austere demeanor had a slightly anticipatory aspect to it. As he arrived at the apartment Rondo appeared at the entrance.

"Finally," said the general, "Einstein has something to show us."

"Well hopefully this will be the answer we've been looking for," said Rondo.

They headed for the pneumatic device that would carry them close to Einstein's laboratory.

"He says that he has found the formula for killing or functionally disabling the humans without effecting the rest of the life forms on the planet," said Rondo.

Titus nodded his understanding.

When they arrived at the pneumatic station, Rondo opened the door, sat down in the enclosed seat, pulled the hatch cover over his head (which hissed when it locked into place), entered his desired destination and waited for a moment. After the room was pressurized and the connecting pathways plotted, the car was sucked into the system and off it went through the pneumatic tubes that ran the length and breadth of the ship. Switches at intersections along the way shuttled the passenger in his airtight car through the appropriate arteries to arrive at the correct destination. It was all determined by the initial instructions that were entered into the car's console. Titus got into the next car and did the same.

As Titus got out of his carriage, Rondo was waiting. They walked together into Einstein's laboratory. After their standard greeting Rondo spoke.

"Einstein, please tell us of the weapon that will solve our dilemma with the earthlings."

Einstein smiled. "It is quite simple actually," he began. "I have developed a microbe, or what the humans would call a virus. The virus has one function only: to destroy genes. In fact, it is quite a feat of gene engineering itself. From the studies that we were able to perform on the human cells that we took from Howard Cooper, the virus should perform the function quite well. What it does is attack and destroy only the genes that are the differentiators of humans from all other creatures on Earth. Our field people captured some apes, which are the humans' closest relatives and tested the differences in their DNA. That difference is what we had to breach. There will be no danger to other forms of life; we also gathered a random sampling of other creatures in order to test it out. What exactly will happen to the humans is not entirely clear. What is clear, though, is that they will lose their ability for rational thought, assuming they think rationally now," he added, snickering, "for speech and the other functions that distinguish them from the other creatures that inhabit the Earth. You see it works only on the brain. They will not change physically but since the brain controls the body, they will act and function differently. Of course we have yet to test it out on any actual humans, but I am certain that we will get our chance very soon," he said, smiling broadly.

"What is the anticipated outcome for the humans infected by the virus?" asked Rondo.

"They most likely will become like an ape or like whatever creature they actually evolved from. I cannot say exactly how many steps back down the evolutionary ladder they will go, but they will most likely become like apes in their behavior or something close to it. The important thing is that they will not have the capacity to communicate, so they cannot transfer information about us to other potentially dangerous life forms. We also know that the infection should take twenty-four to forty-eight hours to work its magic. We included a catalyst in the protein jacket of the virus to help speed up the infection process. The other important area that will be affected besides the brain is the gonads, so that the incapacitated former humans cannot reproduce normal human offspring. We do not know what other effects it will have on them. But they will not be able to communicate as they now do and that is the key. Due to the time constraints, we have not researched this project as thoroughly as usual, but I am confident that we have things under control. The resulting creatures may have a difficult time adapting to the environment that they created in their former condition. In other words, they may become extinct. But that is unpredictable. That of course will be their problem, since it was their own fault. Will that be satisfactory to your purposes?" he asked.

"Yes, absolutely. And what of the environment?"

"It will probably prosper with the source of the pollution gone. Whether it will ultimately survive is anyone's guess. We may have stopped the damage just in time or it might already be too late."

"Wonderful!" said Rondo. "How soon will you be ready to execute the plan?"

"About a week. We are growing the viruses now."

"How will you disseminate it?"

"Since the microbe is highly communicable and therefore easily passed from one individual to another, we need only infect each general area of the globe to successfully complete our task. Any holdouts we will have to track down and administer the germ to them personally."

"What do we do now?" asked Titus.

"Now?" answered Rondo, "we wait for the first lucky humans to be put out of their misery."

It was 5:00 a.m. and the team was gathering for their trip up to the aliens' mother ship. Frank had managed through a prearranged method to contact Howard and Howard to convince Rondo to allow the humans their last chance to plead for their lives. Though hope was slim, it was better than none.

Rondo had time to kill anyway and the meeting would just help him feel comfortable that at least the humans were being occupied and wouldn't be off doing something *inconvenient* that might make things more difficult for all concerned. The last thing Rondo wanted was panic or defensive measures being taken, especially before the virus had a chance to take hold. In short, he didn't want anything to take place that might ruin his neat little plans. And he certainly didn't want the humans sending up any distress signals into space that might attract the attention of some other life forms looking for some sport or conquest.

So, as far as Rondo was concerned this meeting could not come at a better time. It was especially so since the human's had requested it. This way they would not suspect that they were being set up in any way. And how could the humans know that the time they were supposedly buying for themselves was serving two masters.

The aliens did not put any limit on the number of people the humans could send to the mother ship, but the President naturally insisted on keeping the number down to an absolute minimum.

187

The President, his national security advisor, Pamela Wayne, his Chief of Staff, Sid Olsen, General Goodwood (to represent the military), Professor Clearview (for his knowledge of extraterrestrial life), President Radomir (just so the blame could be spread out, if this didn't pan out), and Frank Baker (the President insisted he go, against the wishes of General Goodwood), were set to go. The President thought it might jinx the trip if he broke his promise to Baker. In addition, he thought it would be a lot neater not to leave behind any noisy loose ends.

The ship arrived at the rendezvous point at 6:00 a.m. on the dot. As the saucer shaped ship landed, all those in the party were noticeably impressed.

Radomir stood transfixed and Professor Clearview looked like a kid seeing his first fully dressed Christmas tree.

A door in the ship opened and a human like creature came out and walked directly over to the President, bid him hello and asked him to enter the ship along with his comrades. The President followed the alien and the rest of the party came along.

The President turned to his chief of staff. "It didn't really hit home till now, Sid. Not until you see the damned thing staring you right in the face. Somehow, you think maybe it's a hoax or something, or even a bad dream. But this—God almighty," he said, visibly shaken.

After seeing the President in that state, the blood drained from Olsen's face and he had to hold on to stabilize himself.

When inside they were invited to sit on what appeared to be lounge chairs.

"We will be taking off in exactly three minutes," a voice said in perfect English. Please recline and allow the safety device to engage."

As they leaned back, the armrests came up and snuggled against their bodies, holding them firmly but comfortably. They could see out of the ship in all directions, though they could not see in from the outside (like a two-way mirror).

As the ship rose smoothly into the air, there was no sensation of movement, only the sight of the Earth growing smaller and smaller at an increasingly rapid rate. Somehow, the ship compensated for the weightlessness of space. It seemed as though gravity was still present. The seven earthlings smiled at each other and looked around in silence. Whoever was piloting the ship was not visible to the human cargo heading toward the moon.

A pleasant looking alien inquired into the state of their comfort. Everyone claimed to be fine. The President's demeanor was cool, as was the two in his staff. The general looked uncomfortable. Professor Clearview looked delighted and was taking everything in. President Radomir looked stately. And Frank Baker looked cool while continuing to size everyone up.

The trip passed with small groups conversing among themselves. General Goodwood spoke with Clearview, the President with Wayne and Olsen and to his surprise, President Radomir found Frank Baker quite fascinating.

As docking maneuvers began, everyone, including General Goodwood was rapt. Professor Clearview looked like a kid watching his first circus and Frank acted like this happened to him every day.

The size of the mother ship was overwhelming to the earthlings, with no exceptions. It appeared to them to be an enormous black gleaming sphere, big enough to house a small city.

When all the whirring and whooshing was completed, an alien appeared and asked the earthlings to follow him.

Suddenly a door whooshed open and they followed the alien through the connection. As they filed out into the mother ship, their heads turned to and fro taking in the sights and sounds of this New World.

Everyone walking about the ship seemed occupied in one way or another, no one seemed idle. The demeanor of those walking about seemed pleasant, but they didn't stop to chat with one another or appeared to be wasting time. The visitors had the sense of things getting done. The walls that were not transparent were stark white and perfectly clean. The lights were very bright but not glaring. The floors and ceilings in the hallways were transparent.

They had entered the ship at its equator, its widest point. The inhabitants going about their business did not seem to take much notice of the visitors, which surprised some and bothered others, like Baker and Clearview who were looking for action.

They seemed to be walking a long way. They were heading for the core, the dead center of the sphere. When they reached it, they found a pneumatic elevator that could hold up to thirty people. From this vantage point, they could see straight up to the top and straight down to the bottom of the ship. It was a dizzying sight for someone who was not used to it. The elevator wall, like every wall in the ship, was transparent except when you looked from the outside in. So, from where they stood they could see everything except into offices and apartments.

Everyone stepped into the strange looking elevator, except, surprisingly, Frank Baker. Who appeared for the smallest moment to hesitate? They all wondered, to themselves, if the macho man suffered from vertigo.

Once in the elevator, they were all instructed to stand with their backs up against the wall. The elevator itself was perfectly round and looked, from the outside, like a tin can. As they pushed against the wall, mechanical arms came out and grasped each individual around the midsection. They were instructed by a voice to move the mechanical arms to their waist, to compensate for differences in height. As the arms locked into place, they were held tightly but comfortably.

As the elevator rose with great speed, the lights in the car dimmed to almost darkness. The passengers felt the exhilaration of flying through space, the darkness enhancing a dream like state.

"Now I know what the projectile in a pneumatic tube feels like flying between floors in a department store," said Frank out loud.

The car slowed briefly, before stopping and all onboard felt the sensation of takeoff subside. It stopped smoothly and the doors slid open exposing the panorama of stars and black space.

They filed around the hall, which was at the top of the ship, and up a small staircase, which led to the very roof of the sphere. That is where Rondo waited to greet his guests. They sat in a semicircle behind narrow desks facing Rondo who was elevated just enough to put him in the power position. Looking past Rondo was a gallery of the heavens that took ones breath away. It was like the shootout on Main Street, where the more experienced gunfighter positioned himself so that the sun shined from behind his back into the eyes of his opponent. The earthlings were at a disadvantage and definitely outclassed.

Rondo wore his "Father Knows Best" smile and radiated a warm demeanor. But there was something sinister about his eyes. The blatant tone of the contradictions made everyone particularly uneasy.

"Welcome. Your trip up was comfortable I hope," said Rondo, his eyes softening just enough to make his remarks palatable.

Everyone sort of nodded in unison. He had them hypnotized. "We want your stay to be as comfortable as possible. If anyone has a problem I would like you to let me know personally."

The President, who sat in the middle of the group, spoke first. "I am the President of the United States of America and the gentleman all the way on my right is the President of the Russian Federation. We represent the two most powerful nations on my planet. These people next to me on my right are my chief of staff, Sidney Olson, and my national security advisor, Pamela

Wayne. On my left is the chairman of the Joint Chiefs of Staff of my county's armed forces, General Goodwood. Next to him is Professor Clearview, an expert on outer space and next to him is a civilian observer and friend of Howard Cooper, who helped us communicate with your ship when we set up this meeting."

"Does the fact that President Radomir has no advisors and you have four, mean that he is the smarter of you two?" asked Rondo playfully.

The President could not figure out whether or not Rondo was pulling his leg. He answered cautiously. "It is merely circumstantial, that is all. Since we were the ones contacted, we have better representation. President Radomir was invited to join us out of propriety and respect for him and his nation. He is also a very capable man and we felt that his presence would be to everyone's advantage."

Radomir beamed.

"When you said everyone's advantage, did that include my people?" asked Rondo.

Again, the President didn't know if he was being had.

Just then a little gong sounded. "Excuse me a second," said Rondo, pushing a button on the console in front of him.

The guests could not hear the voice speaking to Rondo.

"I'll be right there," said Rondo into the console. "I beg your pardon, but there is an urgent matter that I must attend to, it will not take more than a moment." He then rose from his seat and walked from the room.

All the guests turned and watched Rondo through the transparent walls. He met a man out in the hall. They seemed to be having an animated conversation. The man appeared to be persisting about something and Rondo appeared to be getting more and more agitated. Finally, Rondo picked him up and threw him crashing out of the glasslike wall of the ship. The man floated right out into space and then was gone. The wall of the ship repaired itself immediately.

The spectators in the conference room were nearly struck dumb. Goodwood turned to the President and said: "He takes no prisoners."

"These people are lunatics," said Olsen, trying to keep his remarks for the President only.

"Quiet," said Frank, "he's coming back."

Olsen looked at Frank as though he were an impudent child talking to him that way.

Rondo walked into the room as though nothing had happened. "Sorry for

191

the inconvenience," he said matter-of-factly.

What the spectators did not know was that what they actually saw was a motion picture created by the use of holography, a three dimensional image in space. What they saw was not real, but the affect on them, was quite real.

They exhibited their uneasiness by little nervous habits that they usually saved for their private times. Radomir rubbed his temples, Olsen and Wayne played with their pens, President Barnes kept pushing back his dirty blond hair to one side and Goodwood rubbed his chin. Clearview kept pushing back his longish gray hair with both his hands and Frank ran his teeth along his thumbnail, more out of anticipation than nervousness. Rondo noticed the affect with gratification.

"I would like to ask a question," said Rondo, bringing everyone's attention back to a single focus. "That object of yours that we retrieved from space, what do you call it?"

"A probe," answered the President. The procedure that was set up was that no one would answer except the President or the one he indicated.

"I see. How do you define the word—probe?"

"To test, to search without really knowing what you're searching for."

"I see. One of your American English dictionaries says the word to probe means 'to search to the bottom, to investigate with great thoroughness.'"

The President wondered why Rondo was nitpicking. He surmised that it was meant for effect. He also wondered if that scene outside wasn't toward the same end.

"So my question is," continued Rondo, "how can you be investigating with great thoroughness and *not* know exactly where the object was ultimately headed?"

"It is only the name we used. We knew where it was headed until it left our solar system. We thought that was clear."

"Nothing is clear with you humans. At least not when you talk about it. What you do is clear. You pollute and poison your planet and cry about the results. You constantly make war on each other, but continually talk of peace and love. Some of you live in opulence while others starve and have no place to live. And you caution your children not to talk to strangers, because you don't trust your own kind, yet, you send up a space probe announcing to the whole universe where you are. You trust unknown species but not your own kind. How do you explain that?"

The President looked dazed. He had no immediate answer. He looked around for help. His eyes came to rest on the professor. Clearview's face took on a very serious aspect; he rose slowly and looked at Rondo, as if he were his student.

He spoke slowly: "We assumed," he paused, "perhaps incorrectly," another pause, "that all life forms that are capable of decoding and understanding our message would be at least as advanced as we pitiful humans," he paused again for effect, obviously referring to Rondo's little speech. "Most likely they would be more advanced, since we recently passed the threshold of technology that would allow for coding, decoding and launching the probe. Since these beings are more advanced technologically, we assumed that they would also be more advanced spiritually as well. Perhaps we were wrong," he said at a faster tempo, and raised an eyebrow as a challenge to Rondo.

"Well said," replied Rondo.

Everyone watched him closely.

"But the simple fact of the matter is that we are in control now. You may be eloquent in speech and you may even win the debate, but we are still in control. You must do better than debate with me. You must convince me why it is in our interest not to end your existence. By the way," he added with a note of irony in his voice, "we would not be cruel about it, we would be quite humane." He lingered on the last word.

Radomir looked at the President. "May I speak?"

"Of course," said the President.

"You are not a barbaric people," he said, with a note of challenge in his voice.

"How do you know this?"

"Because, if you were, you would not be hiding. You would be out conquering," said Radomir, raising his eyebrows and tilting his head.

"This is correct," responded Rondo, with humility. "So what does that mean?"

"It means that it is in your best interest to act civilly. It means that you have a spiritual nature, spiritual enough, at least, to seek peace. With that fact in mind, it would go against that spiritual nature to kill and destroy without sufficient cause."

"Who is to say if the cause is sufficient or not? Or let us say we are obviously in the position to be the judge of that, since we are in control."

"You cannot tell me that you do not have any doubts."

"We all have doubts, but we act anyway."

The President chimed in. "We did not monitor our ship to your planet, we couldn't. We lost track of it when it left our solar system. And as far as signaling others, you are welcome to monitor us for as long as you like. You could not possibly believe that we pose any danger to you."

"You killed one of our people! That is not a great start."

Goodwood leaned over to the President. "The son-of-a-bitch told. Cooper told them! If I ever get my hands on that traitor bastard…his death would be too merciful." He paused. "Let me respond to this."

"Go ahead, General," said the President.

"I will take personal responsibility for that misfortunate occurrence," he said to Rondo. "It was one of my men and I will take personal responsibility. You may take your vengeance out on me personally. An eye for an eye! You should know, though, that my officer was only acting in defense of a fellow officer. But regardless, I offer myself here and now for equal justice. One life for one life. Innocent people should not have to pay for my alleged crime."

"You are quite brave and honorable, General. I compliment your President on the choice of you as Chairman of his Chiefs of Staff. But—I am afraid that it is really not the point. It is the nature of your people as a whole that is my concern."

Frank began to get edgy.

"What does our nature have to do with anything? Don't we have the right to be how we are?" asked the President.

"Not when you disturb our universe!" answered Rondo.

"Maybe a duel would be appropriate," said Frank to everyone's surprise. Combat on the field of honor. Your best against our best," he said, standing up and motioning to Rondo with his hand.

Everyone looked at Frank in horror.

"Do you purport to be that champion, by any chance?" asked Rondo curiously.

"It would be my honor!" responded Frank, bristling.

"Relax, gentlemen," Rondo said to the others, "it is not our way."

"A chance to be the Peerless Warrior! My pleasure indeed," Frank continued.

They all looked at him again.

"Why are you all staring at me? This is not something new. Haven't any of you heard of David and Goliath, Tristan slaying the Morhalt in the epic, Tristan and Isault? In fact or myth this is a tradition with our people."

"It may be a tradition with your people, but we are concerned with survival, not symbolism," replied Rondo.

The President broke in: "We would like an opportunity to show you who we really are and why we should be spared. Please give us the opportunity to show you our best. I invite you to come down and visit our planet as my special guest. You must see that you owe us that courtesy, at least, before you destroy us. One more opportunity."

Rondo pondered for a moment. "You will have five days. I must be back here in six days. That will give you one day of preparation."

"That does not give us much time to prepare."

"I want to see what is going on, not a show on my behalf. A day will give you the chance to clean up a bit, but not too much. Anyway, I must be back to this ship in six days. You may spend the time in between any way you like. That is you choice. That is the most I am willing to offer."

"That is fine," said the President without hesitation. "We appreciate your generous offer."

The meeting was ended and the President asked permission to call down to Earth to prepare for Rondo's visit. The President had General Goodwood call down on the frequency that was set up for such a contingency and tell them that the President needed to speak with his staff. The President told his people that they would be down in the next day with guests, special guests. Everything would be prepared.

They were invited to walk around the conference room and see the sights of their part of the solar system through the glass-like walls.

"Refreshments will be coming soon," said Rondo. Rondo took Barnes and Radomir to one of the viewing windows.

"With this control," he said, "you can turn the ship. It can be rotated three hundred sixty degrees in any direction, without disturbing anything or anyone. There is no up or down, it all depends on your orientation, so relatively speaking no one will even know movement is occurring. Our gravity units keep our feet on the ground. So, as long as we are not in flight or need to be stationary for some other reason, moving this sphere with your hands can change your view. Every time a new viewer uses the sphere, it is put back in the initial position. This is the viewer's starting reference point. You see, it is all relative. As you rotate the sphere the ship is rotated in the same manner."

"Ingenious," said Radomir.

"Yes," agreed the President, with as much enthusiasm as he could muster under the circumstances.

"What is the outer skin of the craft made of?" asked the Russian President.

"It is a ceramic material, which is nearly impregnable from the outside. There are two layers, which are transparent. Between them flows an insulating material that can change color, depending on the purpose at that moment. It can be dark to absorb heat; it can be silver for its reflective properties. We can make the ship invisible to light in the human visual spectrum, to infrared and other energy sources. We can also do other things, mostly of a military nature."

"Marvelous," said Radomir. The President concurred.

Suddenly General Titus appeared. He was introduced all around.

"Yes," he said, when he came to General Goodwood, "we met before."

"My pleasure," said Goodwood.

"General Titus has prepared a little exhibition for us," beamed Rondo.

"Please gather around and look out in this direction," said Titus to the group.

They all came around looking like they were coming to see previews of their own hanging. A less enthusiastic crowd would have been hard to find.

"Look out there," said Titus, pointing through the transparent wall at a fair-sized boulder in the distance. "It's bigger than you think," he boasted. "It's actually three thousand miles away and a hundred miles in diameter. The distance makes it look small from here. This may make it easier to see it," he said, playing with some dials. A part of the wall seemed to turn into a telescopic viewing screen and the object, which actually looked like a rather large meteor or small asteroid, came into focus.

Only Goodwood and Frank seemed particularly interested.

"Because of the power of the weapon and the danger from the debris, it is necessary to detonate it from at least a distance of one thousand miles."

The lights in the room dimmed and the view improved even more. Titus picked up a transmitter and spoke into it.

"Ready for firing," he said. "Fire!"

A fireball flashed and was gone. A moment later, the asteroid began to rumble, then it exploded, spewing tiny fragments in all directions.

Titus explained: "The energy source travels near the speed of light so that it need only be aimed properly, no guidance system is necessary. Not many things travel fast enough to get out of its way in time. The energy wave is attracted by the center of gravity of the object. The objects' molecules are excited and activated, which sets off a chain reaction, almost like your atom bomb. The results, as you can see, are devastating."

"Would you use such a weapon against us, if things turn out that way?" asked the President.

"Oh no," said Rondo, "nothing that crude. This was just for your amusement, nothing else."

You mean for your amusement, thought the President. "What then?" he asked.

"Does it matter?" replied Rondo.

"Maybe not to you."

"Let's hope that it will not be necessary."

The President reconsidered. He did not want to push too hard. He didn't know what he was dealing with and he certainly didn't want Rondo to change his mind about visiting the Earth.

The food came; the guests ate solemnly and retired to their quarters. Their flight back was set for 6:00 a.m. Earth time.

General Titus followed Rondo into his quarters.

"You want to speak with me, General Titus?" said Rondo, sitting down in a chair and waving Titus to also take a seat.

Titus sat. He leaned forward. "Rondo, you must reconsider this trip to Earth, it could be risky. Perhaps they will hold you hostage or kill you as they did M22."

"I believe what happened to M22 was probably unavoidable, due the circumstances. I doubt if they would chance getting us any more angry by trying to hold me."

"We can send guards to travel with you."

"No, I will travel with a small group or perhaps alone."

"That's too dangerous. There may be fanatics among them. Whatever the circumstances, they still could have avoided killing M22 if they really wanted to. I'm sure that they realized even then, that the consequences of their actions could be dire, but they killed him anyway."

"You're right!" said Rondo.

"Good. You're not going then?"

"No, I'm going, in order to raise their level of false security to the point that they would have no reason to try to harm me."

"What do you mean?" asked Titus.

"If I go with a small group as observers they will certainly try to hold me hostage."

"Yes?" General Titus gave Rondo a quizzical look.

"My abduction will serve as their 'ace in the hole' as they say, so this will put them more at ease. But that will of course do them no good since I have given direct instructions to Einstein to execute his plan as soon as the virus is ready. And now I am giving you those same instructions. So you see, my dear General Titus, those holding me will be in no condition to resist us when they become apelike.

"It still sounds a bit risky, but your plan will be executed as you wish."

"I am assured by Einstein that the whole planet will be blanketed with the virus all at once so that my 'hosts' will not have time to take revenge when they find out what we have done to their population.

"I will see that Einstein carries out this strategy in a flawless manner."

"The important thing is that we keep these people calm for the next five or six days to give Einstein time to complete his tests on the virus. It's in stable form now so they do not have to be as careful with it as before. I'm certain that they can make the progress that is necessary to complete the testing on time. I will instruct Einstein to make or beat the deadline at all costs."

"I will see to it," said Titus.

Rondo called the President and told him that someone would be sent around to bring him to Rondo's quarters.

The President arrived, hoping that Rondo had not changed his mind about the visit.

"Come in," said Rondo as the President arrived.

"I hope you called me here to give me good news."

"Yes, in fact, I believe you will find the news quite to your liking. I have decided that I will accompany you down to your planet."

"Wonderful, you will not regret it."

"Yes, we want to give you every opportunity to redeem yourselves."

"I appreciate that. And I don't want to sound ungrateful in any way, but I must ask you why the change of heart?"

"Well," said Rondo, "it's the least we can do. We were quite upset about M22. But now we want to be as fair as we can. And do not blame Howard Cooper for telling us, he and Sandra had no choice. We have ways of getting information that you humans cannot resist. It does not include anything crude like torture. We just know how to work with the mind."

"Cooper himself is not important. What is important is our two worlds understanding each other. If he can help us, that will be fine. And I give you my word that there will be no reprisals."

"I accept your word, Mr. President. And besides," said Rondo with a look of mock sympathy, "what good would it do you to take vengeance on Howard Cooper, who was pressed into service against his will? Especially when your hurting him would be both unjust and counterproductive to the situation."

"All we want is the chance to show you our value as a race; it would be counterproductive to harm anyone. It would help prove the opposite of what we are trying to show. I hereby grant Howard Cooper and his friend Sandra a complete and unconditional pardon and free and unlimited travel privileges as would be the right of any free citizen of my nation."

"Very well," said Rondo. "I look forward to our trip tomorrow."

The President was escorted back to his room.

The picture-phone in Howard's room began to ring. He answered it and Rondo's picture appeared on the screen.

"Howard," said Rondo, "you will be returning with me to Earth at 6:00 a.m. tomorrow morning. Sandra will come also."

"What's going on?"

"The President and his group asked me to return with them for a visit. I have accepted and I believe you can be helpful during the course of the visit."

"Thanks."

"You said you wanted a chance to save your world, well here it is. On this trip, they will be trying to convince me of the value of the human species. This is your last chance. Good luck."

"Wait," said Howard.

"Yes," replied Rondo.

"I would like to return but not with you and the President. It is nothing against either of you; it is just that I believe that I would not be able to add much to your trip. I would just be there to observe, window dressing, as we say. I would like to travel on my own, that is with Sandra and one of your top people, someone who is knowledgeable and can answer questions about your Hidden People."

"I guess that I owe you that much," said Rondo in agreement. "I'll have our historian, Joseph, who is on the ship, accompany you."

"Thank you, Rondo."

"It is no problem."

They broke off communication.

"What was that?" asked Sandra who was awakened from her sleep.

"It was Rondo. He has given us permission to visit the Earth by ourselves, along with an historian named Joseph. This is my peoples' last chance to redeem ourselves."

Sandra looked at Howard. "Yes, I have heard of Joseph; he is famous, but it's probably a trick!" she said. "You and your people are being set up."

"How do you know?" he asked.

"Some things, I just know."

Howard looked at her for a moment. "We have no choice; what can I do? We just have to do the best we can." Then he lay down and closed his eyes. He was in twilight sleep for a while. He tried to shut his mind off to what Sandra said. Then he went out. His dreams began soon afterward.

He was in a zoo, in the primate section, locked in a cage. He tried to get out, but he could not. He called to the keeper. But he did not come. The apes in the cage began to gather around him. They were orangutans and they began crowding in and pushing him. They were becoming abusive. He called again for the keeper to come and get him out, but still no one came. The smell of the apes and the cage was beginning to get him sick. What did they want with him? Why were they bothering him?

Finally, he saw the keeper coming by. He was coming to feed the apes. Howard smiled broadly when the keeper opened the door, but he ignored him. He noticed that the keeper smelled, too. He smelled different from the apes and the cage, but his smell was also strong.

"I'm so glad that you finally came by," Howard said, but the man went about his business without looking up.

"Come on, it's not funny!" he said to the man even louder, but he acted like Howard wasn't even there.

"Look!" he said, this time with anger, "what's the gag?" The man finished what he was doing and opened the cage to leave.

"Well, it's about time," said Howard, and started following the keeper out.

"And where do you think you're going?" shouted the keeper.

"Out of course!" said Howard, "and it's not funny anymore."

The keeper blocked his way. "Get back in there," he said, shoving Howard into the cage.

"What is this bullshit?" shouted Howard back at him.

The keeper slammed the door in his face and locked it shut. "Damned apes!" he said, walking away.

"What's your name? I'll have your job for this!" shouted Howard, grabbing the bars in frustration.

As he stood there, he noticed how hairy his arms were. He looked down and saw that he had an ape's body, too.

"No!" he screamed. "Nooooooo…!"

He awoke in a cold sweat. He sat up in bed. He was relieved that it was only a dream. He had to get some sleep. He had to be at his best the next day and the day after that. After all, he thought, that might be all the time he had left.

CHAPTER SEVENTEEN

It was 5:45 a.m. when Howard and Sandra came to the shuttle vessel that would carry them and the visiting earthlings, back down to terra firma. Howard arrived early so that he and Sandra would not have to make an entrance and face possible embarrassment in front of those who might be harboring hostile thoughts toward them. Sitting there, waiting for the others made Howard think of how it was going to the first show at the movies. Since the theater was empty, you could be in your seat rather than waiting on line outside. And what a show this promised to be.

At 5:55 a.m., the others arrived with Rondo and his two bodyguards leading the pack.

"Howard and Sandra," said Rondo, "they said that you were not in your room when they came for you. I am happy to see that you are here. Never hurts to be early," he said with a little laugh. "Howard and Sandra, do you know everyone?" asked Rondo.

"Not everyone," he said, spotting Frank.

"Frank! How the hell did you get here?" said Howard, realizing that everyone was staring at him. "I don't believe it," he said less loudly, "you are amazing!"

Frank just smiled.

Rondo proceeded to introduce Howard and Sandra to the rest of the group. The President and the others were pleasant; Goodwood was cool.

The ride down was uneventful with Frank smiling a great deal at Howard and looking like the cat that swallowed the canary. Howard and Sandra spoke mostly to themselves and Joseph.

The President, meanwhile, held court as he warmed Rondo up for what was to come when his guest visited the sights on Earth.

They landed in a remote airfield in the dark, so as not to attract any attention. Three limousines were waiting for them. President Barnes and Rondo sat in one, along with Rondo's bodyguards. Howard, Sandra, Joseph, Frank, and by his own request, the Russian President occupied the second limo. Radomir was curious to know what this visitor to another planet had to say for himself. The other four rode in the last car, which gave them the chance to speak out of earshot of the President.

The shuttle vessel was put into a huge hanger and guarded by the tightest security possible without attracting any undue attention. They had arrived at the stroke of midnight, Sunday evening and would leave the same time Friday evening, from wherever Rondo happened to be at that moment. The time between, as far as the President and his advisors were concerned, would determine the fate of the Earth.

The group was whisked unceremoniously into the White House. They all settled into their rooms until the next morning.

The President sat behind his desk in his Oval Office. Wayne and Olsen were pacing up and down the room in front of him. They had to figure out how to show Rondo around without the press getting wind of the situation.

"Sit down, you two. You're making me more nervous than I already am," said the President, looking agitated.

"I know just what they're going to say," he continued in a mocking tone. "Who is this stranger? And why is the President spending so much time with him?"

"He'll have to be shown around by a nobody then," suggested Olsen.

"What if we bring the culture to him?" said Wayne.

"No! No!" said the President. "I will take him around, personally. We will just have to risk the press' reaction. What can they say? How could they possibly guess? Screw 'em! We'll do what we have to do and we'll deal with the press as necessary. We'll just have to take the heat. By the time they get anywhere with this the week will be up."

"Don't worry, we can stall them," said Olsen, now confident.

The meeting went on a little longer before the President told everyone to turn in.

"Okay, guys, let's get some rest," he said. "It's going to be an interesting week."

During the night, Barnes woke up with a brainstorm. They would announce that the President was showing around President Radomir in a surprise visit. This would confuse the hell out of the press and keep them buzzing with wrong guesses long enough, they hoped, to accomplish the goals of the trip. Rondo would just be some unidentified man. How could they know who he was? He would also have the rest of the party: Howard, Sandra, Joseph, and Rondo's bodyguards around when they announced to the press about the world tour.

On Monday, the President's press secretary announced that President Radomir had arrived and would be spending a week with the President visiting certain capitals of the world. The itinerary would include in addition to Washington itself, Moscow, Rome, Paris and London. Rondo's shuttle vessel would ferry them to the capitals to save the travel time. From there, helicopter or car would do fine. Of course, no one would know about the spaceship. It would have to be very carefully hidden.

The President was told that Cooper and his alien girlfriend were just taking some time for themselves and that Cooper would keep in touch if he came up with any brainstorms along the way. The three checked into some ritzy hotel with Joseph in the room just down the hall from Sandra and Howard.

"We must think of something," Howard demanded. Sandra just looked at him with her doe eyes. Monday was not productive; the three walked around the DC area, with Howard asking questions of Joseph, but getting nowhere in the process.

They went to dinner at a French restaurant, for Howard's favorite food, and Sandra tasted frog's legs for the first time but did not like it. "Too fishy," she complained. Joseph liked the chocolate soufflé that he had for dessert.

On the way home they passed a storefront with a sign declaring *Psychic Readings*.

"What is that?" asked Sandra.

"That's when people read the future and tell things about yourself you already know."

"What about things you don't already know?"

"Sure, they should be able to do that, too."

"So why don't we see what the Psychic Reader has to say."

"I guess we have nothing to lose at this point." Howard tried the door.

"They're closed." He noticed the sign that told the hours. "10:00 a.m. to 6:00 p.m. are their hours," he announced to his companions. "We will have to come back in the morning."

Monday was uneventful for Rondo's group as well. They visited the Library of Congress to illustrate Earth's interest in learning, the National Art Gallery for its cultural aspects, the Smithsonian Institute to show man's technical accomplishments, and other museums and places of interest that they were able to squeeze into the day.

They arrived at the White House for dinner before leaving on the next leg of their travels.

"How did we do today?" the President asked Rondo as they sat down for dinner.

"You show promise. Though I will require a bit more convincing."

"This is only the first day and our society is not as old and rich in culture as some of the other stops we will make. If you were impressed at all by what you saw today, the rest of the trip should take you even further in that direction."

"I look forward to it," said Rondo evenly.

Meanwhile, the press was having a field day. Besides the speculations about Radomir and the President, all the major news agencies and some of the not so major ones were desperately trying to track down the identity of Frank, Rondo, and his bodyguards.

At the same time, two citizens were following the events in Washington with greater than casual interest.

"How much trouble do you think we would be in if we blew the whistle on this little charade," Bond asked Foli as they thumbed through the newspaper.

"I think we should leave this one alone," responded Foli. "There are dynamics involved here that we might not be aware of. The consequences may be extremely dire."

"I bow again to your great wisdom, Professor," said Bond, smiling warmly at his colleague. "But all the same, I will keep my options open and my eyes, too. I will be following these events quite closely. No harm in being a concerned citizen is there, my dear professor?"

"Watch your step, Julius."

"Mine and others," said Bond, smiling sardonically. "It's in my blood."

Back in Howard's hometown, Kevin Briggs, Howard's assistant editor and now acting editor-in-chief, sat watching the evening news.

"Hon," he called to his girlfriend, "they're showing pictures of the group that the President is showing around with President Radomir."

"Kev?" she said, closing in on the TV screen.

"Yeah."

"Isn't that Howard in that group?"

"Where?" asked Kevin, jumping up and walking toward the screen.

"HOLE LEEE SHITTT!!!"

"Kevin! Watch your language."

"HOLY SHIT!!! Goddamn it, it is Howard!" he repeated.

"What do you think's going on?"

"I don't know. I'm calling Chief Lynch. I bet that son-of-a-bitch knows something. What a scoop this could be. This will put Arlington and *The Daily Pride* on the map."

"But, Kevin. Don't you think if Howard wanted us to know about this he would have called you or somethin'?"

"I don't really know," he said flippantly, "but I'm in charge now and my job is to sell newspapers. If Howard has a problem with that, he should have called me and told me so. Since I haven't heard from him one way or the other, I'm going to do what my reporter's nose tells me—go after the story."

Kevin picked up the phone and dialed.

"Maybe he is being held captive and he can't communicate with us," offered his girlfriend.

"Is the chief there?" asked Kevin into the phone, while nodding and smiling at his girlfriend.

"He went home," said the voice on the other end.

"What's his number?"

"Can't give it out. Who is this anyway?"

"Kevin Briggs."

"Oh, hi, Kevin. It's Bob."

"Hi, Bob. Look, I need to talk to the chief right now."

"The best I can do is to call him and give him your message. Otherwise, it'll have to wait till tomorrow."

"Can't wait, Bob. Please ask him to call me tonight."

"I'll ask."

"Thanks, Bob. I'll be waiting for his call."

"Keep plenty of popcorn on hand."

"What?"

"Only kidding," said Bob, hanging up.

Kevin sat next to the phone, thinking. About ten minutes later, it rang.

"Kevin here—I mean hello," he said, a little embarrassed.

"Kevin, this is Chief Lynch. Bob Larson told me that you had something important to talk about."

"I do, Chief. Can I come over?"

"I'll be here."

"Thanks. I'll be right over." Briggs hung up, told his girlfriend where he was going, and left.

"Kevin, don't get yourself into trouble," she shouted after him.

Briggs made a face in response to his girlfriend's remark as he climbed into his car. He drove to Lynch's house and parked in the driveway.

Lynch's wife answered the door and directed Briggs to Lynch's den, where the latter was having a beer and watching the basketball game.

"Good game," said Lynch as Briggs entered the room after knocking lightly. "You can shut it off," he said. "Want a beer?"

"No thanks."

"What's on your mind, Kevin? You look like you've seen a ghost."

"That's pretty close. Will Howard Cooper do?"

"Where did you see him?"

"On television. On the news. Did you read about the controversy with our President Barnes showing the Russian President, Radomir, around all the cultural sights in Washington?

"And there is supposed to be an impressive-looking gentleman in the group who no one seems to be able to identify. The government is as tight as a clam's ass about it. According to reports, no one is talking. All the normal sources are dry as a bone."

"So what does Howard have to do with all this?"

"I don't know. I was watching the news and Dolores says, 'There's Howard Cooper!' I look and as sure as shit, it's him. I don't know how the hell I missed him. Funny about women, they can miss something as big as a barn right in front of their faces…"

"So what do you want from me?" he asked, cutting off Kevin in mid sentence.

"You were investigating his disappearance, remember?"

"Sure I remember. But I found nothing. Remember, I was asking you about it then."

"Well, I didn't know anything, then," said Kevin, sounding just the slightest bit contrite.

"Well, I don't know anything now," said Lynch.

"You must have found out something!"

Lynch's mind wandered back to his conversations with Colonel Jones. UFOs, he thought, the big lump of metal that no one could explain that weighed exactly the same as Howard's car, and the strange things that Jones told him about UFO sightings. All that stuff.

"I don't know anything!" he said firmly.

"Chief! You must know something. Anything! Even if you're not certain. This could put Arlington on the map. We'll all be famous."

Lynch looked at Briggs. Briggs looked back with hope.

"No. There's nothing to tell."

Kevin drove home deep in thought. *There's something all right. And I'm going to get it, if I have to pay off his deputy to do it.*

Tuesday, 8:00 a.m. Lynch walked into the office to relieve his deputy, Bob Larson.

"Hi, Chief," said Bob, getting up.

"What's going on?"

"Nothing much. All quiet on the western front," he said, smiling and looking a bit tired.

"Bob, before you go, Kevin Briggs came to see me last night—"

"Yeah, I know."

"He didn't by any chance come around here after that asking questions about anything, did he?"

"Well—"

"What did you tell him, Bob?"

"Well—I didn't think it was such a big deal."

"What'd you tell him, Bob?"

"I told him about the lump of metal."

"What else?"

"That's basically it—"

"What else?"

"I told him that you went to see Colonel Jones out at the base."

"I can't believe it," said Lynch, exasperated. "What'd he do, promise to put your name in the paper—make you a big shot?"

208

Larson moved his head to the side and stuck out his hand in a gesture that said *yeah, I guess*.

"Name in the papers," Lynch repeated under his breath. "You talk to this guy again about Howard Cooper and your name will be in the papers all right—the obituary column. Now get the hell out of here. Can't trust anybody these days," he said, looking pissed. "I'd better get a hold of the son-of-a-bitch before he leaves for the base."

He picked up the phone and dialed Briggs' home. "I hope he's not an early bird," he said out loud. "Hello, Dolores?"

"It's Chief Lynch. Sorry to call you so early. Did Kevin leave yet?...He did? Okay, I'll try him at the office."

He dialed the newspaper office. "That son-of-a-bitch better be there. Hello, Kevin?"

"Yeah it's me."

"I'm glad I caught you. Bob told me that you spoke to him."

"Yeah, I spoke to him," said Briggs, in a matter of fact tone.

"Were you planning to go anywhere special today?"

"The air force base."

"I thought so. Don't go out there. I know I can't stop you. I'm asking you not to."

"Does that mean that you'll talk to me about Howard?"

Briggs made a face and gritted his teeth. "What is it that you want to know?"

CHAPTER EIGHTEEN

They entered the psychic's storefront at 10:05 a.m. She came sauntering through the red curtain as Howard, Sandra and Joseph closed the outside door behind them.

She smiled as she introduced herself. "Gentlemen and young lady, how can I help you today? My name is Madam Cleo."

Howard spoke for the group. "Madam, we have a strong need to know the future. Price is not an issue." They had given Howard additional currency to handle his needs for the week.

"I'm afraid that it does not work that way," she said. "The quality of the reading does not vary with the cost, at least not with any given reader. I will give you the best reading that I can. Who will be first?"

"Can we all sit at once?"

"You may all be present," she responded, "but unless I am conducting a séance or doing a channeling, only one person at a time can be the subject of a reading."

"Then read for me first," said Howard, "and we will see what happens from there."

"Very well, come with me." She showed them through the red curtains and into the back. "Please pull up some chairs for you and the young lady," she said to Joseph. "You sit here," she instructed Howard, seating him opposite her. The table was round, made of dark wood and measured 42 inches in diameter. It was covered with off-white cloth that appeared to have been crocheted many years before, when the color was most likely pure white; it gave the room a slightly musty smell. The room itself was somewhat darkened, which gave Madam Cleo's already exotic look a bit more of a sensual bite.

"What is it that you are interested in finding out?" she asked, drawing out the last word.

"Howard. Did you want my name?" he asked.

"Yes, if you don't mind," she said, "and your friends?"

"Oh, this is Sandra and that's Joseph."

"Very good. Now what is it that you want to know, Howard?"

"Well this may sound peculiar…"

"Try me," she interjected.

"Well I'm afraid I don't really know how this works."

"Just ask me the question and I will guide you," she said reassuringly.

"Where will I be in the next, say, week or two…let's say two weeks from now?"

"Give me your hands," she said, "reaching out." She took his hands and turned them over so that his palms were facing downward and touching hers. "Just let me get a sense of you," she said almost seductively.

Howard waited until Cleo's eye began to take on a dreamy quality. "Are there people in uniform and some important officials involved with you at the moment?" she asked.

"Yes," answered Howard with a note of anticipation.

"Some of these do not think well of you, they suspect your motives."

"That's good," he blurted.

"So you already know this?' she stated.

"Yes, but where will everyone be in two weeks?"

"What is happening in two weeks?" she asked.

"I can't tell you," he said, looking somewhat apologetic. "I rather hoped that you could tell me."

"Well I don't see anything out of the ordinary happening for you."

"Well that's good at least. Is there any way that I can be more certain of that?" he asked.

"How important is this for you?"

"Extremely important and not only for me, but for others as well."

"Then I suggest that you see someone else and get their opinion as well. I can sense that this is quite important indeed and that it could have some far reaching effects," she added.

"Yes," he agreed. "Can you recommend someone? Time is of the essence."

"Well if you have the money, as you implied, and mobility, the best that I know of is called Mobile Moe. He's an old black man and you can find him in Mobile, Alabama."

"Do you have his address and phone number?" asked Howard, as the others sat transfixed.

"I'm afraid that he does not use a phone and I really cannot tell you his address. Very few people know exactly where he lives. He is a bit eccentric, you see. But don't feel bad about it, often the odd ones are the best readers, like great painters or writers or scientists are often odd or even mad, like Einstein or Van Gogh."

"So how will I find him?" Howard asked somewhat frantically.

"Start out on Congress Street between North Water and North Lawrence. And just ask folks where he is. He moves around a bit from café to café. He gives readings for free, but everyone gives him a generous tip anyway. That's the custom. The café owner supplies him with free food and drinks, due to the customers he brings in. There's always folks waiting for a reading. Best time to get him is around 10:00 a.m. Like me, he starts his readings usually about ten, right after he finishes his breakfast coffee."

"Thanks," said Howard, quickly getting up. The others followed.

"Good luck," she said, standing and looking at him.

"Oh, how much do I owe you?" he asked.

"A hundred!" she declared decisively.

"That's not cheap," he said, pulling out a wad of bills.

"I never said that I was cheap."

"And I never asked. But hopefully we're moving in the right direction," he ended, leaving with the other two.

As the sun was going down over Moscow, where Rondo visited that day, a call was coming in over the transatlantic network. The President was called to the phone. It was his press secretary, Charles Maudlin. He took the call and came away with a worried look on his face.

"What is it?" asked Olsen, seeing his expression.

"It was Maudlin. He says some rinky-dink newspaper, out in Texas somewhere, is claiming that the Russian President and I are showing aliens the sights of the Western world. They claim that Howard may have been kidnapped by these aliens and now they're here on Earth. But they don't know why."

"That's pretty accurate," said Olsen.

"Yeah, and this asshole's accuracy will screw us up good. We have to play it cool. Act relaxed and laugh it off. They probably think he's just another crackpot looking for attention. But don't let Rondo or one of his stooges get wind of it. Or we're dead!"

The next day they were in Rome and the press was all over them, though they somehow managed to keep them at bay. Rondo was kept under heavy guard. The reporters were not allowed within fifty feet of him. They sneaked him in and out of buildings, telling him it was for security purposes. They warned him that these so-called reporters could very well be assassins and Rondo seemed to believe it. In reality, he didn't much care one way or the other as long as his people could continue working on their version of the "cure for the human condition:" *annihilation.*

The sculpture and paintings in Rome particularly impressed Rondo. The age of some of the great architecture was also impressive. He asked about the age of the civilization that produced these works. "It's almost as old as ours," he said, laughing.

Suddenly those standing next to Rondo were aware of a beeping noise. Rondo knew, though his hosts did not, that this indicated an urgent message was awaiting his reply. He asked if he could have a room to himself and was led to a small office that was not in use. With his bodyguards standing outside, he acknowledged the communication.

It was Number 2 and the signal from the Hidden Planet was being picked up by the mother ship and relayed down to Earth. Rondo's communicator would have been too weak to pick up the message by itself.

"This is Rondo."

"Rondo, this is Number 2."

"Yes, Number 2. How are things on our planet?"

"We have picked up activity at the outer region of the solar system."

The portion of the solar system that they monitored encompassed a region in a one-billion-mile radius.

Number 2 continued. "We are picking up radio signals and other activity. It may be nothing but we are monitoring it closely and are on standby alert."

"Do you need me to return to the mother ship?"

"I doubt if you will have sufficient time. Unfortunately, things will probably either blow over or get hot before you could reach your command center in the ship."

General Titus will be available to provide assistance. It was farsighted of him to stay behind in the mother ship, thought Rondo.

"General Titus and I will handle it. I will keep you abreast of any significant events as they unfold."

They broke contact.

Number 2 continued to monitor the space. Thresholds were established and different levels of alert were triggered when unknown intelligent life passed those limits.

The inner threshold was sacred and any intelligent creature passing it would never be permitted to return. Those who were not killed in the defensive action by the Hidden People would be relegated to spend the remaining days of their lives as their guests. They would not be permitted ever to leave or communicate in any way with any others outside the planet. The planet had to stay hidden at all costs.

The monitored activities continued their threatening pattern. Alert Level 2 was posted. A military group was sent out to intercept the suspected intruders. General Titus assumed personal command of the operation. Once the next threshold was passed, and if the Hidden People prevailed, there would be no escape for the invaders. A delicate game of cat and mouse commenced.

The intruders might be innocently passing by and might have no idea that this dreary gray planet, where the Hidden People lived, was inhabited. They certainly didn't want to kill or capture innocents, but could not take the risk, innocent or not, that those flying by got too close.

The tactic included dropping behind the strangers so that, if necessary, all escape routes would be closed off. They feared being detected while carrying out this maneuver and thus being engaged prematurely.

The strangers came closer. The alert was moved to Level 3.

There were five levels of alert. Level 5 was full-scale war. This meant that there was an all out attack on their planet. At Level 3, all active military personnel were ready to move.

The strangers were moving in quickly. The alert went to Level 4.

The planet readied itself for attack. All military personnel were on the move. Everyone went to his assigned position. The energy sources for their major weapons systems were put to the maximum level. The defense shields were activated, as all was made ready.

Besides the defensive operations, there was also an escape mobilization plan. Anyone old enough to remember the destruction of their old home planet was particularly distressed by the activation of this precaution.

Rondo's beeper sounded again. He slipped away into a corner. They watched him, but gave him room.

"This is Rondo."

Number 2 was on the other end. "Rondo, we have gone to Alert Level 4. There are eight well-armed ships of unknown origin in sector zone four. We will be attacking presently."

"I have all confidence in you and General Titus to successfully defend our planet," said Rondo.

"Thank you for your confidence," said Number 2. "I will keep you informed."

"Is there a problem?" asked the President as Rondo returned to the group.

"My planet is under attack. I should be there to help in the operation. I am sacrificing a great deal to make good my promise to you and your people. We must proceed with this visit as quickly as possible."

"But everything is ready for the next two days," said the President. "We must have the opportunity to finish our schedule. Our existence is at stake."

"We seemed to share the same problem," said Rondo. "I will do the best to fulfill my promise."

The President did not look very happy.

The aliens continued to advance into the safety zone of the Hidden Planet. The ships that would try to block the escape of the invaders were in place. Only by completely vanquishing the Hidden People would any invaders get out alive. The Hidden People's defense forces would follow the invaders as far as they had to and even use suicidal measures if necessary to prevent the invaders' escape.

One of the scout ships from the Hidden Planet was spotted by one of the alien vessels. The scout ship was pursued and immobilized by a weapon fired by the intruders' ship. The intruders boarded the immobilized scout vessel and the crew was taken to the invaders' ship.

"Master," said one of the invading crew to his captain, "we have the crew members from the alien ship that we spotted."

"Excellent," said the captain. "Bring them to me."

The crew was brought before the captain.

"Who are you and where is your planet?" he asked the highest-ranking member of the group.

The pilot of the crew answered.

"We cannot tell you the location of our planet. It is erased from our memory. The only way that we can return to our planet is to send a certain signal out to our home base and they direct us back from there. But it will do you no good to know that signal."

"Why is that?" asked the captain.

"I have set off an atomic weapon in our ship and before you can have time to escape we will all be blown into another dimension."

The captain's face turned from cockiness to fear. But before he could utter his first command, the vibration of the explosion knocked him to the floor and in a brief instant, all was turned into fragments of what had been.

All the combatants saw the explosion. It was the bugle call to battle, the opening bell of the contest.

The plan of attack for the Hidden People was deceptively simple. They sent out unmanned decoys to draw the enemy's attention. As the enemy's ships followed and destroyed the decoys, they would be funneled through a lane that was directly in the line of fire of the manned ships. The manned ships would fire from a great distance, which would in turn minimize their exposure. It was a method of bringing the target to the projectile. The drones made their runs at the foreign ships, firing without warning. The shots were both visible and lethal. After destroying two of the enemy's ships, they began to run the gauntlet with the aliens in hot pursuit. Two more of the aliens' vessels met their end.

The intruders, with only four ships left, tried another run at the drones. The results were again predictable.

Now there were only two more alien vessels left. The intruders made a run for it, but the Hidden People's security net was waiting for them. The first barrage took out one ship and crippled the second.

The commander of the fleet had a boarding party enter the crippled ship. They signaled back to the commander.

"No one left alive, Commander Bernard," said the leader of the boarding crew. "They were either killed by our blast or took their lives when they saw all was lost. They must have expected the worst treatment in the enemy's hands."

"Just another commentary on the state of so-called intelligent life in the universe," said Bernard. "Let's go home."

Rondo was riding back to his room before the evening meal, when his communicator beeped. It was a rainy evening in Rome as the black limousines sped toward their well-deserved rest after a long day.

"This is Rondo."

"The invaders have been destroyed," said the voice at the other end."

"That takes the pressure off a bit," said Rondo, smiling at the President.

The President smiled back.

"Well done, Number 2. I look forward to returning to our planet."

The communication was ended.

The evening went as well as could be expected. The President was concerned about Rondo's anxiety to leave, due to the close call at his home planet. Rondo was cool. He would play out his cards. Two more days remained.

Rondo retired to his room for the evening. He picked up his communicator and signaled the mother ship.

"This is General Titus," came the response.

"General, congratulations on the performance of your defense forces, but this only emphasizes how vital our mission to Earth is."

"Yes, I am proud of their behavior," said the general. "And as far as our Earth mission is concerned, I'll let Einstein tell you himself. He is here with me. He finally has come out of self-imposed isolation to mingle with the common folks."

Einstein took the communicator. "Rondo, I have good news. We are ready with the virus. They have been grown and are now being packaged for distribution among our friends on Earth."

"I will be back in two days. Wait until then."

"Look at this," said Bond as he and Foli sat in their office, reading the morning paper."

"What's that?"

"This son-of-a-bitch newspaper guy in some stink hole in Texas is getting headlines talking about Cooper and the aliens. Why this guy doesn't know squat and he has already become a damn celebrity. I told you that something was going to pop."

"Why don't you leave it alone, Julie?" said Foli.

"Why? Because it's good business, that's why."

"We're going to bust this damned thing wide open and get the recognition we deserve. Hell, the cat's out of the bag anyway. I can see the headlines: *Private Investigators Chase Aliens in an Attempt to Save Planet.* What do you think, Professor?"

"I think you're crazy."

"Crazy but rich. Did you know that rich people by definition are never crazy? Just eccentric!"

Howard and the crew wasted no time in their search for the psychic Mobile Moe. They had a 14-hour drive in front of them and they wanted to get started as soon as possible. Time was their enemy and they could afford to waste none of it. They drove down US 1 south toward Richmond and picked up I 95. In less than 30 minutes they were cruising down I 85 past Charlotte, NC on their way toward Macon, Georgia. They passed through Montgomery, Alabama, next stop Mobile. Howard let Joseph drive some of the way so he could rest and sit in the back holding hands with Sandra, who seemed to be enjoying the trip. They stopped a few times for food and to relieve themselves and came gliding into Mobile just before 1:00 a.m. ready to get some sleep for the next day's adventure.

Wednesday dawned hot and steamy. They got up, showered and went down for some breakfast. They sat at a small table in the back of a coffee shop that was down the street from the hotel. Howard sat with his back to the wall, in order to check out the scene and take in some of the local color. The waitress came right over and plopped some food-stained menus down in front of them. "What can I get for you folks?" she asked with a distinctly southern accent as she filled their water glasses. She wore a white apron over her tight-fitting jeans with those black cloth and leather shoes with rubber soles that people in her trade often wear. It was 9:00 a.m. and the place was half empty, with most of the breakfast crowd already at or on their way to work.

"Some information for starters, if you don't mind," answered Howard.

"What's that? Say, you folks ain't from around here are you?" she drawled.

"You have no idea," quipped Howard, flashing a rye grin. The others leaned forward and smiled benignly. "Have you ever heard of someone called Mobile Moe?" he asked evenly.

"Why sure, hon, everybody from around here knows about Mobile Moe. He's a big attraction in these parts."

"Do you know where we can find him today? " he asked pointedly.

"Hey, Lionel, where's old Mobile Moe at these days?" she shouted to the counterman.

"He's down at the Dead End Café, but he don't start till about ten o'clock, in case the folks are interested."

"How can we get there?" asked Howard, taking out his ballpoint pen and readying it to write on one of the small paper napkins he pulled from the dispenser in the middle of the table.

"Say, you folks aimin' to get your fortune told?' she asked, looking from Howard to Sandra to Joseph and back to Howard again. "You folks related or somethin'?" she asked, trying to get the who's who among the three.

"No, we're just friends," answered Howard, quickly trying to prevent the others from getting off track or saying some strangely inappropriate things. "And yes we heard that Mobile Moe was the best there is at fortune telling, so that's why my friends and I are here," said Howard, trying to dampen the waitress' curiosity.

"Say," she continued unabated, "how come they don't say much?" she asked Howard.

"They're just tired from the trip. We got in late last night and stayed at that little place up the street, yer know, Flo's Hotel."

"Yer I know Flo, went to school with her younger sister. She inherited the place from her father. A real tightwad he was. Probably still has the first buck he ever made stashed away somewhere. But he didn't take it with him when he kicked the bucket. Could never understand folks like that," she mused.

"Say, Maisy," said Howard, reading the name on her pin, "how did you say we could get to this Dead End Café?"

"I didn't, not yet anyway," she added with a perky grin. "You all are gonna have breakfast ain't yer?"

"Wouldn't miss it for anything" said Howard, flashing a big smile.

"Okay, now on your way out, after breakfast, just make a right turn out the door and that will take you to Congress Street toward North Lawrence. Now you have to go a few blocks and make your right onto Lawrence. Now you don't have to drive or nothin' and I wouldn't advise drivin' anyway, it's tough parking on the street. But after you make the right, you take Lawrence down to Beauregard and make another right. It's on Beauregard about halfway down the block, on the right, you can't miss it. Now what are you folks having?"

They had their breakfast and coffee and headed out and around the block. It was just about 10:00 a.m. when they reached the Dead End Café. It looked quite empty, which was fine, thought Howard, as long as Moe was in. The place looked like an old jazz club with a long wooden bar on the left as you entered. There were tables on the right and in the back was an open area surrounding a bandstand-like area. An old black man, somewhat heavy set and wearing dark glasses and a fancy vest with no jacket, sat at the last table facing the front. A young black man was sweeping up, but laid his broom against the bar and came over to Howard and company as they entered.

"Mobile Moe," blurted out Howard.

The young man pointed to the back, turned and went back to his sweeping.

The old man seemed to be staring straight ahead as they approached. "Sit down," he bade them in a hoarse whisper.

They sat silently, all of them taken by his presence. "Yes I'm blind, in case you're wondering," he announced in a modulated cadence.

"We're here—" Howard began.

"—Yes I know why you are here," he stated confidently, cutting Howard off in mid sentence. "What I do not know is why I heard three of you sit, but only sense the presence of two." The old man reached out. "Let me touch your faces," he commanded as politely as possible. They all leaned into the middle of the small table allowing their faces to be scrutinized by the old man's experienced touch. "Who or what is this person?" he asked excitedly, referring to Joseph.

"What do you mean?" asked Howard, fearing what the old man might know.

"This one," the old man commanded again, this time with agitation, "let him speak," he continued, pointing to Joseph. Howard nodded at Joseph.

"Yes, what would you like me to say?" asked Joseph in perfect unaccented American English.

"What is he?" asked Moe, directing his question toward Howard.

"He's a man," answered Howard, getting a bit nervous.

"He's no man of this earth," declared Moe in a frightening voice.

Howard and the others sat stunned.

"Is he some kind of robot, is this a trick, a joke being played at my expense or maybe some kind of test?" he asked.

"Why no, what's wrong?" responded Howard, somewhat relieved that the old man was not on to Joseph's true origin.

"He or it has no soul!" declared Moe with authority. "That's why I thought there were only two of you. I may not be able to see faces, but I can see souls. This man has no aura, so he can't be a living human.

"Can you help us?" pleaded Howard, trying to ignore Moe's rant.

"Something strange is going on here," moaned the old man.

"It's important," implored Howard. "We drove for 14 hours, all the way from Washington, DC to see you."

"You're here to know if the world will end soon," announced Moe.

"Yes, how did you know?"

"Isn't that why you sought me out, because I know things that others do not? I may not have eyes, but I do have *vision*."

"Yes, of course, please, what is the answer, will we all be here two weeks from now?"

"That depends on you and your friends."

"What can we do?"

"You must go see someone and she will have the answer for you." They sat waiting. "Her name is Hillela Goldstein. She is Israeli and she lives in New York City. She is in a brownstone, in the basement apartment. The address is 328 West 71st Street. Hurry, you don't have much time," he added in a somber tone.

"Thank you," said Howard, taking down the information on the napkin from the coffee shop.

"How much?" he asked.

Mobile Moe waved his hand, indicating no charge.

Howard reached into his pocket and took out three $100 bills and put them into the old man's hand. "They're hundreds," cautioned Howard.

"You're quite generous," stated Moe.

"If you're right, it's worth it and a lot more."

"I'm right," assured the old man.

They got up and started for the door. "If this is a wild goose chase, we're screwed," commented Howard.

"What else do we have?" asked Sandra.

"Nothing."

They retraced their steps back to the car; they had already packed it and were ready to go. "All we have to do, according to the map, is to go back the way that we came and once we get onto I 95 North take that all the way to New York. The last leg from DC should add about another 4 to 5 hours onto the trip. We should make the Big Apple by about three or four in the morning. A few hours of shuteye and we will see what Hillela Goldstein has to say for herself. *And it better be good!*"

The trip was uneventful, by doing 80 to 90 mph most of the way and stopping as little as possible, by 2:36 a.m. they were gliding through the Lincoln Tunnel and into New York City. Coming out of the tunnel, they made a left onto 8th Avenue and traveled north from there. Once they hit 59th Street, Howard made a right turn onto Central Park South. "Always wanted to stay at one of these swanky hotels," he announced to his passengers, "the ones overlooking the park. I hear the view is sensational. He pulled into the tallest hotel he could find on the strip and asked for top floor or highest floor available.

When the bellhop let Howard and Sandra into the room and drew back the curtains they both let out a gasp at the magnificence of the view. After tipping the bellhop, he turned to Sandra. "It's amazing," he told her, standing close as they peered out over the park, "how a little patch of green can look so beautiful surrounded by concrete and steel. But it does." Sandra looked deep into his eyes and nodded her agreement. They went to bed and sleep came quickly to both of them.

"Come to the window," bade Sandra. It was dawn and the sun was just rising over the horizon. From their vantage point, facing uptown Howard and Sandra's window faced in a north easterly direction. "Look, the sun is coming up," she shouted. "It's lighting up the park."

Howard got up, rubbing his eyes, and stood by her side. "Yes, it is a beautiful world, and we have to save it. We had better get some more sleep," he whispered in her ear. "It's Thursday, our last day to find the answer, to solve the impossible age-old riddle. How do you make this corrupt and violent world appear to be worth saving? How do you turn base metal into gold? How do you make a silk purse out of a sow's ear?"

"What are you talking about?" she asked.

"How do you do the impossible?" he asked rhetorically. "What can this psychic possibly tell us that we don't already know? Why are we even bothering?" he asked despairingly.

"Because the old psychic told us to, he seemed to think that there was hope. And because it *is* such a beautiful planet." She turned to him and looked longingly into his eyes. "I don't want to lose my soul like the others. You heard what the old psychic said, Joseph has no soul. They all have no souls; it must be lost when they do the body replacement. I knew I should be afraid, I just could not explain why."

"When the body is gone there must be no place left for the soul to dwell. I guess it goes back to wherever souls come from," he said, sounding dazed and dreamy. "I suppose that makes your people, after the body replacement, not people at all, but some type of robot or android, or something. That must be why you can exist with such a mundane existence.

"I don't want to lose my soul," she moaned, "and become some kind of robot!"

222

"That's why you were afraid," he agreed. "You must have known on some level, your gut instinct was right after all. Let's get some more sleep, we have a big day ahead of us."

They met Joseph for breakfast at nine downstairs in the hotel coffee shop.
"I hope the old lady doesn't sleep too late," said Howard.

They left their car in the hotel garage and walked up Broadway toward 71st Street passing Central Park to their right. They turned left onto 71st heading west toward Riverside Park. The street became a dead end with cars double parked on one side. "Lucky we didn't drive," observed Howard. "How do these New Yorkers live like this?" he wondered out loud.

"Here it is," shouted Sandra, spotting the number on the building. "Moe said in the basement, didn't he? Where would that be?" she asked, looking at Howard.

They went through the gate and found the entrance at the side of the stone stairs. Howard looked around the door and saw a two-inch-long shiny metal object right above the nameplate. "Goldstein," declared Howard, reading the name. He rang the bell and waited.

"Who's there?" a young female voice inquired. "Who is it?" she repeated, sounding impatient.

Howard hesitated. "Is Hillela Goldstein here?" he asked.

"Yes, she lives here," came the answer from behind the door.

"We need to see her, it's important," he continued.

"She's not doing any readings today," said the young woman opening the door just enough to check out her visitors. "She's a little under the weather this morning."

"Mobile Moe sent us," added Howard.

"Mobile who?" she asked with little laugh and a contorted look on her face.

"Another psychic from down south, in Alabama," he added.

"You came all the way from Alabama? All three of you? I guess it must be important."

"It is," said Howard somberly.

"*Bubbie*, can you see some people now?" she called toward the back of the apartment.

"Who is it?" the old lady asked in Hebrew.

"It's three people who have come a long way to see you. All the way from Alabama. They say that it is very important.

223

"Alabama *epes*," responded the old lady. "Okay, okay," she managed in English. "Ask them to wait in the living room, I'll be right there."

"She is my grandmother; my name is Shoshana," she said, introducing herself. I go to school at Columbia University. I am finishing up my doctorate there, in Middle Eastern studies. I will have to translate for you," she continued, showing them into the small living room. It's a little crowded, but we can all fit." she assured.

The old lady came into the room. She wore a house dress and white knitted shawl. She sat in an old armchair and looked around. "*Vos is dos?*" she asked in Yiddish.

"She wants to know who you are," translated Shoshana.

"What language is that," asked Howard, "it sounds a little like German."

"It's Yiddish."

"You speak Yiddish also?" asked Howard.

"Yes, I speak five languages: Hebrew, Yiddish, Arabic, English and Aramaic."

"Aramaic, isn't that an ancient Middle Eastern language?"

"Yes, much of the Old Testament is written in Aramaic, in addition to old Hebrew."

"Let's begin," suggested the old lady in Hebrew.

"My grandmother would like to start," announced Shoshana.

"We were told by Mobile Moe, from Alabama, that you could help us. We need to know about the future." As he spoke the old lady was looking around the room from Howard to Joseph to Sandra.

"*Shimon*," bellowed the old lady.

"His name is Joseph," said Howard in a humble tone, not wanting to offend the old lady by correcting her.

"*Shimon*," she repeated more emphatically, pointing to Sandra.

Shoshana asked her grandmother something in Hebrew, then she and the old lady went back and forth for a few moments in a somewhat heated manner, the grandmother pointing at Sandra, then to Joseph, then back to Sandra again. Shoshana seemed to not be in agreement with her grandmother, while the old lady maintained her resolve.

Howard and the others sat with expectant looks on their faces waiting for the outcome.

"First of all my grandmother did not say that anyone's name is Simon, or Shimon in Hebrew," she added parenthetically. "But she insists that this lady," she said, pointing to Sandra, "is from the Lost Tribe of Israel called

Simon, and the man is without a soul, therefore nothing can be told about him. I know this sounds kind of strange," added the girl, "but this is what my grandmother insists is true, and she is usually never wrong about these things."

"What does this mean?" asked Howard, questioning the relevance of what seemed to be a digression from the purpose of their visit.

"It probably doesn't mean very much to you, it just means that this lady," she nodded toward Sandra, "is descended from the ancient lost Israeli tribe of Simon."

"That's impossible!" declared Howard.

"Why?" asked the girl. "Surely it's *possible*," she said, drawing out the last word.

"Not possible!" insisted Howard.

"Why?" repeated Shoshana. "Unless she's from Mars or something, why is it impossible?"

Howard ignored her question.

"*Shimon*," repeated the old lady.

"So tell me," asked Howard, "what is so special about this lost tribe you keep referring to?"

"As I mentioned," she began, "I study Middle Eastern history and languages, and so I am quite well versed on the subject. According to the Hebrew bible, Jacob, of Abraham, Isaac and Jacob, from the old testament, also called Israel, had twelve sons. The original twelve tribes of Israel were fathered by and named after these twelve sons. Most people have heard of the Ten Lost Tribes of Israel, but in reality, there were only nine. That is, the nine northern tribes that were conquered and dispersed by the Assyrians around 700 BCE. The tenth tribe, Simon, had disappeared long before the Assyrian conquest.

"Simon was the second son of Jacob and his first wife, Leah, and father of the tribe, called after his name, Simon. He and his brother Levi destroyed the entire village of Shechem in retribution for the rape of their sister Dinah. Because of this action, great trouble befell his family. And since Simon brought disgrace and hardship to his family, his tribe was 'divided and scattered' according to the prediction in Genesis. They gradually dwindled in number, and sank into a position of insignificance among the other tribes. It is generally believed that the tribe had been absorbed by the tribe of Judah by the time that they entered the Promised Land.

"But others say, as discovered in the Dead Sea Scrolls, being rejected and scorned by their father Jacob, the tribe sought redemption from other sources. And it is written that one evening in the summer of the year 2751 of the Hebrew calendar, the night of August 27, 1010 BCE of your Christian calendar, a magnificent light appeared in the sky. The light came to earth and 'behold its size was that of a great ship.' And the children of the tribe of Simon, numbering about seven thousand, entered the ship of light and flew into the sky, never to be seen or heard from again."

Howard looked stunned. Sandra looked delighted, then slowly a smiled appeared on Howard's face. "This means they're human!" he shouted.

"This means who's human?" asked Shoshana.

"Never mind," said Howard, jumping up. "That's it, Moe was right, this is the answer," he continued. "I can't believe it. We must go," he announced. "How much do I owe you?"

"You mean my grandmother," replied Shoshana. She questioned the old woman. "My grandmother says that you don't owe her anything, that it was a privilege to be in the presence of someone from one of the Lost Tribes."

"Nonsense," demanded Howard. "You've done us a great service, all of us," he added. He pulled out a large roll of bills. "Here's five hundred," he said. "No wait, here's five thousand, a gift to help pay for your education," he insisted.

"You must be rich," said Shoshana, "but we cannot take so much money, that we did not earn."

"Oh you earned it alright, you and your grandmother," he said, handing her the bills and leaving with the others.

They started walking back to the hotel. Howard turned to Joseph. "You're a historian, is that correct?"

"Yes."

"Do you know anything about the ancient history of your people?"

"Of course. I may not have a soul, as I've been told, but I do have a brain." Howard looked uncomfortable.

"You want to know," continued Joseph, "if what the young lady said about the lost tribe of Simon is true?"

"Yes it could save the Earth and its human population."

"I cannot confirm this, but I can tell you that it is part of our ancient lore that our people were ill and dying out from a strange disease that infected our original planet. We sent out probes all over the galaxy and found a group of people with a rich heritage that was not prone to the same disease and agreed to replace us when we died out. We taught them our technology and traditions and they eventually replaced us and kept our ways alive. If this was your Tribe of Simon, I do not know, but the old lady seemed quite convinced. Let's say it is worth telling Rondo that your people and ours may be brothers."

"We must contact Rondo as soon as possible," insisted Howard.

Joseph bit his lip in a certain spot to activate his communication device. "Joseph to Rondo, Rondo please acknowledge."

"Yes, Joseph," answered Rondo into Joseph's implanted earpiece.

"I have some very exciting news, but we should all discuss this face to face."

"Is it important enough for us to alter our plans?" asked Rondo.

"Yes, you must at least meet with Howard Cooper, Sandra and me before you return or give any final orders as to the fate of the Earth."

"Very well," replied Rondo, "I will cut this trip short so that no overall time is lost and let our meeting be the last event before returning to our ship."

CHAPTER
NINETEEN

"Comrade President," said Nicoli, "there is a call for you."

"Is it important? I am busy."

"It is General Zansky. He says it is urgent."

"Very well, I will take it in the bedroom," said Radomir, picking up the phone in the other room.

They were still in Paris; Radomir was late and planned to catch up with the group as soon as he was ready. "Yes, this is President Radomir."

He listened. "Excellent!" he said into the phone. "Well done, Comrade General."

He finished dressing and came out into the main area of the suite. "Nicki, I just received wonderful news. General Zansky says that they have successfully blocked communications by the aliens. So if Rondo tries to communicate to his ship, to proceed with their destruction of the Earth, that message also would be blocked. The Americans do not know this. They may think that they run the world, but we live in it, too, and have a right to do what we think is best also. At least this may buy us some time. They cannot destroy us twice for fighting back a little. Don't you agree, Nicki?"

"Yes, Comrade President, they can only destroy us once," agreed Nicoli.

The Russians caught up with the tour at the Eiffel Tower.

"Sorry for our late start, Henry," said Radomir to the President.

"It is not a problem," replied the President. "But the trip has been cut short. We must return to Washington this evening. It appears as though the aliens' hostage, Howard Cooper, traveling with two of the aliens, has discovered something that may help us to convince Rondo not to pull the trigger on his plans to destroy the Earth. So, we are all scheduled to meet in my office as soon as we arrive this evening."

"Why wait?"

"We cannot take off with the spaceship until dark and we also need to allow Howard Cooper and company time to arrive at the White House. Don't worry, Uri, I have arranged for the FBI to fly Howard and his friends down to DC and babysit them until we arrive."

Howard, Sandra and Joseph were waiting for the presidential group when they arrived. It was 7:35 p.m. on Thursday evening.

They convened in the Oval Office. Howard suggested that the President keep the group size, for the meeting, down to a minimum; he thought that it might get a bit chaotic with too many personalities in the room at once. The final group consisted of the President, Rondo, Radomir, Howard, Sandra, and Joseph. The President wanted his chief of staff and national security advisor, but Howard convinced him that due to the nature of the information, to start with this group and invite the others in as needed.

"So what is the big revelation?" asked the President, anxious to know the information.

"Actually," Howard began, "Rondo's people and ours may very well be of the same species." The American and Russian Presidents' mouths opened, while Rondo shot Howard a strange look. Then he glanced at Joseph.

"Is this true?" said Rondo, still looking toward Joseph.

"It's possible," replied Joseph. Barnes and Radomir began to smile.

"What does it mean, *possible*?" Rondo asked.

"An old psychic Israeli lady thought Sandra was descended from one of the lost tribes of Israel. And the psychic's granddaughter, a PhD student, said that there was a legend that one of the lost tribes, the one that we are supposed to belong to, was spirited away by some spaceship from another planet."

"When did this *supposedly* take place?" asked Rondo.

"1010 BC," answered Howard. "About 3000 years ago."

"And you believe that this was not a rouse set up by the Earthlings to slow us down or convince us to let them off?" asked Rondo, looking at Joseph.

"It all sounded quite convincing," assured Joseph.

"Why did you not bring the girl and her grandmother, so we could question them?"

"We did not think it would be wise to get them involved," answered Howard.

"Are you kidding, Howard?" demanded the President. "This had better be on the level. We're in enough trouble as it is."

"They can only destroy us once," interjected Radomir.

"Yes, I guess you are right, Uri," agreed the President.

"This is on the level, Mr. President, Rondo and President Radomir; at least that is what they told us. It is not a setup, this is for real."

"Well certainly you do not think that I can just take your word for it do you?" asked Rondo. "If you can prove this beyond a doubt, then you will indeed have our attention."

"Is that all?" insisted the President ironically.

"To be honest, it takes you from no chance at all to some chance. If we are truly brothers, of the same species, then we would be hard pressed to reconsider our actions before proceeding."

"Is that all the assurance that we can get?" asked the President.

"I can give you no assurances," concluded Rondo. "Even if we were the same as you once, we have changed and you haven't. And we must still protect ourselves. Even while on this trip my planet was attacked by hostile forces of unknown origin. We managed to defeat the foe, but we cannot always be assured of success in the future. Staying hidden is our best protection. I will discuss this with my advisors and beam back an answer when we decide. But first, of course we must have the proof. But if you *can* prove it, then I promise nothing will happen until we have full and fair discussions. I give you my word."

"We can have our scientists compare the DNA of one of your people with one of ours," offered the President.

"That is okay," responded Rondo, "we have our own scientists and laboratory in our ship. We will carry out the test."

"Sandra, it must be done with Sandra," insisted Howard. "She has not had a body replacement yet."

"Fine, we will take some body tissue from one of you earthlings and compare it to Sandra's when we get back to our ship."

"I'm not going back to the ship," interjected Sandra.

"Why not?" asked Rondo.

"I am staying here with Howard," she insisted.

"But you and Howard may not last very long here."

"I'm not going back, no matter what," she said, tightly grasping Howard's arm.

"I will not force you," concluded Rondo. "I will take a sample from you and one from Howard then. Whoever said that I was not capable of being a romantic?" he added in a sardonic tone.

The group assembled for Rondo's departure. One of Rondo's bodyguards carried the case holding the tissue samples from Howard and Sandra.

"It actually is quite romantic that our bodies will determine the fate of your world," whispered Sandra. Howard just shook his head.

Rondo had decided to leave as soon as the samples were ready.

A helicopter was waiting. Rondo, his bodyguards and Joseph were being taken to their spacecraft for their journey back to the mother ship. The Presidents, Barnes and Radomir, decided to accompany Rondo to his shuttle vessel in case any last minute questions came up. They hoped that they might have the chance of adding whatever positive spin they could to help sway Rondo's decision in their favor.

While on board, Rondo activated his wrist communicator. "Rondo to mother ship." He waited. "Rondo to mother ship." Again no answer.

The Russian President was getting nervous, remembering that he had neglected to inform General Zansky to unblock the aliens' communication signals. "Maybe your communicator will work better when you get to the shuttle," he suggested.

"No matter," replied Rondo, "we will be at the mother ship soon enough. Remind me to talk to Einstein about this communicator," he murmured to Joseph.

As soon as they returned, the President invited Howard and Sandra to the Oval Office to get their opinions on the prospects for the future. Most of the President's advisors were present. The President turned to Howard. "What do you think are our chances of survival?"

"It's not clear," said Howard. "They will do what is in their best interest. Sentiment is not their strongest suit. But there is always some hope."

"Not very good? Then why did you remain behind?"

"This is where I come from. I couldn't very well live among a people that destroyed my planet."

"Traitor!" yelled Goodwood.

"He stayed behind, General," said the President.

"He's still a traitor, dead or alive. He and his alien girlfriend."

"This is not helpful. And we need all the help that we can get. What can we do now, Howard?" asked the President.

"I asked Rondo the same question before we left his ship."

"And what did he say?"

"He asked me if we knew how to pray."

CHAPTER TWENTY

The shuttle approached the gleaming hull of the mother ship. The trip somehow seemed longer coming back than going. It would be good to end this expedition and get back to their planet, thought Rondo, whatever the outcome.

The docking took place smoothly as usual. The whooshing and whirring of the connections and air seals was music to their ears. They found it a bit strange though, when no one came to greet them as the automated hatch door slid open.

They stood for a moment at the entrance of the mother ship, wondering where everyone was.

Could this be a small joke? Rondo wondered to himself.

They entered the main corridor and heard something going on just around the corner. He sent one of the bodyguards to investigate.

He went down the hall, turned the corner and came back with a smile on his face.

"What is going on?" asked Rondo.

"It looks like they are having sex," he said, still smiling.

"In the middle of the hall?"

Rondo went to see for himself. As he approached, the two "lovers" seemed not to mind that they had visitors.

"What is going on?" shouted Rondo.

The pair, looking startled from his remark, got up and ran off.

"What is going on?" Rondo repeated to his baffled companions.

As they continued into the ship, they found others loitering around, none of them coherent. They tried to communicate with some, but they just made weird noises and ignored Rondo's remarks.

They found some of their people playing with their ape-like habit creatures as though they were on an equal level.

"Einstein!" shouted Rondo. "Where is Einstein?"

They rushed to the lab. He was there, but incoherent like the others. Everything was smashed and thrown all over.

"The viruses!" he shouted.

"Look here in his notes!" yelled one of the bodyguards.

...the people on board are acting strangely. Could it be the result of contamination from the viruses? But how could it be? Even if we did accidentally contaminate the crew, these viruses affect only the human species. It could not affect us. After all, we are not human...

EPILOGUE

According to the Jerusalem Talmud, however (Sanh. 10:6 29c), the exiles were divided into three. Only one third went beyond the Sambatyom, a second to Daphne of Antioch and over the third, "there descended a cloud which covered them"…but all these would eventually return.

Printed in the United States
30991LVS00004B/1-51